When Charlotte Comes Home

May 5, 2007

For Sally,

Lovely and dear librarian.
Thank you for your friendship
and support!!!

When Charlotte
Comes Home

Much much love,

Maureen Millea Smith

MAUREEN MILLEA SMITH

alyson books
NEW YORK

Manufactured in the United States of America.

Published by Alyson Books,
P.O. Box 1253, Old Chelsea Station, New York, New York 10113-1251.
Distribution in the United Kingdom by Turnaround Publisher Services Ltd.,
Unit 3, Olympia Trading Estate, Coburg Road, Wood Green,
London N22 6TZ England.

First edition: May 2006

06 07 08 09 10 **a** 10 9 8 7 6 5 4 3 2 1

ISBN 1-55583-934-7
ISBN-13 978-1-55583-934-5

Library of Congress Cataloging-in-Publication Data is on file.

Cover photograph courtesy of Jupiterimages BrandX/ David Papazian Photography Inc.
Author photograph by Susan Makepeace

For Dan and Kerry

All Souls' Day: The Day of the Dead

THE DAY BEGINS in Washington, D.C., where my sister, Sarah, attends All Souls' Day Mass before going to the National Geographic Society, where she works as a map librarian. Her two sons, Christopher and Aleph, who are both in college now, are with her this All Souls' Day. Antonio, her husband, has dropped them off at the church on his way to Ronald Reagan Airport. In the back of the sanctuary, Sarah turns the pages in the book of the dead, touching the black letters of two names with the tips of her fingers as if to say, "Hello, you're not forgotten. Please don't forget me," as her boys watch. Then she brings her fingers to her lips to kiss them before kneeling in genuflection, like a half curtsy. I have watched her do this. It is a soft little dancer's movement. The brush of her fingers—the tactile—making the dead alive to her once again. If it is a new church, precipitated by a move in the District, or if she is out of town on business and is attending Mass at the church closest to her hotel, she inscribes the names in that church's book, knowing that our dead will be mixing with a whole new set of souls.

As the sun moves westward toward Omaha, my father, Morgan, and my brother, Laurence, awaken to walk to the Cathedral of St. Cecilia to attend the earliest Mass on All Souls' Day. They hold hands on their short walk to the church. Morgan holds hands to give strength and the balance to Laurence. Laurence would hold hands with anyone—the postal carrier

1

or his supervisor at Long John Silver's. It is in Laurence's nature to hold hands—one of the many surprising blessings of people with Down syndrome. Morgan and Laurence do not look into the book of the dead, although the names are there. It would be far too emotional an act for them. One time I showed them the names there in the cathedral's soft darkness, the letters lit by candlelight. They wept. Their day together ruined. The now-bachelor lives of these two men were disturbed beyond control. When my taxi came to take me to the airport that afternoon they stood on the curb of Thirty-eighth Street in a mix of emotions.

"Maybe," Morgan whispered as he hugged me, "you could visit us, Fred, when it is not All Souls' Day."

TWO HOURS LATER the sun breaks into day at my house on the Avenida Barcelona in San Clemente, where All Souls' Day is called the Day of the Dead. I stand looking out of my bedroom window at my former wife, Hetty, my lover, Thomas, and my daughters, Claire and Ellen, fifteen and eleven, respectively. They wait for me around Hetty's aged red Volvo station wagon. Three surfboards are secured with bungee cords to the Volvo's roof. My daughters hold bunches of marigolds and Thomas holds a picnic basket full of breakfast. Hetty holds the cooler. They stare at my window as I stare back at them, reaching for my gentleman's handkerchief and knowing that it is time to leave for the mission church at San Juan Capistrano. They stand in the middle of the softening jack-o-lanterns that decorated our yard for Halloween. My fingers drum the top of a gilded table. The table's four legs resemble those of a heron. At this moment the table is my beloved object and I am afraid to leave it and its constancy. I am hesitant on All Souls' Day, having looked for the sun long before Thomas awakened.

Loss has bred both hesitancy and the permanent stain of sadness into my character. At times it has germinated a false sense of wisdom and a false sense of destiny, hence my marriage and my divorce. But loss has its byproducts. My daughters, and Hetty herself, who came back into my life at a time when despair had taken over. Hetty represented to me what eleven-year-old girls become—the intoxicating reality of beautiful women. Moreover, she understood my sadness, and I, hers. Sadness is a difficult breeding ground for intimacy. We could not teach each other joy.

My friend, James Day, once told me, "Life is short, Fred. Be brave, cut Hetty free." But I held on to Hetty, hoping that we could become our parents. Our girls would have halcyon childhoods, as I remembered mine. Most of all, I stayed with Hetty because I loved her, something she never quite believed. "Good God, Fred," James used to say. "May I quote Tina Turner? 'What's love got to do with it?' You two argue like cats and dogs. You're incompatible personalities." When the time came, it was hard to admit that James was right.

I was in graduate school, studying art history, when James turned up on my doorstep in Berkeley, needing a room. I opened the door that rainy afternoon in 1975 and he walked back into my life like sunshine, duffel bags and all. Proximity melted the chill that had surrounded our friendship during his years in the navy. Moreover it bred an unspoken forgiveness between us. I did not realize how lonely I had been until I saw him asleep across the room from me on that first night. As my roommate, James anointed himself my father-confessor, giving me advice on all topics, liberally quoting rock music lyrics as philosophical support for his point of view. James never gave up on debate. It led him to Berkeley's Boalt Hall and the law, and eventually to a very happy life in San Francisco.

I watch as Thomas guffaws while Ellen hoots and Claire chortles. They sound like a flock of seabirds. I can see Hetty smiling. Thomas is a roly-poly, horribly dressed man who does not take me, nor the fact that he is gay, all that seriously. He sleeps comfortably with my sadness by ignoring it, as best he possibly can. He makes me laugh. "Pull on your face, dear Eleanor Rigby," he will say, dragging me out into the day. Thomas shuts the door to the Camry that propels me onto the highway and into the parking lot of the Orange County Museum of Art. Hetty is now closer to Thomas than she ever was to me. Her friendship with Thomas allows her to forgive me most of my flaws. It is the byproduct of her loss.

On the nights, on the very worst nights, when my sadness leaves me anxious and shaking, Thomas holds my hand and says to me what he said to me on our very first night together: "So tell me your story, Fred Holly."

I tell it all. Again. It began with the colic. Charlotte was born with the colic.

Colic

MY SISTER CHARLOTTE was born in 1959 with red hair like my mother's, and the colic. She was our parents' fourth and final child. I was seven at the time of Charlotte's birth, my sister Sarah six, and our brother Laurence, who was born with Down syndrome, just past two. "Colic," as Morgan would say, "was not in the plan."

Charlotte cried sixteen hours a day the first five months of her life. My parents tried a vast number of possible cures—a change in my mother's diet, a change to formula and then back again to breastfeeding, no noise, and then soft music with warm baths—but nothing consoled Charlotte. The gut-wrenching pain that ruled Charlotte's cries took over our lives. Peace arrived only at the moments when Charlotte, so exhausted from hours of crying, fell asleep in Mom's arms. Only Mom's arms. Charlotte cried even harder when Morgan picked her up, or anyone else. I remember those months of second grade as laced with a kind of dread that dispersed only as we walked toward Saunders Elementary School, and picked up again like the stickiness of a spider's web as Sarah and I returned home.

On the fourth Saturday of Charlotte's life, Mom told Morgan that she couldn't survive the colic with three other children underfoot every weekend.

"Do something with your children," she ordered him, pointing at the three of us in our pajamas while red-faced Charlotte wailed in her arms.

"What, what should I do, Eileen?" Morgan said back to her in frustration, throwing his arms into the air and dusting the kitchen table with the ash of his lit Marlboro.

"Sign them up for classes. I want all of you out of here. Everywhere I turn there is some child asking me for something while this one is screaming." Charlotte wailed as Mom danced her around the kitchen.

In desperation, Morgan enrolled me in Saturday morning drawing classes at the Joslyn Art Museum and Sarah in ballet lessons at the Lana Beth Boyer Dance Studio. He and two-year-old Laurence would spend their Saturdays ferrying us between the museum and the studio. Morgan stood as the lone male amidst the stage mothers in Lana Beth's foyer, pulling rubber bands and ribbons for Sarah out of an old bowling-ball bag loaded with Laurence's diapers and bottles of milk. During those weeks he learned to braid Sarah's hair and to wrap the ballet slippers' pink satin ribbons around her tiny ankles. At the Joslyn Morgan relaxed. He sat on the vast front steps of the museum, smoking Marlboros with the small coterie of Omaha's bohemian parents. They lingered together as their children drew, painted, and pinched seemingly endless pots in the museum's classrooms.

It was on the Joslyn steps that a piano teacher named Annie Little offered chalk to two-and-a-half-year-old Laurence, showing him how to drag it across a limestone step to make a line. Laurence was enchanted with the chalk and with Annie's brown skin. "Cocoa," he said over and over again when Annie guided his hand through those first lines, Morgan told me. He drew lines across every step and over Morgan's wing-tips. The following Saturday when Annie taught him how to draw a square, Laurence touched her cheek with his left hand, imprinting her brown skin with the chalk dust of his fingertips, and bringing to her face a dazzling smile. I watched him do this as I stood with Annie's identical-twin sons, Joshua and Micah, showing Morgan our latest pencil drawings for his approval.

I loved going to the classes, not because I was a particularly gifted art student but because it gave me access to the museum and its collections. I believed the Joslyn to be a magical place—sane, quiet, and filled with treasures. The slap of my tennis shoes against the Joslyn's marble floors thrilled me. On a sunny Saturday morning, the Floral Fountain Court inspired in me a sense of awe about architecture—of what a builder could build and what a person could dream. Its atrium was so high, and I felt so very small. I sounded out the Latin words embedded into the ceramic tiles of the court's floor–"Ornat, Pictvra, Artis, Dominum"–feeling exotic and foreign.

Moving from gallery to gallery as the volunteer docents told our classes the history of each painting and statue, I opened my imagination to the world of art. It was in the Joslyn that I developed the habit of falling into paintings. The play of color and light would pull me into a canvas, leaving me for a time still and outside of myself. There I would float across thick ridges of oil and pigment, slipping into a landscape, or onto the beauty of a figure.

What I realized at the age of seven was that I wanted to go to all those places beyond Nebraska to find other museums. Moreover, I wanted to find, collect, and catalog art objects. I wanted to grow up to be the boss of a museum. With the hubris of all seven-year-old boys in 1959, I believed that I could grow up to be anything I wanted to be. I would be in charge of all the statues, prints, and paintings. I would boss the curators and the nice old lady docents and make sure that the people who visited my museum obeyed my rules. I imagined myself in a suit like the one Morgan wore to his job at Mutual of Omaha, wearing heavy shoes and with a deep strong voice. I imagined looking at every object every day in my museum.

TO THE DISMAY of most of my elementary school teachers, I would write "museum boss" as my career of choice rather than football player, firefighter, train conductor, or doctor. Only in fourth grade did I learn the correct term for my aspirations: museum director. In fifth grade, my teacher, Miss Finley, called Mom at her job as a receptionist in the Medical Arts Building downtown.

" 'Mrs. Holly,' " I overheard Mom mimic to Morgan that evening when I was supposed to be in bed, but was sitting on the landing to the kitchen stairs, hoping to find out why my teacher had called, " 'don't you think it's a bit *queer* that Fred wants to be a museum director?' "

"Queer, Morgan, that woman must have used the word 'queer' three times. As if I didn't know what she was getting at. So I told her that Fred had been taking art classes at the Joslyn for years, thinking she would drop it. And do you know what she said to me then, Morgan?" Mom paused, and I heard Morgan strike a match.

"I have no idea, Eileen," he said to her, inhaling on his cigarette.

"She said, 'But, Mrs. Holly, Fred isn't even that good at art.' So I told her, 'Miss Finley, Fred loves the artwork. That's why he wants to direct museums. He appreciates art. He has the eye.'"

" 'But doesn't that worry you, Mrs. Holly? That he has the *eye?'* She says it like, Fred has the evil eye. Good God, Morgan, where do they get these teachers?"

And then I heard Morgan begin to laugh and say, "Don't worry so much. Fred's fine."

"Well, these teachers never call you at work, do they? You'd feel differently if they got you on the phone at the office with their insinuations. When it comes to teachers, it's as if all these kids sprouted out of my head with no help from you, Morgan Holly." Then the sound of water drummed into the kitchen sink and quickly, very quickly, she turned it off and spoke again.

"You have to teach Fred to be a boy. Fred behaves like a little man. He talks like a little adult."

"Is that so bad?" Morgan said this as I thought the same thing from my perch on the landing.

"Fred is not a man. He is an eleven-year-old boy. A very good eleven-year-old boy, but he sticks out and the teachers notice."

"What's so wrong about wanting to be a museum director?"

The question stood there between Morgan and Mom and me. What, I thought to myself, is so wrong about wanting to be a museum director? I wanted to be a museum director. I didn't want to be a baseball player or president of the United States or a fire fighter.

"He's not like the other children in the neighborhood. He's smart and good and he's..."

"Fred observes and he takes stock."
"People notice him, Morgan."
"He's a kind child, Eileen."
"The world is not always a kind place to people who are different."

UNTIL THAT MOMENT, I had never thought of myself as different. I thought of Laurence as different. For me he was the standard of how unique a person could be and still be a person like all other people. Laurence's differences always helped me feel more normal than normal. Supernormal Fred. In the darkness, a heated anger spilled down my chest into my belly and it began to churn. I wanted to scream, "I am not Laurence. He's the retarded one. He's different. I'm normal." For whatever normal was, I clung to it as the definition of me in my eleven-year-old mind. Laurence was retarded and I was normal. As suddenly as I wanted to scream those words, I was ashamed of even thinking the word "retarded." It would have been like calling Laurence spaz or idiot or jerk or moron. I was trained to say, "My brother has Down syndrome." My guts turned against me and I hated myself.

Why my anger was directed toward Mom and Morgan and not Miss Finley, who had clearly impugned me by using the code word "queer," I'll never know. I understood as I listened to them that she was hinting at me being a homosexual. Miss Finley knew that if she called Mom, she would get just this response. If Miss Finley had called Morgan at his desk in the middle of the Mutual of Omaha tower, there would have been no discussion. He would have thanked Miss Finley, quietly, and never spoken of the matter again. It would have disappeared. Vanished from the reality of our existence. Instead, Miss Finley shot at the soft underbelly of Mom's worry and struck a bull's-eye.

Morgan nor Mom ever spoke of the matter to me. Nor did they discourage my love of the Joslyn or my dream of being a museum director. I noticed, however, a change in our mail. Mixed in with Morgan's rose catalogs and actuarial journals, the *Smithsonian* began to arrive monthly as did *Sports Illustrated*. One magazine delighted me and the other surprised me. I read both of them, as did Sarah and Morgan. Morgan taught all four of us—including James, my best friend who lived next door—how to catch a ball and swing bats and rackets.

When James came into my life, I connected it to Charlotte's colic. The changes that her colic brought into our lives, it seemed to me, had the purpose of bringing James into my life. Without Charlotte there would have been no colic. Without Charlotte's colic there would have been no lessons. Without lessons there would have been no James. Without James, I was certain, as only an eleven-year-old boy can be, that my life wouldn't have been worth living.

James

ON THE LAST Saturday of a very hot August in 1960, before I was to start third grade, Sarah and I stood on the driveway, leaning against the doors of Morgan's Studebaker. Laurence faced us, swinging a pail full of colored chalk while he sucked his thumb. The three of us were waiting for Morgan to finish his coffee, after which he would grab the bowling-ball bag and Charlotte's hand, and lead her down the back steps, past his rose garden, and to the car. A door slammed at the blond-brick house next to ours, and I looked up to see a woman in white high heels and a pink summer dress with a tall boy about my age in navy blue shorts and a white shirt. The sandy-haired boy carried two sets of shoes by their strings. They were our new neighbors who had moved in the week before, but then had immediately left town for four days. The woman crossed her yard onto our driveway, waving to us.

"Good morning," she said in an accented voice, "I am Mrs. Day and this is my son, James." The boy offered his hand to Sarah, then to me, and finally to Laurence, who handed him a piece of chalk. As we said our names, James responded to each of us, "So nice to make your acquaintance," in a voice ever so slightly inflected with his mother's accent. I stared at the two sets of shoes James carried. They were brown and black tap shoes. Folded into one of the black tap shoes was a pair of black ballet slippers. His mother continued to speak in her foreign accent.

"Lana Beth Boyer told us that your family goes to her dance studio every Saturday morning, and we were wondering if James might go with you today, because I must drive downtown to meet with more movers." As she said this, Morgan pushed open the screen door with Charlotte holding one of his hands and the bowling-ball bag in the other. Mrs. Day walked toward Morgan and Charlotte. We could hear her introducing herself to them.

"How long have you danced?" Sarah asked James.

"Four years," James said, "First in Indianapolis, and then in Libertyville outside of Chicago. My mother danced in Durham and she always wanted her children to dance. So I am her only child, and I dance."

"Where's Durham?" I asked him.

"Durham's in England, but there's also a fairly well known Durham in the state of North Carolina," he told us in a polite voice.

"Wow, your mom's from England," I said.

"Yes."

"Have you been there?" I asked.

"Three times, but I can't remember the first time because I was a baby."

I was amazed. I dreamed of visiting Italy, France, and New York. They seemed as far away to me as Mars. Hearing James say the word "England" made me think of Jupiter. Almost with an ache, I knew I wanted to go there. And I wanted to touch James, the way I secretly touched the gilded frames of my favorite paintings at the Joslyn, or rubbed my cheek against bronze statues when docents and guards weren't looking. It was the way I memorized the things I loved. I believed that fine particles came off the objects onto me. The particles were the magic that would propel me out of Omaha and on my way into the world and to my museum. Standing there with his tap shoes thrown over his shoulder, James seemed like an emissary from the great world I hoped to join.

As I considered James, Charlotte broke away from Morgan and tumbled across the grass on her chubby legs, running to Sarah. Dropping her pink shoe bag, Sarah scooped up Charlotte and introduced her to James.

"Charlotte," she told her, "this is our new neighbor, James Day."

Laurence pulled his thumb out of his mouth and said, "Charlotte, James Day."

James said, "Such a lovely child," and reached out to touch Charlotte's red curls while Charlotte buried her face in Sarah's blouse.

At eight, I thought it was odd to hear James describe Charlotte as a child, as though the rest of us already belonged to the adult universe, and even odder to hear a boy use the word "lovely." Only later did I realize that James probably did think of himself as an adult, alone in his big blond house with his polite and very adult parents, and that his own language was a unique variation on his mother's. He'd abandoned any hint of the flat tones of his father's Indiana upbringing for the soft nuance of his mother's words. For, I would come to learn, as much as James loved his father, he was his mother's son.

When Charlotte peeked at James from the security of Sarah's arms, he winked at her, making Charlotte giggle and hide her head while Sarah laughed. Then James turned and winked at Laurence, who blinked back at him a dozen times in his attempt to wink one eye. Still sucking his thumb, Laurence put down his pail of chalk and covered his left eye with his left hand to create a one-eyed blink for James.

Morgan and Mrs. Day were murmuring as they crossed the lawn. When they reached us she gave James a brisk "Cheerio," and kept on walking back to their new house while we piled into the car. Morgan was going to drop me off at the museum and then take everyone else to the dance studio. Sarah sat in the front seat of the Studebaker with Charlotte on her lap. James and I sat in the back with Laurence between us. All of the car windows were rolled down, creating a gritty wind tunnel effect throughout the Studebaker. Morgan played KFAB on the radio at full blast over the sound of the air. We all sang along to Nat King Cole's "Mona Lisa." James sang in the perfect tones of a young boy's soprano. Laurence kept repeating the words, "Mona Lisa, Mona Lisa," long after the song was over and we were well into the crop report. I noticed James was looking at Laurence when Morgan pulled into the parking lot of the Joslyn to let me out.

"Fred, we'll be back later," he told me as I pushed open the passenger door.

Standing in the sun, I was watching Morgan circle the Studebaker around the parking lot, when James's head popped out of the side window, and he called out to me, "Good-bye, Fred." His thin arm waved with an enthusiasm that caught me off guard. I yelled back to him, "Good-bye, James," imitating ever so slightly the way his mother said his name, tasting their accent on my tongue, and liking its exotic sound in my eight-year-old ears. For a moment, I wished that I was going to dancing lessons with them.

Later, after they picked me up, while James was using the men's room at King Fong's Cafe, Sarah whispered to me, "He's a great dancer. He's the best dancer I've ever seen." There was an awe and honesty in her voice that made me stare at James when he returned to the booth to tear apart his egg foo yong and eat it, two egg rolls, and an extra helping of fried rice with a ferocious hunger.

"**WHAT DO YOU** do now?" James asked us as Morgan pulled into the driveway of our house on Thirty-eighth Street.

"It is our tradition, James, to take afternoon naps while Mrs. Holly goes shopping," Morgan told him as he inhaled on his Marlboro.

Mom stood by the side of the driveway in a yellow straw hat with three jet black feathers jutting out of its brim. Her red hair was pulled back and under at the nape of her neck. She wore an emerald green summer dress, white pumps, and white gloves. A small yellow linen purse dangled from her left arm.

As the car doors flew open, Mom spotted James.

"And who is this, Morgan? The changeling child you keep in that garden of yours? A young stray picked up off the streets? Or have I been miscalculating our brood from the very beginning?" Mom smiled as Morgan lifted a sleeping Charlotte off Sarah's lap; then he handed Mom the Studebaker's keys.

"This is James Day, Eileen, our new neighbor. He, too, takes dancing lessons and will be accompanying us on our weekly excursions."

"I am happy to make your acquaintance, Mrs. Holly," James said, offering her his hand.

"And I am delighted to meet you, James," said Mom, shaking his hand while Laurence grabbed her green skirt and rubbed its soft material against his face. "It's nap time, Laurence," she told him, disengaging his hands from her skirt. "You go on with Morgan now."

We all stood to watch as Mom backed the Studebaker down the drive and pulled out onto Thirty-eighth Street, and with two toots of the horn, she was gone. Laurence waved to her.

"Do you want to stay for naps?" I asked James, embarrassed by the fact that I still took them, but wanting him to stay anyway. "You can call your Mom and let her know you're over here."

"Sure, I'll take a nap," James said.

"After naps, I'll show you our attic, where I practice dancing," Sarah volunteered as we walked up toward the house.

THE SHADES WERE drawn in the bedroom that I shared with Laurence. An electric fan whirred in the center of the floor, pushing around the warm August air. With his thumb in his mouth, Laurence climbed into his bed and fell onto his pillow to sleep. I gave James my bed. Curling up on the floor on a sleeping bag, I was too drowsy to say much to him.

"Fred?" James said from the bed.

"Yeah," I answered.

"I don't mean to be rude, but is Laurence all right?"

"Laurence was born with Down syndrome, but he's all right. You'll get used to him. He'll surprise you," I said.

"Surprise me?"

"Yeah, Laurence is sweet-smart. I mean he's pretty smart in a really sweet way. It always happens when you don't expect it. It's nice."

"Nice," James repeated after me. I could hear the sound of sleep in his voice as I began to drift off. Then he asked one more question.

"Why do you call your dad 'Morgan'?"

"We always have," I told him. "I don't know why." And then I was asleep.

The Attic

JAMES LOVED THE attic of our house on Thirty-eighth Street. It had been built in 1907 as a small ballroom for the original owners, who later lost their home in the stock market crash of 1929. Subsequent owners called the ballroom an attic because it was unheated. Documents left by the builders indicated that warmth from the first and second floors would rise, heating the ballroom somewhat, if not adequately. "Dancers," they wrote in their notes on the house, "will create all the heat the ballroom needs." As the fourth owners of the building, Mom and Morgan saw the attic as a playroom and a storage space. They visited the third floor only to collect the Christmas decorations, store blankets for the summer, or pull out our summer clothes. Up there, we were left to our own devices.

Built into the attic's cedar walls were latches that opened doors into a series of cedar-paneled closets stuffed with the meaningful debris of our lives—baby shoes, christening gowns, school art projects, and pressed flowers—boxed and put away. The closets were a great place to hide on rainy spring evenings with a book and a flashlight, or to tell ghost stories to Charlotte and Laurence, who were willing to be scared. Morgan had sanded and waxed the ballroom floor of the attic and erected a used ballet barre near the windows so that Sarah could practice there.

After our naps that Saturday afternoon, we took James upstairs to the attic. Even its stifling heat did not dampen his enthusiasm. He picked up Charlotte, and danced her around the floor.

"Charlotte," James told her, "we will put on pantomimes, and you will be Little Red Riding Hood and I will be the brave woodsman who will save you. Fred will be the Big Bad Wolf and Sarah will be Grandmother. And Laurence will be your brother, waiting for you to come home."

Charlotte giggled, touching his cheek, while Sarah, Laurence, and I watched them dance through the attic's oven-like air. Putting Charlotte down, James pulled Sarah into the center of the floor, saying, "Wait here, wait here," then ran down the steps to the second floor to return with his brown tap shoes. Pulling them on and tying their looping brown laces, James tapped his way across the ballroom floor to Sarah, the tail of his white shirt flapping over his shorts. Grabbing her hand, he led her through a soft shoe, his steel taps disturbing dust motes that floated upward to the exposed rafters. Holding Charlotte and Laurence's hands, I watched as they danced.

Determined to follow James, a red-faced Sarah sweated through his maneuvers as though her life depended on it while he smiled with a peculiar and intent ferocity. It was obvious to me that James loved to dance and that he possessed a kind of skill that no one else exhibited in the many recitals I'd attended at the Lana Beth Boyer Dance Studio. I was too young to understand what James meant to my shy sister, or how it must have felt to Sarah to have a partner. With her braids flapping against her thin camp blouse, Sarah tapped her imaginary shoes after James until he whirled into the center of the attic floor and fell into an exhausted heap, where she tumbled after him, to our applause.

Over the years what James and Sarah created on the old ballroom floor of our attic might have left me feeling estranged, except that even at eight, James understood the dangers of leaving someone out. He understood the power of inclusion. How he came by his knowledge of getting along in a strange and foreign land was always a mystery to me. For a time, I believed that Serena Day had instructed her son in some sort of English charm school of her own making. But it was also apparent to me that behind James's extreme politeness was an actual goodness. James believed in doing good.

As in the rest of America, Omaha's yards in the 1960s were littered with the spawn of the baby boom. Once we were potty trained and threatened within an inch of our lives with all the tales concerning the danger of strangers, we were sent into a children's jungle dominated by larger families and bully boys. The four Hollys and the one James were a small army against the conquering hordes of children in our neighborhood. James could dodge and feint with the best of them, but he was never a bully or provocateur. He would do no harm.

On that first Saturday afternoon, James jumped up from the attic floor saying, "I have an idea. We can do *Harold and the Purple Crayon* as a pantomime. I'll be right back." He ran down the attic steps in his tap shoes and out the front door, and returned five minutes later with the small, purple, hand-sized book. The five of us trouped out of the attic's heat down the kitchen stairs and out the back door into the yard. James read the story aloud to Laurence and Charlotte, the three of them sitting on the wooden bench next to Morgan's rose beds. Sarah and I spread ourselves out on a blanket in the grass, staring up at the cloudless blue sky to listen once again to Harold's story as locusts called out the end of summer and the sun moved deeper into the west.

<hr />

IT TOOK UNTIL mid-September for us to pull the pantomime together. First we assigned parts. Laurence wanted to be Harold because he loved to draw lines, and I would be the narrator, because I couldn't dance. James and Sarah choreographed two dances to open and close the show set to forty-five records played on our three-speed player. Since the choices were limited to the songs that were within our combined collections of forty-fives, Sarah and James chose Bobby Darin's "Mack the Knife" and a gravel-voiced rendition of "Me and My Shadow" by an Englishman named Berkeley Thrive that Serena's brother had sent from Durham.

It took a great deal of effort to convince Laurence to draw throughout the narration. He loved drawing with chalk on the sidewalk, but it was hard for him to drag the purple crayon to any great effect across the white sheets of Mutual of Omaha scrap paper that we taped to the attic's cedar walls. Often he would become frustrated halfway through the story, dropping the crayon to suck his thumb. Finally Sarah thought of the idea of a purple Magic Marker. Laurence loved the squeaking sound and the flowing sensation of the marker's ink against the white paper. Once holding the Magic Marker in his fist, Laurence then refused to stop drawing his lines and squares for the final tap-dancing routine.

All Charlotte wanted to be was a fairy princess who twirled in circles across the ballroom floor. Wearing an old ballet outfit of Sarah's, a cardboard crown covered in aluminum foil, and a wand made out of Sarah's baton and curled ribbons, Charlotte opened and closed the show by twirling around in circles until she was giggling and dizzy. She would only stop twirling when she heard a loud round of applause, cheering, and whistling. If we didn't applaud soon enough she would twirl until she got sick. So for Charlotte, applause began with the first lift of her baton.

After many afternoons and evenings of practice and set design, James declared the show ready for an audience. We wrote formal invitations to our parents, who trouped up the stairs to the attic on a cool Friday evening in late September with highballs in hand and a plate of saltines smeared with pimento cheese carried by Morgan. The last adult up the attic stairs was Ronald Day, James's father. Built like a fireplug, Mr. Day wore a brown pinstriped suit with a vest and pocket watch. His reading glasses rested on the freckled skin of his bald head.

After taking his handwritten program from Charlotte, he asked her, "Might I touch your wand for good luck, dear?"

Charlotte offered him the beribboned end of the baton, nodding her red curls.

"Thank you, Charlotte. That is your name isn't it?"

Charlotte's head bobbed again.

"Could you escort me to my seat?"

Charlotte looked at Mom, who said, "Take Mr. Day to his seat, Charlotte."

Mr. Day wrapped all of his fingers around Charlotte's hand and followed her across the ballroom floor to his assigned folding chair. Sitting down, he smiled at her and sipped his highball. The show delighted the parents. Mr. Day called out, "Brava, bravo" at the end, saying of the dancing routines, "I think Omaha has produced another set of Astaires." This praise brought a gleaming smile to James's face. We all wandered downstairs so that the parents could have another drink and the children could enjoy lemonade.

As the Days were about to leave that evening, Morgan said, "Wait, for one moment, please," and he slipped out the kitchen door with his clippers. Minutes later he returned with an armful of roses, and offered them to Serena Day.

"They are the last of the season," Morgan told her.

"Thank you so much," Mrs. Day said, burying her face in the red and pink and gold petals.

"The English are mad about roses, Eileen," Mr. Day said to Mom.

"Well, Morgan can keep her in roses until she's insane," Mom said. And then all the adults looked at each other and burst out laughing.

Serena Day

SERENA DAY WAS like no other mother in our neighborhood. First, because she was English, and second, because she was the only mother of an only child for miles, but most important, because Serena Day was an interior decorator. For weeks after the Days moved into their house, plumbers, carpenters, and electricians filed in and out of the building as she remodeled and redecorated its interior. Everyone in the neighborhood observed the changes with a sense of vested anticipation, for Serena was the neighborhood's first career woman. In the sunny study on the south side of the house, Mrs. Day set up an office, where she hosted the neighborhood ladies for coffee on the opening day of her business, in early December.

At dinner that Friday night, as Mom served the tuna casserole, she burst forth with descriptions of the Day residence: "Serena's house is gorgeous, Morgan. The dining-room table was covered with a green cloth and centered in the middle was a huge Waterford vase filled with long-stemmed red roses. There were swags of evergreen hanging off the mantelpiece and up and down the staircase off the foyer. She put pots of blooming paper white narcissus on every coffee table and her Christmas tree was a tower of poinsettias," Mom said, pausing to smile and hand Laurence his plate before continuing.

Looking at us, she said, "Kids, you wouldn't believe it. The rooms smelled as good as they looked," but then Mom looked back at Morgan. "And Morgan, almost every stick of her furniture is secondhand and Serena does the refinishing. Agnes Maher kept asking her, 'Serena, where did you get this piece?' and Serena would say, 'Oh, at the Goodwill' or 'at the Hadassah shop,' or 'at the St. Vincent de Paul,' in some place or another. And in her basement, she has a whole workshop set up. She can actually use those tools. And do you know what else, Morgan? If a customer wants a piece out of her house, Serena sells it to them. She has sold three of her dining-room tables to customers who wanted them. Can you believe? She says she can always find another table."

Listening to Mom's description of the Day house, I felt a twinge of jealousy, because James had never invited me to their house. Our friendship lived on at the school playground, after school in our attic, or outside on the sidewalks and lawns of Thirty-eighth Street. Staring at my casserole, green beans, and orange Jell-O, I understood I had been denied access to a castle and its treasures. I longed to wander through the rooms and touch its objects. Looking up from our scratched farmer's table to the kitchen walls covered with years of finger paintings and gold starred homework arranged around a *Mutual of Omaha Wild Kingdom* calendar, I saw that our house seemed shabby in contrast. Eating Friday night tuna casserole off white Melmac plates with fading blue flowers felt like an act of destitution. My museum-boss dreams dimmed a bit in the face of the fact that I hadn't been invited into James's house. How would I ever get out of Omaha, I thought, as I swallowed an oily lump of tuna, if I can't even get into my best friend's house?

<hr />

"MY MOTHER HAS a gift," James said to me on the day before Christmas break as we walked the six blocks home from Saunders Elementary School.

"What's that?"

"She has the eye."

"The eye?" I asked him. For a moment, I wondered if Serena wore a glass eye, something I'd heard of but had never seen.

"You can put any group of objects in front of her, and she can place them in a beautiful organization."

"What?"

"It's uncanny. She can be talking on the telephone and I can put a yo-yo, a box of Crayons, and a pink sponge in front of her and she'll arrange them in some great pattern, or even a lovely pile," James said. "That's the eye. She can see where objects need to go so that they can work together."

"While she's talking on the phone?" I asked him.

"Yes, it's rather amazing. Her fingers just start placing things, fanning out the crayons, balancing the sponge, drawing out the yo-yo string. She can't stop until she has created some design. Dad likes watching her even more than I do."

"Would she do it for me?" I asked him.

"I think so. It's not something people know about her. But it's something her clients learn. Even the first time she walks into a potential client's house, she automatically begins moving the furniture around. She can't seem to help it."

"Well, maybe sometime I can stop by your house to see what she's done there. Then I'll get an idea of what she does. How she has the eye." I said casually to James, adding, "I can stop by any time it's convenient."

"Well, what about now?" James asked me. "She should be done for the day and working on the billing."

"Sure," I said with a pounding heart.

Even then, I felt simultaneously foolish and thrilled at the prospect of entering James's house, of seeing the Days' things. It came from that yearning born in the Joslyn for the beauty of objects and the power they held over me. It was more than being drawn to beauty. Instead, I was drawn to unexpected beauty—how light and placement and a willingness to see could change everything. I understood from Mom's description of the Day house that this was something I shared with Serena. Even in third grade, I knew that my interests were peculiar. Other little boys my age were not lobbying their parents for more art lessons. They were collecting baseball cards or building forts. Nor would I ever be foolish enough to mention that my desire to be a museum director was really born out of my love for the art housed in a museum. Somehow I mentally predicated the ordinariness of my dreams, at eight going on nine years of age, with the idea of wearing a suit such as the one Morgan wore every day to my museum. I saw my "bossing a museum" as businesslike and manly, like wearing wing-tips. Having James Day, the tap dancer, as my best friend seemed to make it all the more normal to me. I was like James. James was like me. Thus I saw us as normal and everyone else as different.

One spring day when I was in seventh grade, Annie Little found me in the Joslyn staring at the painting *Le Printemps–The Return of Spring,* by William Adolphe Bouguereau. Spring was a gorgeous nude woman, perfect in every detail, surrounded by the cherubic angels called *putti.* She was then what I hoped all girls looked like outside of their clothes—pink, creamy, and beautiful—and not like my sisters. Modestly erotic, *The Return of Spring* was the great art of my junior-high years.

Annie looked at me staring at the painting and said, "Fred, honey, you can do anything you dream, but you'll be a lot safer pursuing those dreams outside of Omaha. When you're good and successful, then Omaha will want you back. But, baby, you can never be a prophet in your own land."

Both James and I understood that we could be different in Omaha if we never talked about it. We could be different in Omaha if we planned to leave. Everyone would accept what we did if we did it out of town. Somewhere far away, where we would not embarrass the city.

My friendship with James Day meant that there would be at least one person besides Sarah who would know my dreams. It meant that when I was forced into the wilderness of the world outside Omaha to survive on locusts and honey, I knew that James would be there, too.

THE DAYS' HOUSE was everything Mom had said, and more. In every nook and cranny there were artfully placed things. Stones from streams juxtaposed against pine cones. Miniature bundles of sweet-smelling grass were cornered into bookcases. Tucked all over the house were birds' nests surrounded in gold foil and silken ribbons. Inside them were blue fragments of robin's eggs and the blown-out speckled eggs of bantam hens. In the upstairs bathroom was a glass bowl containing an ostrich egg the size of a cantaloupe melon, surrounded by three emu eggs the color and size of avocado pears.

James and I ran from the foyer and up the house's central staircase, which was swagged in evergreen just as Mom had reported, to his bedroom at the head of the stairs. We dropped our books onto his single bed, which was pushed against the wall beneath a window. The bed was covered in a woolen blanket broken into squares of brown and blue. Across the room next to the closet was a maple desk and an oak ladder-back chair. Above the desk were framed pictures of dancers—Fred Astaire, Gene Kelly, and George Balanchine. Out of habit, I ran my hand over the bedspread and then moved to the desk to slide my finger down its grooved pencil well. I leaned against the ladders of the chair and stared at the black-and-white photographs of James's heroes.

"Come on," James said, "let's go see Mum, and then get some cookies." Before we walked out of the room, James lifted the lid of his desk and grabbed a deerskin bag of marbles, three unsharpened number two pencils and an unused Pink Pearl eraser.

We found Serena Day in her sunroom office, punching numbers into a large adding machine with a ribbon of white paper spilling onto the floor. She wore heavy black-frame glasses and there was a small furrow between her brows. "Boys," she sighed, looking up from her work, "the numbers always win. The profit is all in the numbers." James went up to her and put his arms around her shoulders and kissed her hair as she rested her head against his chest. "Sweet thing," she murmured to him. Releasing her, James put the bag of marbles, the three pencils, and the Pink Pearl eraser down on the desk. Absentmindedly Serena picked up the deerskin bag and poured the marbles into the triangle that she'd made of the pencils. As she talked to us, Serena began to sculpt and shape, looking back and forth between us and the miscellany on her blotter. I found it lovely to watch her hands move the marbles, separating them into rows of complementary colors and playing with the balance of the eraser.

Asking us about our day, Serena created patterns of marbles and then piles of marbles before tearing them apart to begin again. Was our teacher still reading *Charlotte's Web* to us? Did we think Wilbur would survive? How far were we into our multiplication problems? And did we think there would be any snow for Father Christmas? Father Christmas, I learned, was her name for Santa Claus. While we answered and watched, her hands kept assembling and reassembling the objects.

Decades later, in Minneapolis, I was invited to observe visiting Tibetan monks create a multicolored sand mandala. Watching the shaven-headed men in their saffron-colored robes use their gnarled hands to create deft perfection with grains of sand, readying their pattern for ritual destruction, all I could think of was Serena Day, and the moments in that sun-filled room when James and I would plant objects on the green felt of her blotter to watch her tapered fingers move, build, and tear down as she sought some soothing organization. It became for me almost a religious obligation to observe Serena unawares, a note from God about my place in the world, telling me that things and beauty mattered.

James took us one at a time into his house. The rambunctiousness of the Holly children was too much initially for the Days to entertain as a group. On Thursdays, Sarah drank tea in the dining room with James and his mother. Once a month, for an hour, Serena would play chopsticks at her piano with Laurence before serving him chocolate chip cookies. And as Charlotte grew up, she would eat lunch in the kitchen on Wednesdays or Fridays with Serena and Willa, their cleaning woman, entertaining the women with chatter and her peals of laughter, which would roll out into extended giggles.

On Saturday evenings at sunset, Morgan and Mom would disappear into the Days' blond-brick house as James made his way across his lawn and our driveway to spend the night. The five of us would watch television, eat popcorn and cookies, and finish the evening drinking 7-Up flavored with grenadine and laced with maraschino cherries. Our mothers were beautiful on Saturday nights. They wore panty girdles under silk sheath dresses whose hems lingered at the bottoms of their kneecaps. Their dresses spanned a rainbow of vibrant colors. The two women muted nothing when they dressed for Saturday night at the Days' house. A dress was never pink when it could be fuchsia or maroon when the choice could be scarlet. There was nothing drab about our mothers as they dressed up for the bridge or charades or dominoes that they played after drinks and dinner.

Sarah and Charlotte thought that Mom and Serena Day looked like the women photographed in magazines, and when they pressed this point to James and me, showing us *Vogue* and *Harper's Bazaar,* we were forced to agree. Our mothers' hair was set and teased to be frozen confections. Their lips were painted in the boldest of reds, and their fingernails, lacquered to match. Stiletto heels gave them a tippy-toed walk, both alluring and childish. As the four of us Holly children waited for James at the back door, we would watch Mom lean into Morgan as the two of them walked across the lawn. The cloud of her White Shoulders cologne wafted backward and through the screens. Mom looked young next to Morgan. His hand would slip around her waist, clasping the silky softness not claimed by bra or girdle.

The Days' house on Saturday nights was a universe set aside for adults, where children were neither invited nor wanted. Only fire, burglary, or medical emergency were causes for interrupting this singular weekly event. When Mom and Morgan returned to find the five of us asleep in front of the RCA's flickering test pattern, little did we understand the sophisticated rituals of shy adults' sexual habits. They plopped us onto toilets and slipped us blind with sleep into our beds and sleeping bags to return to the pattern of their evening, which only later did I come to understand.

During my high school years, when I began to sneak out of the house after they'd gone to bed, I realized what they did on Saturday nights as we slept. I would listen, as I crept down the hallway, to Morgan's warm grunts and Mom's coos. My own footsteps were shielded by the squeak of their old bedsprings and their sleepy ecstasy. In the early hours of Sunday morning, it seemed to me that they were like birds after a plumage dance. How much, I thought, it took them to get to that awkward intimacy of sex. The dress, the scent, the liquor—all the building up for the possibility of tearing down—to act out what I am sure was unspeakable for them. Standing in the hallway,

I was embarrassed by the unexpected knowledge that my parents still copulated, or "did it," as teenagers put it then. At fifteen, knowing that they did it made sex seem far less sexy to me. I believed that when I finally did it, it would be smooth and elegant and perfect. The cooing, the grunting, and the humping bedspring were sounds I connected with their being old and not too good at it.

On the summer Sunday mornings of my boyhood, Morgan always placed roses on the breakfast table next to Mom's plate. Sitting in her lavender bathrobe with her face washed clean of makeup and her hair pulled back, Mom would blush, saying, "Thank you."

And Morgan would put his hand on her shoulder and say to her, "I think the roses are looking good today, Eileen."

She would squeeze his hand, blushing even deeper, and say something like, "They're lovely, Morgan. They're always lovely," and then drop his hand and grab the newspaper, fanning it out in front of her pink face.

During the many times of my sneaking back into the house just before dawn, I would think of the roses, and of this exchange. How Mom's blush would extend to the very roots of her red hair. I would sleep through breakfast and Mass, to wake up to lectures on my faithlessness to the faith and hints that my bad habits could lead to serious trouble. I would promise to pray and improve, taking whatever punishment they would dole out and laughing inside at their morality, their worry, and about the secret of what I considered to be their nighttime indiscretions. I was as callow as only a teenage boy could be.

Only decades later did it seem to the me that my siblings and I were products of all that manicured beauty and longed-for intimacy on Saturday nights. Our embryos were what came of the passions of two shy people coupling. What my father could say in roses, but could not speak of. And I was happy for it.

1962

ON THE FIRST day of summer vacation in 1962, James and Serena flew to England for six weeks. When I learned of their pending trip, in April, I was certain that they were going to invite me along. Where this bizarre notion came from I do not know, but I held on to it up to the very last moment before Ronald Day drove his family down Thirty-eighth Street to take them to the airport. Standing with the rest of my family on the front steps, dressed in khaki pants and a navy blue golf shirt, with my teeth brushed and hair slicked back, I was ready to leave. Hidden in the coat closet off the foyer was Morgan's brown leather suitcase, in which I had packed my tennis shoes, shorts, swim trunks, and a toothbrush, all the things I believed I would need for six weeks in Durham, England. Prepared in my mind was my feigned surprised acceptance speech at the last-minute invitation that I expected from the Days. My fantasy scenario had changed with each week as the hoped-for invitation to England had not materialized. I woke up on that first Thursday in June, longing for this exchange:

"Oh, we couldn't think of leaving without, Fred," I believed Serena would coo.

"How about it, Fred, old boy?" Mr. Day would ask.

"Fred's my best friend in the whole world," James would declare. "I won't go to England without him."

None of it sounded like the Days, but it was a type of scenario that I had seen on television shows. Desperate as I was to go to England with Serena and James, I was willing to hang my ten-year-old imaginative cap on just about anything. Waving my arm at the rear window of Mr. Day's Chevy

29

until it ached, I realized that they were gone, and I was about to spend almost a whole summer without James. I followed Morgan and Mom up the steps and back into the house while Laurence and Charlotte continued to scream, "Good-bye, bon voyageeeeee, good-bye, bon voyageeeeee." Waving their arms, they giggled at the empty street.

Sarah stopped me in the foyer and asked, "Do you want to pull out the sprinkler and run through it with the little kids this afternoon?" I looked at her as though she were asking me to fly to the moon.

"Fred, are you okay?" she said, tossing her braids back and forth, looking concerned.

"I don't feel so well. I think I'm going to lie down for a while."

It was true. I didn't feel well. My stomach and head ached. Sarah watched me climb the stairs. In my bed, I stared up at the spidery cracks in our coved ceiling. Tears rolled out of the edges of my eyes. It was only seven-thirty in the morning, and the summer already felt ponderously long. Someone pushed the door open. It was Laurence. He stood in the doorway for a moment sucking his thumb, and then he crossed the room to the closet. Dragging James's sleeping bag from the closet floor, Laurence pulled it up over himself as he lay down on his twin bed across from mine. He continued to suck his thumb while he rubbed the silky edge of the bag against his cheek. I could hear Morgan flushing the toilet as he prepared to leave for work. Then I fell asleep.

Hours later, I woke up to Mom's hand on my cheek.

"Sweetie," she said to me. I looked over to see if Laurence was still in bed. He was gone. James's sleeping bag was on the floor next to the bed, and that's when I saw it. There beside the sleeping bag was Morgan's suitcase. Mom saw me looking at it.

"Sarah found that it the closet. It looks like you have some things to put away."

"They must be Morgan's," I told her and looked up again to the cracks on the ceiling.

"You know, curiosity is a wonderful thing. There's nothing wrong with dreaming."

I didn't say anything.

"But a trip to England costs a great deal of money. Serena rarely gets to see her family. They have to save for two or three years to afford to send Serena and James. That's why they don't buy Ronald a ticket. It's very expensive and he can't be away from work for more than a few days."

"I wanted to go." It was all I could think to tell her.

"I know, honey."

I could feel the tears welling up again, and I tried to hold them back.

"We'll make it a nice summer, Fred."

"But I'll miss him. Whose gonna play with me?" The tears spilled.

"Everything's going to be fine. I've got it all planned," Mom said, hugging me.

The next Monday, Mom took us bus riding to show us the ropes of our summer. I would take summer art classes at the Joslyn on Monday, Wednesday, and Friday mornings, and would stay after to work until noon volunteering in the gift shop. I would ride the eastbound bus on Dodge Street to the museum and take the westbound bus back home. Sarah and Charlotte would ride the westbound bus on Dodge Street to the Lana Beth Boyer Dance Studio on Tuesday and Thursday mornings for lessons.

On Tuesday and Thursday afternoons, I was given the job of walking Laurence to Annie Little's house for piano lessons. Annie thought Laurence had potential because he would so willingly mimic any kind of physical activity, if asked to do so. Mom was thrilled that Annie would consider teaching Laurence, who was to enter the Madonna School, a private school for the disabled, that fall.

Annie had told Mom "that she believed in each person's potential," and it was a balm for Mom's soul.

"Finally," Mom declared that evening at dinner, "Laurence will have something of his own." Then Mom and Morgan began searching for used pianos.

Annie and her husband, Abram, lived five blocks from us, on Webster Street, and only three blocks away if I cut through the Duchesne College campus, run by the Religious of the Sacred Heart. In 1962, the nuns were still cloistered, and all the mothers in the neighborhood, including mine, instructed their children to stay off the college's property. I always asked Mom why

"Well, they're praying when they're not teaching, Fred. And if every Tom, Dick, and Harry walked through the campus, it would disturb their prayers. They pray for us. That's their job, and our job is to leave them alone so that they can pray. So I don't want to hear that you're cutting through their property. And neither does Morgan."

While Annie trained Laurence in piano by having him repeat everything she did on the keyboard until he could play a song, I played basketball in the backyard with her twin boys, Micah and Joshua. Micah and Joshua were fine athletes and much better than me. Playing a half an hour two days a week with them considerably improved my basketball game, but soured my attitude. Micah and Joshua were best friends. Thirty minutes of hoops with them reminded me that James was gone. I missed James as I missed shots, and as the summer passed the missing evolved into an unspent anger. My game improved, but my grudge against James did not. Laurence would pound the keys of "Mary Had a Little Lamb" and "Row, Row, Row Your Boat," and I would sink shots to the approving shouts of "Way to go, man," from the twins, thinking of James in Durham, and all those places and things and people that he would see without me.

Looking back, it was not a bad summer. Morgan bought a family pass to the Elmwood Park Swimming Pool and he took us there every day after work. I regularly jumped off the high board and saw my first bikinis with real high school girls actually wearing them. A Japanese woman named Reiko Kato taught my art classes—two weeks of origami paper folding, two weeks of calligraphy, and two weeks of throwing pots on motorized wheels, which she fired raku style. Mrs. Kato told me that I showed great promise, and I believed her. The old ladies in the gift shop let me use a box cutter to open the cartons of merchandise—something Mom would never have allowed, if she had known about it. I loved the smooth rip and tear of the cutter, and took great pleasure in unloading the boxes of note cards and the palm-sized bronzed replicas of the Degas ballet dancer that the store sold. It would have been a great summer, if James had only been part of it.

On the day James was to return, Laurence and I left late for his piano lesson. I turned toward Duchesne College to cut through the campus to save time.

"No."

Laurence balked at the edge of the campus.

"Come on," I said, pulling on his hand.

"No, Fred."

"We'll be late if we don't cut through."

Laurence began to walk the regular way and I followed him, refusing to hold his hand in retaliation. When Annie Little opened the door, Laurence began to bawl.

"Laurence, what's wrong?"

"Fred's s'posed to hold my hand so I don't get run over, but he wouldn't hold my hand."

"Fred?" Annie looked at me.

"We were late. He wouldn't hurry." I felt like pinching Laurence. Instead, I kicked the cement step with my tennis shoe and stubbed my big toe.

"Well, you walk home, holding Laurence's hand. I would rather have you late than have Laurence upset. Now go round back and play with the boys." Annie took Laurence by the hand and firmly shut the door in my face.

When Micah saw me he called out, "Hey, Fred, isn't James coming home today?"

I nodded.

Joshua looked at me, "You're happy aren't you? All you talked about all summer was James."

Micah tossed me the ball. I couldn't remember talking about James.

"No, I didn't," I said, aiming for the basket, but missing.

"You and James Day are like Siamese twins," Micah said, catching the rebound.

"Yeah, separated at birth. You two white boys even look a little alike," Joshua added.

"Let's play horse," I said, wanting to get away from talk of James. My chest hurt. My solar plexus felt bruised as though all of the summer's emotions were pushing out. I could hear Annie playing "Twinkle, Twinkle Little Star," and then she played only the first few notes for Laurence to hear and watch. Then Laurence played the "Twinkle, Twinkle" notes over and over again. When he stumbled on a key, it felt as though someone was poking at the bruise in the center of my chest.

So we played horse. Micah and Joshua made every shot and I missed all of mine.

Maybe if, when I was ten, I had understood the word "bereft," I would have finished that particular Tuesday with some dignity. But I understood so little then. My emotions existed in a great gray field that I understood as one feeling–bad. I felt bad. Anger, sorrow, jealousy, and loneliness were springing leaks with the thud of each missed shot off of the Littles' backboard.

And then I heard Annie calling me: "Fred Holly, it's time to take Laurence home."

"Hey, Fred, bring James on Thursday and we can play teams," Micah said.

"Yeah, James," said Joshua. "He can tell us all about his trip."

"Now, hold Laurence's hand, Fred, and tell your folks we're working on 'Twinkle, Twinkle Little Star.' Tell them he's doing fine, and that I might have found them a used piano. Tell your mom to call me."

I nodded, grabbing Laurence's hand.

"You be nice now."

I nodded again, adding, "Thanks for the lesson, Mrs. Little."

I held Laurence's hand all the way up to the Duchesne campus, and when I stepped onto its forbidden lawn, Laurence stayed planted on the sidewalk, saying, "No, no, no." So I picked him up–Laurence was small for five–and carried him onto the lawn and down toward the alley of oaks. That's when Laurence began to scream, "No, Fred, no." After that there was no hiding from the nuns, or the earnest coeds. They all turned to stare at us, and I began to run. The louder Laurence screamed, the faster I tried to run, but couldn't, because of the weight of him. The coeds saw us and began to shout, "Put that little boy down." Nuns poured out of the doorways and from behind the trees. A tall girl with a blonde beehive hairdo began to chase us. The others followed, and then the nuns joined into the chase. "Should we call the police?" some girl shouted, and a nun bellowed, "Put that little boy down, young man."

"No, no, no," Laurence screamed as his legs kicked me. I could hear the rattle of rosaries and the huffing and puffing of the nuns who themselves ran against the tangle of their habits, summer heat, and Omaha's high humidity. The blonde girl was gaining on me when I started my steep ascent up the grass-covered hill to Thirty-eighth Street. Halfway up the hill, I could see Mom, Sarah, Charlotte, James, and Serena Day at the crosswalk.

One of the nuns shouted, "Put that poor boy down, you little heathen," just as Mom saw me. As they all saw me.

Behind me, the blonde girl yelled at Mom and Serena, "Stop the kidnapper."

"Oh, I'll stop the kidnapper all right," Mom shouted back, running down the hill with Charlotte at her heels. She grabbed me by the collar of my shirt as the sweating, huffing blonde reached us. "Fred Holly, what do you think you're doing?" She hissed at me as she took Lawrence from my arms. At this point, Laurence was bawling as though he had been kidnapped. It was then that I really saw James. He was at least an inch taller and brown as a nut.

"James," I called out, overjoyed to see him. Mom stepped in front of me, effectively blocking me from the gaggle of nuns and outraged coeds who were comforting Laurence and patting Charlotte's red curls.

Mom led with an apology: "I am so sorry. I've told that boy a hundred times to stay off your property. You can be certain his father will hear about it. Keep him in your prayers, dear sisters, his life won't be worth living once Morgan Holly learns about his shenanigans."

At that moment, I didn't care if my life was worth living, or what Morgan or Mom thought, or the nuns or the coeds, or the Pope, for that matter. James Day was standing on the lawn by the crosswalk and I ran to him as Serena and Sarah walked down to Mom and the crowd below. I was in pain from running, but my solar plexus now felt as though it might burst from joy.

"Hey, Fred, I missed you." James said and gave me a slight punch in the shoulder.

"Me, too," I said, giving him a playful slug back.

"What's going on?" James asked, faking a jab to my cheek.

"I cut through," I said, faking an upper cut.

"Got caught, eh?" His fist flickered by my chin.

"Wouldn't have if Laurence wasn't such a baby," I said, faking a slap, and making him take a step back.

As Mom and Serena reestablished diplomatic relations with the Religious of the Sacred Heart, the punches, slaps, and jabs kept coming closer and closer to reality. To my surprise, James put me into a headlock and pulled me down onto the hardness of the late-summer ground. Then we began to grapple in earnest. We weren't fighting so much as refusing to let go—rolling over from one side to the next—Fred on top and then James on top, grunting and saying things like, "Glad you're back," and "I missed you." Before either of us knew it, we were rolling down the hill toward the people below. It was Charlotte who saw us. She shrieked so loud that the crowd turned their attention to the hill in time to part as inertia kept us in motion. James and I rolled through them, stopped only by the level ground of the cement sidewalk that bordered the parking lot.

Bruised, sweating, and bleeding on the hot cement, I felt happy in a way that I had not felt for six weeks. In our grappling, I sensed that James had missed me, too.

"You boys, look at you boys," our mothers kept clucking as they apologized again to the nuns and the coeds, pulling us up to our feet. "What are we going to do with the two of you?" They made me apologize to the assembled nuns for trespassing on their campus, and then they made James and me apologize together for wrestling. The nuns nodded knowingly as though to say, "This is why we don't teach boys."

Mom threatened me all the way home, but I paid no attention to her. I just stared at James and asked Mom if he could spend the night.

After dinner and before James came over, Morgan took me with him to cut roses. It was my job to hold a long, flat wicker basket into which he deposited both the flowers and the deadheads. In silence, we moved up and down the rose beds.

Finally Morgan stopped, lit a Marlboro, and said, "So what did you learn today, Fred?"

I thought for a while and then said. "I missed him, Morgan, but I never knew he would miss me, too."

"Ah, you learned that your feelings are not the only feelings in the world. You're not alone, son. It was a long summer for James, too. What else did you learn?"

"Watch out for nuns?" I looked up at Morgan. The sun was coming down behind him. At his back the world was gold and red and orange.

"Ah, but you should have learned more. You should have known more."

"Known what, Morgan?"

"To stay off the campus. You know the neighborhood rules. You terrified Laurence. Don't do it again. Leave the nuns alone and be kind to your brother. He has to be able to trust you and we have to be able to trust you with him, because there are judgments Laurence can't make. So you have to do what he knows is right. You knew you weren't supposed to be on the Duchesne campus, and so did he. Don't get so wrapped up in your own feelings, Fred, that you become a little shit." Morgan tossed the cigarette to the ground, stubbing it out with his work boot.

Then I felt shame. Shame was a readily identifiable emotion for me. It felt both black and clear. Morgan and Mom held expectations for the rest of us when it came to Laurence. Once I complained bitterly about having to clean up after him, and Morgan said, "Fred, you are an extremely gifted human being. I expect you to share those gifts with your brother. Someday you will understand."

I hated it when Morgan said, "Someday you will understand," because it was no more my fault that I was what I was than it was Laurence's fault that he was limited by Down syndrome. Our family's common goal of keeping life as normal as possible for Laurence conflicted with the fact that Laurence wasn't normal. Our parents' expectations for both Sarah and me were that we were to take the extra steps to help make life better for Laurence by including him in our play. There were times I resented Laurence, and for that I always felt shame. Shame and resentment grew to be hinged feelings for me. It was rare for me to have one without the other.

On the Tuesday that James returned, I was ashamed of how I'd treated Laurence. The shame was so overwhelming that evening in the rose garden with Morgan that it crowded out the resentment.

Dog Days

THE NEXT WEEK, the Madonna School counselor visited our home to observe how Laurence, who was then five, interacted with the rest of the family. To the great surprise of Morgan and Mom, her report centered on Charlotte, who was three and a half. "Charlotte," the counselor wrote, "spends so much time with Laurence that she does not understand how normal children will react to her play. She continually speaks for Laurence and finishes his sentences. She dominates him. Her language and gestures are uncanny imitations of her eldest siblings. Charlotte needs to associate with other children of her own age, either in your neighborhood or through a nursery school program, to learn the give and take of non-parallel play before she enters kindergarten."

Mom's reaction to the report was swift. She enrolled Charlotte in a nursery school program that would begin in September and she also enrolled her in a preschool art class at the Joslyn. The class was called Dog Days, a name that aptly described those last two weeks of August. Both Sarah and James were committed to classes at Lana Beth Boyer's studio, to which Serena would drive them. Mom told me that I would be taking Charlotte to the art museum, because she needed to be home with Laurence, who would not understand why he couldn't attend Dog Days, too. Nor would three-and-half-year-old Charlotte. "This is your chance to redeem yourself, Fred," she told me. Mom arranged it so that I could volunteer in the gift shop while Charlotte finger-painted in the education room and learned how to play with children who were not of Laurence's temperament and background. I took seriously my responsibility for Charlotte. I listened to all Mom's warnings about safety, and why it was important "to socialize Charlotte," a new phrase in our family's lexicon.

On the first day of her art classes, Charlotte wore a yellow sunsuit and carried a brown paper bag that contained graham crackers and raisins for her midmorning snack. Charlotte held my hand as Mom and Laurence walked down Thirty-eighth Street with us to catch the bus. Her small hand perspired as she gripped my fingers like a vise. On the bus she continued to hold my hand while staring out the window at Mom and Laurence as they walked home. She sat as close to me as she could without climbing into my lap.

"Fred," she whispered, "why isn't Laurence coming?"

"This is for you, Charlotte. You will love it. I love all my classes at the museum."

"But why not Laurence?" She looked up at me. Her blue eyes were solemn. She squeezed my hand even harder.

Dodging her eyes, I looked down on her head. It was a tangle of red curls, sausages of hair that my fingers longed to pull and spring. "Sarah and I don't do everything together."

"But Laurence and I do," she said, looking up at me. This time I couldn't break from her gaze. Or from staring at the freckles that covered her nose and cheeks. Even at ten, I realized that Charlotte was a cute kid.

"You know that next year Laurence is going to the Madonna School?"

"Yeah," she said.

"Well, you won't go to that school. You will go to Saunders like Sarah and me."

"Why not?" She asked.

"Why not what?" I answered.

"Why won't I go to school with Laurence?"

"Because the Madonna School is a special school for kids like Laurence. At Saunders, there'll be kids like you."

"But I am like Laurence. He likes macaroni and cheese and I like macaroni and cheese. I like applesauce and he likes applesauce. He sleeps with a monkey and I sleep with a lamb. We both like Captain Kangaroo."

"Charlotte, you know that Laurence has Down syndrome, right? Kids with Down syndrome learn differently. You don't have Down syndrome so you will learn like Sarah and me."

"Can I get Down syndrome?"

"No," I said so loudly that some ladies turned in their seats to look at me. The bus was hot and dusty. The windows were open and the air smelled of asphalt and diesel exhaust. Charlotte and I were the only talkers on the bus. I had learned over the summer that talking about the weather was the great neutral topic of bus riding. Talking about heat, however, only made it seem hotter. Silence was a cooler state.

"Why not?"

"Because you have to be born with Down syndrome. It's not like mumps or the chicken pox."

"Well, I want to go to school with Laurence," she said, looking away from me.

"Remember how long it took for Laurence to get potty trained? Remember, he used diapers even after you didn't?"

"Yeah." She looked up at me as the bus hit a bump on Dodge Street and then grabbed me by the chest to steady herself.

"Well, it's always going to take Laurence longer. There are some things he'll never be able to do. You're going to be able to learn things that Laurence can't learn. Down syndrome makes it harder for Laurence to learn."

"Oh," she said, and then climbed into my lap. She looked out the window and began to pull on the longest of her red curls. For a time she didn't say anything.

"Will he get to drive the Rutabager?" Charlotte called the Studebaker the Rutabager.

"No, Laurence will never drive the Rutabager."

"Will I?"

"Sure you will. Morgan'll teach you how to drive the Rutabager."

"So I'll drive Laurence in the Rutabager?"

"Yeah, you can drive Laurence in the Rutabager."

She was quiet for the rest of the ride.

On the walk from the bus stop to the museum she asked me, "Are these kids going to be like me or like Laurence?"

"Like you."

"Will they be nice?"

"If you're nice, they'll be nice."

Charlotte smiled. "I'm nice."

"Yeah, you are Charlotte. Just remember to share, even if other kids don't share. Not all kids are as nice as you."

"I'll share."

The museum was a dark and cool relief from the already heavy heat of the morning. I walked Charlotte to the education room, where mothers in pedal pushers and summer dresses were dropping off their children. Two of the kids were crying as their mothers tried to coax them into the classroom. I showed Charlotte where to put her snack and walked her to the small tables and chairs set up for the preschoolers.

"I'll be back at eleven-thirty," I told her. "Stay in the classroom until I get here."

Charlotte nodded and I turned to leave.

"Fred," she said, "you need to kiss me."

"What?" I asked her.

"You need to kiss me. Mom and Morgan always kiss me good-bye."

The chairs were filling up with three- and four-year-olds. I looked around, wondering how I could leave Charlotte without kissing her in front of all these kids and their mothers.

"Well," I said, hesitating.

"You need to kiss me," she said again and much louder. I could hear the dangerous sound of tears in her voice. The threat of full-fledged bawling forced my hand.

As I bent down to kiss her cheek, I could feel a warmth rising up my neck and over my face. It may well have been the fastest kiss ever kissed, but nonetheless it was a kiss that Charlotte greeted with a smile.

"Bye, Fred," she said.

"Bye, Charlotte," I told her, skirting the mothers, who were cooing, "What a sweet big brother."

~~~

THE GIFT SHOP MANAGER assigned me the task of unpacking boxes of notecards and attaching price tags to them in the shop's crowded storage room. The room was dim and warm, but I was glad to be away from the scrutiny of cooing mothers and the eyes of the munchkins of the Dog Days class. It gave me time to come up with an explanation for Charlotte as to why I wasn't going to kiss her good-bye anymore. "First, of all," I planned to say, "I am not Morgan or Mom." To me, it seemed like a logical beginning that Charlotte could understand. Lost in thought amidst cardboard boxes, I was startled when Mrs. Kato called to me that it was almost eleven-thirty and time to go.

Charlotte was waiting for me in the classroom. Her lip was trembling as she stood there with one of that morning's paintings.

"I was nice, but everyone isn't as nice as me," she whispered to me in the throng of mothers picking up children.

I knelt down beside her and whispered, "What happened?"

"The teacher said that I needed to let Andrew paint his own painting. But I was just trying to help. He needed more red."

"Do you like Andrew? Is he nice?" I asked her.

"Yeah."

"Then why don't you let him do his own painting and you do yours."

"But I was trying to help him."

"Well, sometimes people just need to learn on their own."

"I always help Laurence."

"Yeah, you do," I conceded, not knowing what else to say.

As we walked out the door, Miss Prin, the Dog Days teacher, called out, "I love your paintings, Charlotte."

Charlotte stopped in the doorway and smiled.

I whispered to her, "Say thank you, Charlotte."

Charlotte whispered to me, "But she wasn't nice to me."

"Well, she's being nice now. Say thank you."

Charlotte stood her ground, saying nothing.

"Thank you, Miss Prin," I called back to her.

"It's so good to see you, Fred," Miss Prin said, waving to me. "Charlotte's a chip off the old Holly block."

I waved back, giving her a shy smile.

"It will be fun tomorrow, Charlotte," Miss Prin said. "We're going to make puppies for Dog Days."

"Bye, Miss Prin," I said, taking a step into the corridor.

Charlotte turned in the doorway and stepped back into the classroom. "Can I make a puppy for Laurence, too?"

"Who's Laurence?" Miss Prin asked, walking toward the doorway as mothers and children navigated around us.

"Laurence is my brother," Charlotte said. "He has Down syndrome. So he's going to the Madonna School, but I can't go to the Madonna School because I can't catch Down syndrome. It's not like mumps or chicken pox. You have to be born with it. And he'll never drive the Rutabager, but I will."

All the mothers paused to listen to Charlotte. For just a moment, they stared at me. During that moment, I grew warmer than I had been on any August day.

"Of course, you can make a puppy for Laurence, Charlotte," Miss Prin said, breaking the silence all around us and bringing the mothers back to movement and their children.

"Thank you, Miss Prin," Charlotte said, and then walked out the door to take my hand.

Charlotte fell asleep in my lap during our hot ride home. I carried her and her finger-painting off at the bus stop, where Mom and Laurence were waiting for us. Mom took her from me, cooing as she did, "How's my baby girl?" Laurence held my hand and stared at Charlotte's painting all the way home.

EVERY MORNING OF Dog Days, I kissed Charlotte good-bye. They were the fleetest of brotherly kisses. These kisses were witnessed with delight by the mothers of the Dog Days students. I did not have the heart to make my speech about kissing, but I practiced it within the confines of my imagination and the gift shop storage room for all ten days. On the bus rides home from the museum, Charlotte would crawl into my lap and fall asleep. Her sweaty curls would flatten against the cotton shirt that covered my thin chest. There was not a day after the first morning that Charlotte did not make something for Laurence. Nor did she ever stop trying to help Andrew. It became apparent to all concerned that we could socialize Charlotte only so far. Charlotte would always be Charlotte.

The Rolling Stones: Omaha, 1964

MORGAN HATED ROCK 'N' ROLL. And I loved it. I loved it even more because Morgan hated it so. (He even hated Elvis, something Mom could never understand, but he did.) After the summer of 1962, James Day brought British rock 'n' roll home over the Atlantic Ocean and unlocked something in me. Something that was all mine. Something I could never share with Morgan or make Morgan understand. The sound, the rhythm, the slick-to-sloppy look of all rock 'n' roll musicians appalled him. With the music, I was transformed. No longer the oldest child in a family with a retarded brother, now I was alone and free in a solipsistic world created in the attic on my portable record player playing at full volume, until Morgan came home from Mutual of Omaha to shout, "Turn that goddamn noise down," and I returned to the planet Omaha, pissed off at Morgan, wanting to yell back, but not daring to do so. Instead, I turned the music off, angry, sullen, and wounded by the fact that he could not hear what I heard.

When I listened to the music, that music, in the music, I could be free. As testosterone spread its oily little dominance over me, the expectations of Mom, Morgan, Sarah, Charlotte, my teachers, even Laurence ruled that I would be a good, trustworthy, smart, hardworking, honorable boy, but through rock 'n' roll I could survive. I could sing and jump and dance and howl so that I could face the day and the world and all those expectations. I would walk Laurence to Annie Little's house and play basketball with the twins or, on winter days, sit in the anteroom to her studio and listen to her train Laurence on the piano. Whenever Laurence played well, Annie would end the lesson by playing some long beautiful piece for him—Bach, Bartók, Gershwin—something that would take my breath away, but leave me longing for my records.

James Day returned to Omaha a foot soldier in the British rock invasion. He found in me a willing acolyte to his service. Guided by his uncle Ian, Serena's younger brother, he was a guerrilla warrior for the new sound. Uncle Ian spent the summer introducing James to the British music scene. His letters were filled with detailed lists of what we should try to buy in albums and forty-fives. Uncle Ian also sent James copies of London music magazines, black-and-white photographs cut out of tabloids, and posters he'd torn off the sides of pub walls. We decorated our bedrooms and the cedar walls of the attic with these artifacts. For me, James's Uncle Ian was a genius and a visionary. Over the years we learned from Uncle Ian of the Beatles, the Rolling Stones, Cream, Humble Pie, the Who, Genesis, the Kinks, Yes, the Clash, the Sex Pistols, and learned that Eric Clapton was God. Even after Berkeley, James would share word of Uncle Ian's pronouncements on the world of rock music in his letters. Ian's long faithfulness to the rock and pop form taught me a broad and catholic approach to music—listen to everything, try to love it all. Over the years, my love of rock 'n' roll expanded into the Americas, but in my heart, I would always have a special place for the music groups of the British Isles; I even accorded the one-album wonders such as the Fine Young Cannibals, a special reverence, because of their link to Uncle Ian's Britain.

It was in 1964 that Ian notified us that a group called the Rolling Stones was coming to Omaha in June and that we could not miss seeing them. Both James and I knew that it would be a tricky negotiation to get permission to attend the concert. We hit upon a plan of asking our parents at a barbecue that Mom and Morgan were having for the Days on a Saturday night in mid-May. The five children were to eat with their parents on card tables set up next to the early-blooming roses in the garden, and then the adults were going to retire to after-dinner drinks and bridge while we watched the

Saturday night movie on NBC.

James brought the letter to the barbecue.

"Mum," James called out to his mother, who was in a yellow linen dress, sipping a gin and tonic and watching the men grill steaks.

"Yes, dear," Serena said over the chuckles of Morgan and Ronald Day.

"Uncle Ian said in his letter that Fred and I should go see this group called the Rolling Stones. They're coming in June. Uncle Ian says they're cutting edge. That we must see them. That they are going to be famous. Like the Beatles. Look, it's in his letter." James showed Serena her brother's recommendation.

"Oh, not the Beatles," moaned Ronald Day.

"I hate the Beatles. I would like to put them out of our misery," said Morgan. The two men chuckled. Mom was tying Laurence's shoe when she heard Morgan and Mr. Day laugh. An uncomfortable look came over her face. She double-tied the bow, sending Laurence off to play with Charlotte.

Mom spoke up. "Well, if Serena's brother thinks the boys should see the concert, maybe they should." Then she tapped her foot three times as if to say to the men, "Pay attention." "James's Uncle Ian was certainly right about the Beatles. They are world-famous."

"It is rather amazing that England is leading the way in music and fashion right now," Serena said rather primly.

"That's right," Mom chimed in. "There isn't a magazine that hasn't written about the Beatles. Look at Twiggy. Girls all over Omaha are trying to look like her."

"Maybe the boys should go to the concert," said Serena, clinking her ice cubes. "I really do trust Ian about these kinds of things."

Ronald Day snorted. Serena Day turned in profile to look at her husband. Her lips were pressed together.

"Well, Morgan, Ian's a bit on the creative side, but he does seem to know this music stuff. I certainly can't make heads or tails of it myself," Ronald said, clearing his throat and pinkening.

The ball was in Morgan's court, and everyone knew it. No one said a word. Sarah was looking back and forth between us and the adults, calibrating the points that were piling up between the men and the women. It was obvious to me that she was considering whether she would have any leverage to come along. We all knew that Morgan would never say a word against Serena's brother, because Morgan may have hated rock 'n' roll, but he worshipped Serena Day. Laurence and Charlotte even stopped running around to stare at the four silent adults.

Finally, Morgan spoke, "Well, it sounds as though Eileen and Serena are going to take the boys to the concert, Ronald. I'm sure it will be educational for all of them."

"Can I go, too?" Sarah shouted.

Serena sipped her gin and tonic, and then Mom grinned.

"Sure, we'll take the boys to the concert," Mom said.

"Of course," said Serena.

"Can I go, too?" Sarah asked again.

The men stood at the barbecue, smirking, as though Morgan had played a trump card. Serena winked at Mom. Mom looked at the men and back at Serena, pursing her lips as though to say, "They'll see."

I didn't say a word. Neither did James. It was a done deal. The adults didn't speak at dinner. Their manner was polite, but frosty as they cut their steaks and passed the potato salad. We knew the real conversation would take place later in their bedrooms as each wife took her husband to task. Before the four adults left for bridge, Morgan excused himself and went into the house, returning with his small pair of hand clippers and the flat wicker basket. He walked past the card tables and began clipping away at the early-blooming bushes. Deadheads and stems piled up on the brown wicker while we all stopped to watch Morgan from our seats around the tables. Ronald lit a cigar. Mom and Serena sipped their gin and tonics. There was precision to Morgan's work, and when he finished, he paused to present the stemmed roses to Serena. They were yellow, fragrant, and only beginning to open. Mom smiled. Ronald chuckled, and Serena bent her face into the flowers.

"Oh, thank you. They are lovely," she told him.

"Isn't it time for bridge?" Morgan asked.

Mom said, "Fred, put those deadheads on the compost pile and put your father's tools away." She waved her hand at me. I jumped like a butler. It was the first time an adult had addressed me throughout the dinner. The four of them stood up, pushing back the card chairs to meander across the Days' driveway. The little kids tagged along. Charlotte held Ronald's hand and Laurence held Morgan's.

"Don't forget to do the dishes," Mom called out over her shoulder. The sun was coming down. The four of them looked young and sporty. The men wore Van Heusen sport shirts and khaki trousers. Our mothers were in sleeveless linen dresses that broke at their knees. Mom's dress was lime green, and Serena's was a butter yellow that nearly matched the roses she carried. In the light from the dying sun, our parents looked elegant and in charge.

As we collected the bowls and plates, Sarah said, "I want to see the Rolling Stones, too."

"You can't," I told her.

"Why?"

"Because you're not invited."

"Who said I'm not invited?"

"I did," I said, looking at James.

"Well, I'm going to ask Mom and Mrs. Day," Sarah said, tossing one of her braids, then marched up the path to the back door with all the plates.

"Girls," I mumbled to James, but he still didn't say anything as he followed Sarah with the platters and salad bowl.

On Sunday, Mom and Serena told Sarah that she could go to the Rolling Stones with us. For days, I fought with Mom about Sarah, when I wasn't bickering with Sarah about the concert. I didn't want Sarah to go, because in my twelve-year-old mind, the Rolling Stones belonged to James and Uncle Ian and me. Sarah was eleven, a girl, my younger sister, and by these definitions alone, she was hogging in on my band, my best friend, and my music.

"Sarah goes, or no one goes," Mom finally said to me. "I don't want to hear any more about this, Fred Holly."

After Mom threw down that gauntlet, I refused to speak to Sarah. Who then refused to speak to me. A week before the concert, James told me he wouldn't go if Sarah and I weren't speaking.

"I won't have any fun, if you and Sarah are like this," he said in the attic after he and Sarah had practiced a new tap routine. Sarah ended it with sticking her tongue out at me and flouncing down the attic stairs in an angry thunder of metallic clicks.

For a moment in the morning light of the attic I thought about not speaking to James, too. Everyone seemed to be bent on ruining the concert for me. My vision of James and me, dancing in the aisles of Omaha's Civic Auditorium on June 13 was beginning to take on a fractured look. The moms were never part of my imaginary equation. Having to take Sarah along made the whole event seem to me like going to a circus, or a children's play, not a rock 'n' roll concert.

I considered taking a stance against James and Sarah, the moms, and our fathers. A stance for my dream of James and me, in T-shirts and blue jeans, with our bangs combed down over our foreheads, dancing in our Beatle boots and the black leather jackets we did not own but longed for. I believed in my dream of the music and how it would sound and how the whole band would look down off the stage and know that James and I were cool. Cool in a way that boys with sisters and mothers in linen dresses could never be.

In my heart I was a rebel. My heart was covered in black leather and a lit cigarette dangled off my heart's lip. I wanted to be free of chaperones and sisters and mothers and rules and fathers who stood around and made fun of the Beatles and Elvis and the Rolling Stones. I was tired of Perry Como and Bing and Johnny Mathis and Frank Sinatra. Of neatness, melody, and punctuated rhythms. All of this burst in my chest as James toweled sweat off his face from the tap-dance practice. I turned to him, ready to declare myself against Sarah and the moms, until I looked into his eyes.

James Day's eyes were dark blue, like the marbles that we traded at school. They could sparkle in happiness and open up like an ocean. But when I looked into his eyes that morning all I could see were clouds. For the first time, I noticed how blue can go to black in the human expression.

"Fred, I'd rather not go, if you and Sarah are going to fight," he said with troubled eyes.

"Sarah and I fight all the time. We fight over the bathroom and over who will get the first piece of pie. You've been watching us fight for years."

"But, I've never been in the middle of the fight. And I would rather give up the Rolling Stones than live through this anymore. You both want me to take sides. I can't. I won't. You and Sarah are both my friends." He looked at me steadily with his stormy eyes. My eyes broke first.

Hearing him say that Sarah was his friend, too, was like the pain of a thousand cuts. A stab. I stood there torn between breaking off with James altogether and not going to the Rolling Stones. In those seconds, I considered my life alone without James, without any friends, without ever speaking again. The prospect felt bleak and dangerous. I was mad at him and Sarah and the moms, and especially Morgan, who had dealt the card forcing the moms and, ultimately, Sarah on us and on the Rolling Stones.

I turned on James then, ready to tell him that I didn't care. That I didn't give a shit or a damn or even a fuck about his feelings. All the filthy words I was never allowed to say for fear of Mom clipping me halfway across the kitchen came to me in a rush that morning in the attic. But again, I looked into James's eyes and could see pools of tears in his clouded whites.

There is that knowledge between boys and men that if a friendship breaks, no matter how deep, or long, or what amount of unspoken love stands between them, that it breaks permanently. Forever. Shattered. Unmendable. We were there, James and I. I stood at the edge of my words and our friendship and the silence that could go on forever between us, knowing somehow that I didn't want to live without him as my friend.

"Okay," I said, looking over his shoulder at a picture of the Beatles on the *Ed Sullivan Show* that I'd torn from a magazine and taped to the attic's cedar wall. "I'll drop it. It's okay that Sarah's coming. The most important thing is that we'll get to see the Rolling Stones. Like your Uncle Ian says, we'll be on the cutting edge. They are the music." Then I punched him in the shoulder. His eyes brightened. The tears receded. He punched me back playfully.

With no comprehension of the feelings that drove it, I stepped back from the abyss of life without James. I didn't understand that I loved him. Or how rare it is to have a friend like James to love.

THE ROLLING STONES were everything Uncle Ian promised. They were blues-laced rock 'n' roll at its most louche and most frightening. They dressed in black and leather. Their full young lips sneered in half smiles and full leers. They were the figures of Morgan's nightmares. James, Sarah, the moms, and I were there in the small crowd of fifteen hundred people in the Civic Auditorium that could have held four thousand bodies. Dressed in our Beatle boots with our bangs slicked down and plastered onto on our foreheads, James and I looked ready to join the band. Our practiced sneers kept giving way to smiles of sheer delight. Our mothers were there in their lime and yellow linen summer dresses. They wore white gloves and white pumps, and carried white straw purses that matched their white straw hats. Sarah was round-eyed at the sound and the grinding sexiness of the band. Her sundress was white eyelet and she wore white patent leather sandals. Her braids swung back and forth like a pendulum to the rhythms.

Halfway through the concert, Mick Jagger pointed at Sarah from the stage and shrieked, "Little white girl, I love you," and she blushed so deep and so red that the whole band laughed. A group of white girls all dressed in black from head to toe and group of Negro women all dressed in linen sheath dresses like the moms', but in stiletto heels, turned in chorus and sang to Sarah, "Little white girl, I love you." Blushing even deeper, Sarah laughed and danced into the aisle. James and I followed. The moms sat on their folding chairs, stiff, appalled, and frightened.

Mick Jagger screamed, "Where in the hell are we?"

And all the fifteen hundred voices in the cavernous hall except the moms screamed back at him, "Omaha."

"Well, Omaha, we're gonna play it loud." Then everyone in the auditorium, but our mothers, screamed like banshees and the Rolling

Stones played it loud.

The moms were silent as we walked back to the Studebaker under the orange glow of the city's green gas lamps. People kept calling out to Sarah, "Hey, little white girl," and Sarah would smile and wave to them. James and I kept dancing and playing our imaginary guitars. Ripping through words and chords, we continued to press down on our bangs, hoping to cover our foreheads.

"What will we tell the men?" Serena asked, looking across the front seat as Mom adjusted the rearview mirror of the Studebaker.

"We'll tell them they were loud."

"Will that be enough?"

Mom snorted. "More than enough. If they wanted to know so much about the Rolling Stones, they should have come along." Then she revved the engine and the black leather jacket on my heart loosened toward her, softening its rebel stance, if only momentarily. My heart's lip lit its cigarette, blew white smoke rings to Omaha's starry skies, and sang all the way home.

Charlotte

THESE ARE ALL the things that I never tell anyone about my sister Charlotte. She was ten and going into fifth grade the fall of my senior year in high school. All summer long, she had made raids on my room, borrowing my records without asking so that she could play them in the attic with her best friend, Hetty. Charlotte sometimes scratched the records. She sometimes forgot to put them back into their sleeves and in their correct place on the shelf above my bed. I would find them in the attic on the player, turning around and around and around. Sometimes she borrowed change out of my top drawer so that she and Hetty could buy ice-cream bars at Bogart's Drug Store. The change was always a permanent loan. When I discovered evidence of her transgressions, or if I was able to get Laurence to implicate her, I would pick her up and not so delicately press her against the attic's cedar walls, threatening her within an inch of her life while I accused her of playing my records and stealing my change. Not once did she cry. Never did she give in. Every time, she denied my accounts of her wrongdoing, yelling right back into my face.

"You're so full of it, Fred Holly," she would scream at me, her freckled face going deep red and her blue eyes challenging my very presence as she dangled from my hands against the wall.

"Just leave my stuff, alone. Keep your dirty little paws off of it," I would say, giving her a shake.

"I didn't touch your stuff."

"Charlotte, don't lie," I'd say back to her, always appalled at her ability to plead innocence when she was so clearly in the wrong. The turntable was still spinning and Hershey's Kisses wrappers were scattered across the floor.

"Did you ask Sarah? She loves Hershey's Kisses," Charlotte continued in her self-defense from her precarious position on the wall. "Or maybe James stopped by," she added. But she never implicated Laurence, knowing that that would push the situation into the realm of real falsehood for me, and in my eyes, real sin.

Our relationship that summer of 1969 seemed to be based on her transgressions, my accusations, and our moments of yelling at each other. In my memory, her red hair is fanned out against the brown knots of the attic's cedar walls. She was chubby and compact, the way little girls are before their bursts of growth. As I held her against the wall she seemed small to me.

Thirty years later, my body still remembers the flush of anger at the discovery of a scratch on my *Let It Bleed* album. I still have that Stones album, scratch and all. It has moved with me all over the United States, from dormitories to apartments to first houses to fourth houses, existing within my vast collection of albums as a memory of Charlotte in vinyl. What I didn't understand then, in that last summer I would spend with Charlotte, was how little time I did spend with her. How little attention I gave to her and Laurence after I entered high school. Three decades and graying hair have taught me what little children, and those you love, will do for attention.

In the summer of 1969, I worked at the Joslyn Art Museum doing odd jobs—anything a curator, a docent, or the head janitor, Herb Pepper, asked of me. Sometimes I spent hours cutting open boxes, and other days I cut the grass. At night, James, Micah, Joshua, and I would take off in James's Galaxy 500 to places unknown, going farther afield in Omaha than we had ever gone, to listen to the radio and drink beer in parks, and dream our dreams together. Late at night we would drive east into Iowa over the Missouri River, paying the toll at the Mormon Bridge, to discover the signals of radio stations in faraway places. Voices from Little Rock, Arkansas, Cincinnati, Ohio, and Casper, Wyoming, would reach us. They were as foreign and exciting to us as those of visitors from another planet.

Our parents were upset about the Vietnam War in the summer of 1969. Morgan and Ronald Day were uncomfortable with the notion that within months, both James and I would have to register for the draft. That their sons could be drafted, sent to a war that few people seemed to understand and where they could ultimately die, frightened them. They wanted Vietnam to be a good war like World War II, in which Americans served and died to save lives and freedom. Morgan and Ronald were Nixon supporters, as were most people in Nebraska, but Serena and Mom were not. Their Saturday nights grew far more verbal, with the women accusing the men of automatically being for the war if they were for Nixon. James and I could hear them arguing as we quietly pushed the Galaxy 500 down the drive so as not to be noticed as we made our way into the night.

Both of our fathers had served in World War II and seen action. They used the word "serve," with an earnest gruffness. Like rock music, the idea that a boy would seek refuge in Canada or apply for conscientious objector status was repellent to them. I refused to worry about it that summer. Maybe it was because I was among a generation that had already effortlessly dodged so many bullets—polio, the red measles, tuberculosis, diphtheria, tetanus. I understood the power of antibiotics and the luxury of vaccinations. My health was a product of the times: a confluence of wealth, research, and serendipity.

Unlike my parents' and Ronald and Serena Day's childhoods, my childhood had never been interrupted by war, poverty, or economic depression. The cratered streets of a war-torn England were the nursery of Serena's experience. Morgan grew up hard in the thirties, standing on Omaha's street corners late into the night, waiting to pick up some work shining shoes, selling newspapers, or cleaning up after a fruit vendor. He did this from the time he was eight not only to earn his keep but also to help out his maternal grandmother, who raised him. Morgan saw World War II and its draft as opportunities. After the war, the G.I. Bill provided an education, giving him his profession as an actuary. Morgan's experiences were the stories of my childhood, but they were not my childhood. I was a child for far longer than either of my parents. I grew up with the security of the Mutual of Omaha paychecks that came each month on the tenth and the twenty-fifth, and Mutual of Omaha health insurance that paid for my pediatrician and all the scrapes and illnesses of my youth. I saw dentists and ophthalmologists, wore braces, got glasses. Every day in 1969, brochures arrived in the mail from colleges all over the United States. My life was not my parents' lives. Everything their children experienced—health, safety, education, robust economy—was new and foreign to both Morgan and Mom.

I did not believe that I was going to die in Vietnam, or anywhere else, for that matter. This was not because I related the war to my health or good fortune or my place in the universe. My belief rested solely on the fact that I was seventeen years old. At seventeen, my body raged with potency. I didn't believe I could die. I didn't believe in death. A sense ran through me that anything was possible. I believed in the likelihood of my not getting drafted at all. In the end, Vietnam was a numbers game, and I was the son of an actuary who was ready to toss the dice.

Morgan found my attitude wanting.

"There are boys dying in Vietnam," he said to me that spring as we tipped a wheelbarrow to dump a mixture of compost and manure at the base of the rosebushes.

"Morgan, that doesn't mean I'm going to get drafted. Or even if I were to get drafted, it doesn't necessarily mean I'll end up in Vietnam. I'll apply for a deferment."

"Deferments are unfair," he said, looking up at me from where he knelt, spreading out the foul-smelling mixture around a bush. "In World War II, no one would have thought of not serving. Everyone served, except farmers and the Quakers, but the Quakers went to work camps and the farmers grew food. College boys went to war."

"Well, Morgan what do you want me to do? Get drafted? Enlist?"

"Fred, I want you to have a plan."

"That is my plan. I'll register, see what my draft number is, and go on from there. If it's a bad number, I'll apply for a college deferment. If it isn't, I'll go to college like I've always planned and not worry about the deferment."

Morgan stood up, lit a Marlboro, and pushed his glasses back up on the ridge of his nose.

"You'd never go to Canada would you?"

"Why do you always ask me that?"

"I just want to know."

"It's the guys at work, isn't it? None of them have sons, so they pick at the bones of my skeleton and your honor, wanting to know what I'm going to do."

He looked away from me and I knew it was true. "But you wouldn't go to Canada would you?"

"Damn it, Morgan, if I ever hear that those guys at the office had a pool on my draft number or what I would do, I swear, you'll never see me again. I hate the way they examine my life and my choices as though they're public property."

Morgan's colleagues knew everything about us. They knew our birth dates, they knew our birth weights, and they gambled on everything. Probability was their bread and butter. No pregnancy passed without a collective pool. They gambled on the minutes a colleague would be late to work, factoring in his stop for a ten-cent *Omaha World-Herald* and his wave to the clerk of his dreams. They could gamble on something as simple as Cornhusker football, but they would rather gamble on how many times Marlin Perkins would use the word "Jim" in an episode of *Mutual of Omaha's Wild Kingdom*.

Mom once said, "Those guys would gamble on how many angels could fit on the head of pin, if only they could get an angel's measurements."

Morgan had responded. "We would, but first we'd have to factor in a belief in angels. And actuaries are unlikely believers in the intangible."

"But would you go to Canada?" Morgan persisted.

"Would you rather have me dead in Vietnam or alive in Canada?"

"Well, what if they stop giving out college deferments and you get the wrong number?" he asked, blowing a smoke ring toward the sunset.

"Then I'll try and enlist in some branch of the service where I won't get killed in Vietnam."

Morgan sighed and took a deep puff on the Marlboro.

"Or I'll go to Canada," I said, grinning.

And he began to choke, "Goddamn it, Fred."

"Well, that's pretty much my plan."

"That's no plan. You have to have a plan."

***

VIETNAM HAUNTED MORGAN. Every time we were together, he would ask what I was going to do. At dinner, in the garden, at night as I was walking down the hallway to bed, he would stop me, or I would find him staring at me. He worried about my situation almost constantly that summer. Many times the conversations moved down bad and bumpy roads, leaving Morgan and me shouting at one another. I tried to disappear as much as I could, taking extra hours at the Joslyn, or staying out until I knew everyone would be asleep.

One night at dinner after watching the battle footage of a particularly gruesome television news report, Morgan started in on me again. It was a very hot night. We were in the kitchen, eating bacon, lettuce, and tomato sandwiches with the fan on and the lights off.

"Fred, boys are dying over there," Morgan began.

Mom gave him a warning look.

Sarah whispered, "Morgan, please don't."

Charlotte and Laurence watched Morgan and me like we were a Ping-Pong game.

"I know that, Morgan," I told him, biting into my sandwich, hoping that he would stop before he got started.

"You have decisions ahead of you."

I nodded, my mouth full.

"Your life depends on these decisions, son."

"Yes, Morgan," I mumbled as I swallowed.

"You could die, Fred."

Sarah and Mom looked shocked. I felt as though someone had punched me. My bite of sandwich sank into my stomach like a greasy piece of lead.

"Stop this right now, Morgan Holly. Enough already. I won't let you say another word," Mom hissed at him.

"Is Fred going to die?" Laurence asked, his lip quivering.

"Fred is not going to die," Mom said, bending over Laurence at the end of the table and wiping bacon grease off his chin. "But this conversation is going to stop. I am making it a rule of our house that we never discuss the Vietnam War at any meal again. Ever."

Morgan looked grim. "Eileen, I'm only trying to point out to Fred the gravity of the situation. He isn't taking anything seriously enough."

"We will not discuss this now, Morgan. You're frightening the younger children."

Unable to finish my sandwich, I slipped it onto the plate, waiting for dinner to end, so that I could escape into the summer night, away from Morgan and his questions.

"It's the music. It's Fred's goddamn music. All that rock-'n'-roll shit."

"Morgan, don't use that word at my table."

Morgan glowered at me, but I didn't say a word.

BACK THEN, I didn't say a word because I knew that my silence upset Morgan more than my words. My silence was evidence of all the things that Morgan suspected me of—revealing a nonchalance about patriotism, a disrespect for my elders, and worst of all, an optimism about my future. Morgan distrusted what he could not control, and he believed that worry—constant, diligent worry—was the coin that the gods subtracted from humans for their protection. Confidence was the coin of fools. It was flying too close to the sun.

ONLY ONCE DID Charlotte really get back at me during our hot summer of confrontations. I had her pinned against the attic wall. The scent of grape juice, graham crackers, and the baby powder that Mom made her wear to fight heat rash floated off her like a cloud. She smelled like a kid. A little kid.

"Fred, you don't care about anything but yourself and your music. You can just go die in Vietnam for all I care," she said to me.

I looked into her flashing blue eyes and put her down. An album was spinning around and around and around on the turntable. I put the needle down on a groove. The Beatles sang, "She loves you, yeah, yeah, yeah," and I covered my face and sobbed to its poppy sappiness. Charlotte stood behind me in the heat of the attic.

"Fred," she said, "I didn't mean it."

"Charlotte, just go. Leave me alone."

Whatever I was facing at the dawn of my eighteenth birthday, it was nothing that a ten-year-old child could understand. But Charlotte understood far more than I did that Morgan's words carried weight with me. Hearing him through her hurt more than hearing him.

"I'm sorry," she said in a small, scared voice as I crumpled to the floor, pressing my face against the dusty floorboards.

To my great surprise, Charlotte kissed me on the crown of my head, before leaving me alone to cry in the attic. Her kiss lingered there. It brought about the beginning of a truce between us. I began to ignore missing change and she began, more often than not, to return my albums to their white sleeves and protective covers and place them on the shelf above my bed. Our flare-ups seemed to settle more quickly after that. She was a child who always wanted to help. Who believed in the power of a kiss. There on the floor with Morgan's frightening specter of war unleashed through Charlotte's words, I knew how much I did not want to die. I knew how much I loved my life, and, even then, Charlotte's place within it.

In Love

WE WERE ALL in love in September of 1969, or wanting to be in love, or denying that we were in love, or denying that we wanted to be in love. It was all Romeo and Juliet for us at Central High School, on its hilltop post overlooking downtown Omaha. Central was our citadel of longing and dreams. There, I was still a man-child who could plan a life undefined by my future draft status. The teachers refused to see the boys as only fodder for war and the girls as merely the recipients of broken hearts and pregnancy. For the teachers' dreams were linked to ours. In quiet and subversive ways, they pressed on a contained discussion of a future for us undetermined by the Vietnam War. They planted in us the seeds of hope that we could pursue dreams beyond the scope of our backgrounds and our beliefs. They pushed us relentlessly to work hard, but that never stopped us from falling in love. The teachers' dreams, our dreams, and love all commingled, floating up and down the boys' stairs in oily hormonal clouds to waft over to the girls' stairs, meeting bursts of fragrance mixed with longing that sometimes penetrated the smoking denizens of the faculty lounge. Scent and sensation pierced our teachers, leaving them sadly bewildered by desire.

I was in love with Arianna Isaacs. She was the daughter of a rabbi and captain of the debate team. James and Sarah were both debaters. I was not. Arianna was in love with Micah Little and Micah was in love with Arianna. All the students and all the teachers knew that they were in love. Many students, probably most students, felt that their love was ruinous. Black girls harangued loudly in the bathrooms about white girls stealing the best and the brightest of Omaha's Negro society. White boys, particularly Jewish boys, predicted Arianna's ruin if she ever *did it* with him.

"No white guy is ever going to marry her, if she's done it with some colored boy," a guy named Stan told me at the urinal underneath the Benson High School stadium during a September football game. It was two weeks after their love affair became public in the school's parking lot.

"Micah's my friend," I told Stan. "He's a good guy from a good family."

"Don't be a fool. Of course, he's a good guy, but he's black as the ace of spades. Rabbi Isaacs would have a heart attack if he knew. Hell, Micah's mama would probably kill him if she found out, if Micah's old girlfriend doesn't kill Arianna first. Jesus Christ, this is Omaha, for God's sakes, not New York."

"People have no right to say who another person can love," I told him, leaning away from Stan and his smell of Aqua Velva, piss, and pragmatism.

"God love ya, Fred, you're such a fucking dreamer," Stan replied as he took leave of me and the bathroom to get back to the football game being played above us, where Micah and Joshua were stars of the team.

"You tiny dick-brain," I whispered to Stan's urinal. The roar from the field filtered down to me, alone in the boys' john. I stood there, believing in my defense of Micah and Arianna because it was my defense, too. I loved Arianna to the point that it hurt. It was a foolish love, not because Arianna's father would have loathed a Catholic boy any more or less than an African Methodist Episcopal Negro boy. No, that was not why. It was a foolish love because Arianna did not love me. She felt nothing for me. Not friendship, not debate team spirit. We barely knew each other, except to say hello in the halls, or to nod when I walked into a tournament to watch Sarah and James debate.

To be quite frank, I would not even have noticed Arianna at the debate tournaments except that James was the match that lit Arianna Isaacs's flame. It was his way with girls. James liked them. I believed it was from all those years of tap dancing, where he lived his life in the studio as the frequently lone male. He understood the ways of girls' language and the peculiar nature of their feelings. The smells of girls, their enticing movements, never affected James. He teased them and talked to them as naturally as he did to me. For James, a girl would light up. I could watch a girl become her finest self there in the hallway, or in the classrooms that made up the arenas of debate team competition when James said hello.

During the February of our junior year, I slipped into a classroom to watch James debate when Arianna Isaacs called out to him in a fake English accent, "Oh, Jimmy, old boy."

And he responded, "Yes, darling, my tea cozy, my crumpet," in the purest of English accents. One that he rarely used, or at least not around me.

The two of them bantered back and forth. I watched Arianna at ease with James. Her playfulness, the extreme silliness that James brought out in her, struck me that afternoon, and something inside me split. Arianna began to spill into my consciousness. The opening continued to widen and I noticed her everywhere. More and more of her presence pushed its way into my world until I longed to touch her as I did the bronze toe of a statue or the gilded frame of a painting at the Joslyn.

Arianna Isaacs became my secret longing my senior year. The girl I fantasized about at night in my bed while I listened to the thrum of Laurence's breathing and the purring of Tiger Cat. In the drowsy halfway point between wakefulness and dreams, I lived those nights with the comfort of boys and men: If there was no Arianna to touch there was always something on me to feel. Meager pleasure though it was, it brought me solace without hope.

Knowing that my love was fruitless, I placed my hope in Micah, who, like James, also awakened something in Arianna. For if Arianna did not love me, I wanted her to love Micah. When I saw them standing together in the parking lot next to Annie Little's tan Ford Fairlane while Joshua stood a respectful two yards away, waiting to drive home, Arianna blossomed. I watched her come alive in a far more vivid way than when she was with James. There was a rare and unique happiness between them during those public moments in the parking lot. We all stopped—students and teachers—to glance obliquely and sometimes boldly at the pair.

Love between them seemed to be a long, musical conversation. Rifts of words focused on the telling of stories. Stories about church organs with broken pipes and cantors with laryngitis were shared there on the crushed white gravel of the Central High School parking lot. Statements, declarations, and questions were put forth with frequent references to "my papa" or "my mom." Whether the sun shone down on them or the blustery Omaha winds blew them about, Arianna and Micah stopped in the parking lot daily by the Ford Fairlane, within the safe demarcations of school and language, to be with each other. They were in love.

One day during the first week in September, as James and I were standing in the parking lot next to his Ford Galaxy 500, waiting for Sarah, James said to me, "I worry about them, Fred," and he looked toward Micah and Arianna.

"Why? They're in love," I told him, turning to look at James, whose eyes were troubled.

"But it's a taboo love," James said, shaking his head.

"What's taboo about their love?" I asked him.

"It's hard to be different," James said. "It's hard to live in the open when society's against you."

"Like you would know about that?" I challenged him.

"Try tap dancing as an extracurricular activity, Fred, and see the look on people's faces when you tell them."

"Well, maybe you just need to fall in love and see what it's like," I told him.

"So you're an expert on love now, Fred?"

"Well, almost as much as you are, James."

He laughed. I could see Sarah walking out the door, waving to us.

I believed that if James could fall in love, he would understand Micah and Arianna and have hope for them, too. I believed that I lived alone in the world of secret longings and love.

Kidneys

LATE IN THE afternoon of the third Thursday in September of 1969, as Sarah and I were eating Jell-O, green beans, and macaroni and cheese laced with chunks of hot dogs, before leaving for the Central High School football game being played that evening against Creighton Preparatory High School—our archrival among the private schools—Charlotte walked into the kitchen. Her cheeks were flushed and puffy and she was whining, "Mom, I want to go to the game with Fred and Sarah."

"Charlotte Anne Holly, we have been over this a thousand times. You are too young to go to the game with Fred and Sarah. Someday you will be in high school and then you will go to high school football games. Let me see your cheeks."

Charlotte wandered over to bury her face just below Mom's right shoulder. Mom put her arms around her, kissing the crown of her red head. Charlotte's hair looked rich and lush compared to Mom's, which was fading. Strands of white sprouted next to the hair that she kept a faint orange with the help of weekly henna rinses.

"Why can't you and Morgan take me? Other parents go to the games. Laurence wants to go, too."

"Because Morgan and I are old fogies. And because I have to work tomorrow and you have school. Let me see your face." Mom pushed Charlotte's shoulders back and cupped her cheeks.

"Sweetie, you feel a little warm; maybe there won't be any school for you tomorrow." Mom peered at her. "And you look a little puffy. I wonder if you have the mumps." She put the back of her right hand on both of Charlotte's cheeks. "Well, Morgan will have to take you to Dr. Jensen's in the morning. Sarah and Fred can watch you in the afternoon, because they'll be home." The teachers in the high schools were doing an in-service day so we were starting the weekend early.

"Not Dr. Jensen," Charlotte whined. "He gives shots."

"There aren't shots for mumps," Mom said.

She hugged Charlotte again and then walked across the kitchen floor, and opened the back door to step out. From the window we watched her cross the backyard to where Morgan was working with his rose bushes, getting them ready for their ritual winter burial under bushels and bushels of fallen leaves.

"Take me to the game, Fred," Charlotte persisted.

"No, Charlotte, you heard Mom," I told her.

"Sarah, please make Fred take me to the game." Charlotte threw herself onto Sarah's lap. "Please, please, please."

"Oh, honey, I'm sorry, but Mom and Morgan don't want you at the games. They want you to stay home. Fred and I never went to high school games when we were ten. Besides, sweetie, you're sick. I'll get you some 7-Up." Sarah gently lifted Charlotte out of her lap to stand up and headed toward the pantry. Charlotte sat down in Sarah's chair.

"James won't mind if I go," Charlotte continued as Laurence walked into the room. I got up from the table to get a plate for him.

"Charlotte, you're sick, and if you weren't sick, you'd have school tomorrow," I told her, avoiding any discussion of James, who I knew would take both her and Laurence to the game if asked.

"You're mean, Fred, you're always mean to me."

Laurence sat at his place at the end of the table, staring at Charlotte and me, looking puzzled by the conversation.

"I know. I'm the meanest guy in the whole world. I'm a rotten, mean, bad guy who ruins your whole life," I said, placing the plate with Laurence's dinner in front of him. "Do you want some dinner?" I asked her, as I looked out the window again. Morgan was leaning on his pitchfork, smoking a cigarette. Mom was still talking to him. Sarah walked in with the green glass 7-Up bottle. I handed her the bottle opener.

"Can I have pop, too?" Laurence asked.

"No," Charlotte shouted. "I'm sick and you're not. You can't have any."

Laurence looked crushed at this reception.

"I always share," he said.

"Now look who's being mean," I said, putting a plateful of food in front of her.

"I am not mean. I'm sick." Red-faced, Charlotte screamed this at me as Sarah opened the 7-Up bottle. Over Charlotte's head I could see Mom walking back to the kitchen. Then Charlotte started to cry the heaving sobs of a child who is growing out of control.

"Look, Charlotte," Sarah said, "we'll take you to the homecoming parade. We'll get permission from Mom and Morgan and you can sit in the front seat with James."

"Me, too?" Laurence asked.

"Not you, Laurence, just me," Charlotte shouted through her sobs as Mom came through the kitchen door.

"Laurence goes if you go, Charlotte," I said, holding out for the hope that Mom and Morgan would say no to homecoming, too.

"I hate you, Fred Holly, I hate you," Charlotte shouted and then the tears flowed like a river down her florid face with its outsized orange freckles.

"What's going on here?" Mom asked, startled by the scene as Charlotte sent her plate of food spinning across the table and bolted from the kitchen.

"She's mad because she can't go to the football game," I said.

"And she doesn't feel well," Sarah added.

I bent down to pick up the plate. Macaroni, bits of hot dog, green beans, and the orange Jell-O were strewn across the red and green linoleum tiles.

"Did you tease her, Fred?" Mom asked.

"Not really," I said.

"Sarah, did he tease her?" Mom looked to Sarah.

"No, Mom, Fred didn't tease her. Charlotte's just mad about the football game."

Holding a spoonful of Jell-O, Laurence looked up from his plate and said, "Hetty's going."

"What?" I asked him.

"Hetty's going to the game with her mom and dad. Charlotte told me."

Charlotte told Laurence everything.

"If Hetty walked off a cliff, I swear, Charlotte would follow," Mom sighed. She took the glass of 7-Up from Sarah. "I'd better go talk to her."

<hr>

THE FOOTBALL GAME was at Creighton Prep's field. When I was in sixth grade, Morgan took me on a long walk. We walked to the Cathedral of St. Cecilia and then back to Dodge Street, walking east past the Mutual of Omaha tower all the way downtown, only to walk back home again. It was several miles of walking where Morgan smoked and said nothing. Puzzled and exhausted, I was thrilled to turn onto Thirty-eighth Street and make our way home. Serena Day waved to us from her desk in the sunroom as we walked past their big blond-brick house. After we waved back, Morgan spoke.

"Would you like to go to Creighton Prep for high school?"

"No," I said. James then walked into Serena's office. He gave us his big, long-armed wave.

We both waved back to him.

"Why not?" Morgan asked, dropping his cigarette to the cement and grinding it into the apron of our driveway.

"No girls there," I said, "I like girls."

"Is that the only reason?"

"Well," I told him, "James won't be there. He's not Catholic. I want to go to school with him."

"No other reason?" Morgan asked.

"Well," I said, pausing to think. We stood there on the driveway for a few minutes so that I could think. Morgan lit another cigarette. What finally occurred to me was to ask Morgan a question. "Who's the most brilliant guy you've ever met?"

"Saul Kripke," Morgan said without a moment's hesitation.

"Where did he go to high school, Morgan?"

"Central High School."

"Well, then if Central High School was good enough for Saul Kripke, it's good enough for me."

"Well, your mother was wondering if you might like a more religious education. She was wondering if you might like to give the Jesuits a chance."

"Where did you go to high school, Morgan?"

"Central High School. But that's not the point," he said, pushing his glasses up the bridge of his nose before inhaling on the Marlboro.

"I get enough religion at the cathedral on Sunday. I don't want to spend every day with a bunch of priests. I'll go to Central with James and Sarah."

"Your mother might be disappointed."

"Don't let her make me go there, Morgan."

"It isn't hell."

"It would be for me," I told him.

I THOUGHT ABOUT Saul Kripke at the game that Friday night. How Morgan and a group of actuaries and statisticians once hosted a lunch for Saul Kripke on a Sunday at the Omaha Athletic Club, when he was just thirteen. It was a story I had heard several times. After they ate their kosher chicken, the men started to ask Kripke questions and all of them ended up writing out long mathematical problems for him to solve on the athletic club's white tablecloths. This went on for three and a half hours, with the thirteen-year-old Saul Kripke moving from table to table solving the problems. The men bought the tablecloths from the club manager to keep as souvenirs. Morgan was stunned by the boy's mathematical gifts. "It was like meeting Einstein," he'd tell us. Teachers at Central, mathematics teachers especially, talked about Saul Kripke the whole time I was in high school. Saul Kripke was, and is, brilliant at symbolic logic—a higher form of calculus. It seemed to me that Kripke left a kind of sheen on the old walls of Central High School. The polish of his acme was something I was ready to believe in far more than the Jesuits. I felt saved by him.

But there were always girls to consider as I stared down at Arianna Isaacs, who stood along the sidelines to watch the game, putting herself that much closer to Micah Little. Most of the time, Arianna didn't come to the games because she was at Sabbath services. Since this game was on a Thursday night, she could watch Micah play. And I could watch her. I loved girls and I felt no desire to ever attend schools that did not admit them. I could not imagine spending every school day without girls. Looking across at our opponents with their blue sweaters and letter jackets and male cheerleaders, I shuddered. For me, living day in and day out in large crowds of boys would be like living at the stockyard. I could only imagine the farts, the stink from deodorant that was never applied, the bullying, the ragging, and the horrible things that a bunch of horny boys would say about girls. I looked at Sarah, glad that she was far away from all those Creighton Prep boys with their smells and their thoughts. Sarah, of course, was staring at the hundreds of boys with a look of mixed fear and curiosity. Beside her, James was watching the game. He once told me that he didn't think Creighton Prep would be that bad. I told him he was crazy.

At half-time, the bands filed onto the field and James elbowed me.

"I need to speak with someone over there." He pointed at the wall of Creighton Prep blue.

"Over there?" I repeated, not quite sure I'd heard him correctly in the first blaring moment of trumpets, trombones, tubas, and drums.

James was already climbing down the aluminum bleachers.

"I'll be back for the second half," he called up to me.

"I wonder where he's going," I said to Sarah.

"Oh, he's going to see his coach from debate camp. He's sitting over with the Prep kids. They all go to debate camp," she said to me, pointing at a clump of boys surrounding a tall, blond man who was laughing.

"Who's he?" I asked.

"His name is Neil Mahaffey," Sarah said.

"And he's a debate coach?" I asked.

"About eight years ago, he was one of the best debaters in Nebraska and then he debated at Northwestern. Now he's trying to decide what to do with his life. He finished at Northwestern and he's thinking about law school or the priesthood."

I started to laugh, and Sarah looked at me like I was a little crazy.

"You mean this guy actually says things like, 'Oh, it's either law school or the priesthood' "? I asked her.

"Well, not to me. He says things like that to James, who by the way takes Neil Mahaffey very seriously, and then James tells me these things. I am not on Neil Mahaffey's good side because I didn't go to his debate camp last summer. Whenever I see Neil at debate tournaments he reminds me of how much better I would be as a debater if I 'had gotten less sun over the summer and more coaching.' "

"What a prick! Why would James like a guy like that?" I asked her.

"Well, because Neil Mahaffey never speaks that way to him." Sarah's eyes were watching James on the outskirts of the crowd of boys that surrounded Mahaffey. "More important, Neil never speaks that way to me around James. He only speaks that way to me when James isn't around. Ask Arianna. He does the same to her."

"What's the deal?" I looked at Sarah in her red Pendleton jacket and gray pleated miniskirt. I couldn't understand why anyone would treat her that way.

"Neil makes cracks to Arianna and me about how girls belong pregnant and in the kitchen, and not at debate tournaments. Once Arianna and I mentioned it to Mr. Lyons, our team sponsor, and he took it to Neil. Neil told him 'he couldn't imagine what could make two girls fabricate such a tale.' That's what Mr. Lyons said to us."

"So did Lyons believe him?"

"Not exactly, but he didn't believe us, either. And that was the calculated point of it all, Fred. Whenever Neil is around Mr. Lyons now, he is ever so nice to everyone from Central. But he's a real prick to Arianna and me if we happen to run into him alone in a hallway at a tournament. He doesn't like the girls."

"Do you mean he's queer?"

"No, I mean he doesn't like women. I mean he lives his life enjoying the missionary position. Neil Mahaffey knows how to conduct himself so that he can get away with just about anything. The underbelly of debate strategy is learned calculation. Neil calculates his risks. It's what he teaches in his debate camps. He can teach you how to do it. All facts, no feelings. Neil teaches a disrespect for feelings."

I looked at James, who had penetrated the blue sweaters and was speaking to Mahaffey. James was smiling and animated. I could see that he really liked the guy. The drums on the field sounded like thunder. I waited for them to stop before asking Sarah my next question.

"But why would James like a guy like that?" I asked Sarah.

"For God sakes, Fred, James is a tap dancer." Sarah said this with more than a note of exasperation in her voice.

"So he tap-dances." I shrugged my shoulders.

"Down there James is a guy the way Micah and Joshua are guys on the football field. Mahaffey talks strategy with them. Dancers don't use the word 'annihilation,' every other minute like Neil Mahaffey does." Sarah looked uncomfortable when she said the word 'annihilation.'" The tubas oompah-pah-pahed while I thought.

"James has been always a guy in my book. Lots of guys tap-dance. Fred Astaire and Gene Kelly are guys. What's the big deal? Micah and Joshua don't think anything of James's tap dancing," I told her, not really understanding all the guy distinctions she was making.

"Yeah, but Micah and Joshua are Negro guys at an almost all-white school that has never welcomed Negroes. So they probably relate far more to tap dancing than you might think."

There was a crescendo of horns.

"But Sarah, why didn't James ever mention Neil Mahaffey to me before? I'm his best friend." I could hear a plaintive note in my voice. For a moment I felt unsteady, the way I did the summer James went away to England.

"I don't know. James is funny about Neil." Sarah paused. The teams were coming back on the field while the bands were marching off. James was climbing up the bleachers. "James wants to be the best in debate. At the state tournament last year, he told me, 'I need to shine at something, Sarah.' Neil makes him feel like he's shining, I guess." As he reached us, James's pant leg got caught on a jagged piece of aluminum, causing him to stumble forward. Sarah and I grabbed him, breaking his fall, and he grinned.

"Thanks, you guys. I don't know what I would do without you," he said.

"Who were you talking to?" I asked him.

"My debate camp coach," James said, his eyes again on the game.

Our team kicked off. James focused on the play. I did not know how to ask him more questions and he did not volunteer any information. I kept staring at Neil Mahaffey, who was cheering on Creighton Prep. He was blond and tall and handsome. Then I would sneak glances at James, trying to see a change in him. But I couldn't. He was James to me. Taller and stronger, but still brown-haired James. It frustrated me that I could not see the connection between Neil Mahaffey and James. Or feel it. But when Central beat Creighton Prep, I was happy. To me it felt as though our football players had beaten Neil Mahaffey.

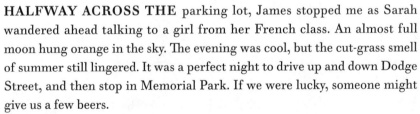

HALFWAY ACROSS THE parking lot, James stopped me as Sarah wandered ahead talking to a girl from her French class. An almost full moon hung orange in the sky. The evening was cool, but the cut-grass smell of summer still lingered. It was a perfect night to drive up and down Dodge Street, and then stop in Memorial Park. If we were lucky, someone might give us a few beers.

"Look, Fred," James said, "my debate coach invited me to go out to eat with him and talk strategy. Would you mind taking the car home?"

"But you're supposed to go out after the game with Sarah and me," I told him, hearing a heatedness in my voice.

"I didn't expect to see Neil here," James said. "There's just some debate stuff I would really need to talk to him about. It's a lucky thing for me that he was here."

"Yeah, but James, the whole plan was to celebrate after the game if we won. It was a big game. We beat Prep."

"Look, I'm sorry. I didn't think you would care."

But James didn't look sorry. He looked irritated.

"James, get the lead out," I heard someone shout from the other side of the parking lot. I turned to see Neil Mahaffey standing next to a tan Volkswagen bug. He was waving at James. James gave him his big-armed wave in return. Then he turned to me.

"Please, Fred. Take the car home and leave the door unlocked at your house. I'll let myself in. We'll go out tomorrow night." He handed me the keys to the Galaxy 500 and started to sprint around the cars and clumps of bodies until he reached Neil Mahaffey. I watched James smile and climb into the passenger seat of the Volkswagen. I could feel myself flush. A feeling that might have been jealousy or anger or despair washed over me. I didn't know the name for the feeling. I still don't. Tears pricked at my eyes. I was so startled that Neil Mahaffey, whoever he was, had appeared in my life, and that James had left with him, and not with me. The whole evening was not the evening that I'd expected. I knew there was no possibility of me walking away from James, or our friendship. Our friendship was beyond the point of ending. It would be like leaving my arms or my legs or my eyes behind me. I felt alone for the first time. I hated that sensation, especially among the hundreds of people walking past me in the parking lot.

I found Sarah sitting in the back of the Ford Galaxy 500. James had left the convertible top down.

"Where's James?"

"He went to a party with Neil Mahaffey," I told her. "Why don't you sit up front. I hate to play the chauffeur."

"No, James is best at that," she said. There was a cautiousness to her tone.

"I told Micah and Joshua that we'd do something with them after the game. I told them we meet up with them at school."

I didn't want to go then, but I drove downtown to meet the team bus. Sarah and I watched from the car as the players piled off holding their helmets and cheering. Joshua's girlfriend, Lily Baker, hugged him. I could see Arianna Isaacs standing with a bunch of girls. Micah blew her a kiss. She caught it in cupped hands, bringing her fingertips to her lips. With her arms folded across her chest, Annie Little stood by her Ford Fairlane, watching the trajectory of Micah's kiss.

Joshua and Lily came up to us.

"Hey," Joshua said, "it's a partying night. Mom brought us the car." Annie was talking to Micah, who was looking toward Arianna.

"I think we're gonna head home," I told him. Sarah's eyebrows arched, but she didn't disagree with me.

"Where's James?" Joshua asked.

"He saw his debate coach and they decided to talk over strategy," I told Joshua.

Joshua shrugged. "Are you sure you don't want to go out? There's a party not far from here."

"Tomorrow could be a long day. I told the janitor at the Joslyn that I would help him tear down some crates tomorrow morning. And something's up with Charlotte, mumps or something. Our folks might need me to pick up Laurence from school, so we'd better go home." Sarah and Lily were watching Annie Little tap her index finger angrily on Micah's sternum as Micah shook his head. Joshua turned his eyes from me to them.

"I think my brother might need me. Call me, Fred. We can go out tomorrow. Just the guys." Joshua's hand trailed a wave as he and Lily walked up to Annie and Micah. Arianna and her friends watched the mother and son from under the spitting glow of a street lamp. Their arms had fallen to their sides, and their animation, the giggles and tiny shrieks of waiting girls, had died. Arianna looked solemn, and my heart, always so full of her, cracked a little. For a moment I forgot James and wondered about love and my love for her, and how it could bring her no solace in the face of a mother's wrath.

We drove home in silence. I parked the Galaxy 500 on the side of the

Days' driveway and pulled the convertible hood down snugly, just as James always did. The light was on for us and the front door, unlocked. We left it unlocked with the light off for James. It was not late.

I grabbed a pack of Marlboros from Morgan's carton in the kitchen and Sarah poured us each a rum and Coke. Mom and Morgan never drank rum. They kept it at the back of the liquor cabinet for guests and they were not completely puzzled by its flow level when, on the rare occasion, they went looking for it. Morgan didn't want us smoking, because he saw the daily toll that tobacco took on life. It was there in his actuarial charts, but he himself couldn't stop. "Please don't be like me," he would say to us, "please don't smoke." Sarah and I were secret, rare smokers; we didn't even do it with James. Like incense, the burn of Marlboros linked us to the primal, smoky scent of Morgan that must have calmed us in the womb. Drinking, I think, if it didn't get out of hand, never frightened Morgan. "Discipline the drink Fred," he would tell me, "or don't drink." What Morgan didn't want to see was the Irish monkey clinging to our backs—the vomit, the drunkenness, the nasty waste of it all—the thread, linking us back to dirt, famine, and poverty on a craggy, mythical island.

We sat out on the bench next to Morgan's roses. The garden smelled of soil and manure and the faint sweet odor of crushed blossoms. For me, late September was a sad time, as a few bushes kept blossoming in the Indian summer and Morgan piled up the falling leaves to bury them. I hated to see the end of the roses. When I was little I couldn't believe that they would ever bloom again, buried alive as they were under the weight of manured compost and what seemed like tons of leaves. "Have some faith, Fred," Morgan would chide me. But I noticed the death toll each spring. Certain bushes died over the winter for the myriad reasons roses die, but Morgan would replant every summer with the faith of an optimist, thankful for all that had survived.

"You know," Sarah said, inhaling on her Marlboro, "I love him. I think I've loved him from the very first day."

"Who?" I asked, my mind still on the roses and James sprinting across the parking lot and the joy-stripped look on Arianna's face.

"James," she said, blowing a series of smoke rings.

"James," I said back to her, wondering for a moment who James was, wanting to believe, of course, that Sarah meant a different James. A James I did not know.

"On the night of the *Harold and the Purple Crayon* pantomime and we danced to 'Me and My Shadow,' I thought to myself, 'This is the boy I will marry.' I thought that God had lifted James Day out of Libertyville, Illinois, to put him next door to me. I thought that we would just keep dancing. Marriage would be holding hands and dancing forever."

I took a big drink of Coke and rum, and said, "James?" again.

"Yeah, James."

"I didn't know," was all I could think to say.

"You, Fred, are not good at picking up on the details. Whereas I realized months ago that you were head over heels for Arianna Isaacs, you never even thought that I might like someone."

"You knew about Arianna?" I asked, looking straight at Sarah, who had curled her legs under the pleats of her woolen miniskirt and buttoned the red Pendleton blazer around her black turtleneck against the cool of the evening. She looked back at me evenly, holding the cigarette in her elegant way with the first two fingers of her right hand.

"Fred, you practically drool when you see her. You're pretty transparent about your feelings, at least to me. Every year for the past three years, you have had a crush on an unattainable girl. You rarely go out with anyone, but you're always in love."

I felt pithed, like a butterfly pinned but not yet dead. My crushes, I believed, were private. Having Sarah speak of them, revealing them to be both public and scrutinized, was embarrassing.

"Does anyone else know?" I asked Sarah, hoping that she would answer negatively.

"Sure," she said. "James, Micah, and Joshua," and she paused before adding, "and Arianna, of course."

In a gulp, I finished my rum and Coke, attempting to fend off the heat of my embarrassment. I felt warm everywhere and my palms were perspiring.

"Sarah…"

"You're always in love with someone you can't have. Or something. Arianna thinks you're weird because you barely speak to her. The docents at the Joslyn think you're adorable. Morgan sent me in to get you one Saturday, and one of them said to me, 'Oh, you're the little curator's sister. Fred's just so cute.'" The words came out in a rush at a nervous pitch. She looked into the darkness that was the rose garden. Her hand trembled, shaking the Marlboro. Cigarette ash fell to the ground.

What she said cut too close to the bone for me. Adorable and weird were not inspiring adjectives.

"Sarah, what about James? What do you want?"

"I want him to come walking across this yard to offer his hand in marriage to me on bended knee. I want him to dance me across the driveway under that big harvest moon forever and ever and ever. What do you think of that? 'How likely,' as Mom would say, do you think that is of happening?" Sarah looked away from me and up at the orange moon. Wisps of clouds were floating by it.

"Well, as Mom would say, 'When pigs fly.'" I didn't know what else to tell her. There was nothing in what I knew about James to indicate to me that he saw in Sarah anything more than a friend. A sisterly friend at that.

"God, don't you know it," Sarah said, still looking at the moon. "Sometimes I hate and love James Day so much, all at the same time, that I don't know what to do." She hiccoughed a giggle and then began to chortle. When she was heaving with laughter the tears came. I tossed my cigarette into a watering can. It sizzled as it met the surface of the water. Then I put down my empty glass and hugged Sarah. I didn't know what else to do. "Do you know what the worst thing is?" she whispered into my ear, her arms locked around my bent back, "I hate Neil Mahaffey. I can't help it. The hate seeps around in me and sometimes it spills out on James." Then she cried again.

VERY LATE THAT night James slipped into the bedroom and curled up on the floor in the sleeping bag and pillow that I had thrown down there for him. I woke up and so did Laurence's cat, Tiger, who was asleep at the foot of Laurence's bed.

"What time is it?" I hissed to James.

"Go back to sleep," James grumbled from his fetal position in the sleeping bag.

I grabbed our alarm clock and read its luminous dial.

"Jesus Christ, James, it's four in the morning."

"Go to sleep, Fred, you're not my keeper."

"Who is this Neil Mahaffey, anyway?" I asked him, feeling very awake then.

"Just a guy. Come on, please let me go to sleep." James sounded tired, almost plaintive.

I shut up, and lay in bed asking myself over and over who Neil Mahaffey was as I listened to Laurence talk in his sleep while his cat purred. He said, "No, no, no root beer," three times. James's breathing was quiet and he was still, curled like a shell on the beach. I was jealous of his sleep and considered for a moment waking him up and forcing him to talk to me. But I kept hearing the plaintive note in his voice. When I finally fell back to sleep, it was so deep that I didn't know where or who I was when Morgan shook my shoulder and whispered, "Fred, wake up. I need to speak to you in the hallway."

I looked across the bed. Laurence and the cat were up and gone. It was light. On the floor James was burrowed into the sleeping bag, his face buried in the pillow. I followed Morgan out into the hall in my briefs, hoping not to see my sisters and wishing I could pee.

"Fred," Morgan said, "I need to take Charlotte to the hospital."

"What time is it?"

"It's eleven-thirty. We saw Dr. Jensen at nine. Listen now. You need to be here to meet Laurence's bus. Your mother is going to go straight from work to Children's Hospital. Sarah's coming with Charlotte and me."

Dazed, I stood silent for a moment before asking, "Why are you taking

Charlotte to the hospital?"

"She has a problem with her kidneys."

"Kidneys?" I asked Morgan, too tired to be certain what a kidney was. I stood there, cold in my briefs, needing to pee, and then I heard Sarah said, "What about your pink pajamas?" and Charlotte saying, "No, those are too babyish, Sarah. Remember to call Hetty after school for me. Tell her to get my homework assignments. Ask her if I can borrow her white go-go boots for school on Monday. Tell Hetty to call me at the hospital."

Hetty

CHARLOTTE'S BEST FRIEND was a girl named Hetty Carmichael, whose father was the rector of St. Barnabas Episcopal Church on Fortieth Street. They became best friends in first grade when Hetty verbally pummeled a boy named Mitchell Abington for making of fun Charlotte's red hair.

"What would Jesus think of you, you shameless sinner?" is what Hetty said to Mitchell on the playground of Saunders Elementary School in front of their thirty-seven classmates, or at least that's the quote Charlotte produced for our dinnertime conversation that evening. From that moment on, Hetty became Charlotte's heroine, best friend, and the ruling theologian of her universe. Jesus was the major player in Hetty's world, and he came into her life not by virtue of her father's profession, but through the auspices of her maternal grandmother's Baptist congregation in a tiny town called Sparkman, Arkansas. An only child, Hetty spent three weeks of every summer in Sparkman with her mother, Helen. Helen's conversion to the Episcopal religion of her husband and to civil rights activism did not stop her from returning to the Baptist church of her youth to partake in the long, hot hours of summer Sunday preaching. Helen could have driven the short ride to Arkadelphia for an Episcopal service, but she chose the hellfire and brimstone of her childhood minister, because it was through him that she had been saved by the Jesus who led her to sit down at a Dallas bus stop beside the giant of a young man who would become her husband, Harry Carmichael. Jesus started for Helen in Sparkman, and she wanted Jesus to begin there for Hetty, too. All of this she told to Serena Day, who was a member of St. Barnabas. Serena told it to Mom, and Mom told it to us.

Hetty's proclamation to Mitchell Abington as quoted by Charlotte made everyone look up.

"Pardon me, could you say that one more time, Charlotte?" Morgan asked her. "I'm not quite certain that I heard what you said."

"Mitchell called me 'Charlotte, Charlotte, ugly red spider,' and then he called me 'mashed red bug guts,' and I was going to hit him when this new girl named Hetty said, 'What would Jesus think of you, you shameless sinner?' When everyone started to laugh at him, Mitchell started to cry and he said, 'I'm no shameless sinner, Jesus loves me.' And then Hetty says, 'Jesus does not love it when people make fun of the way other people look.'"

"Who's Jesus?" Laurence asked.

"God's son," Charlotte answered. "But in Catholic churches people are far too involved in ceremony to pay attention to Jesus like they should. That's what Hetty said."

Morgan's eyebrows were halfway up his forehead and his glasses halfway down the bridge of his nose as he shook a Marlboro out of his pack, lit it, and asked her, "Charlotte, how did Hetty come to know so much about the Catholic church?"

"Well, Morgan, her dad is a piscopal rector."

"A what?" Mom asked.

"Hetty's dad is a *piscopal* rector," Charlotte said again with emphasis.

Mom and Morgan looked at each other.

"Do you mean he's an Episcopal priest, Charlotte?" Mom said.

"No, I mean he's a piscopal rector at St. Barnabas Church." Charlotte screwed up her nose as she always did before digging in her heels.

"That's pronounced 'Episcopal,'" Morgan said looking at both Sarah and me, because we were by now grinning from ear to ear.

"I am so proud that you did not hit Mitchell Abington, Charlotte, because you did promise me that you would stop hitting him this year." Mom jumped in to ward off an argument on the pronunciation of the word 'Episcopal' before Charlotte completely dug in her heels.

"I did not promise not to hit Mitchell Abington. I promised not to hit Mitchell Abington if he quit teasing me." Charlotte's memory often differed on the finer points, and she would argue her interpretation of them to the death.

Mom looked at her. "You, Charlotte Anne Holly, are to hit no one, teasing or not. If Mitchell teases you, I will call his mother, but you are not to hit him. Do you hear me?"

Charlotte's nose was screwed up almost between her eyebrows.

"Charlotte, answer your mother," Morgan said.

"Yes, but– "

"No, buts," Mom said.

CHARLOTTE AND MITCHELL Abington had come to blows twice in kindergarten, with Mitchell the worse off for his effort. Charlotte's resorting to blows might have been accepted if she were a boy. I had been in a few schoolyard scrapes that were broken up by teachers who saw very little harm in the fisticuffs. But Charlotte's sheer domination of Mitchell on the playground brought down on her the wrath of Mitchell's mother, the kindergarten teacher, and the Saunders Elementary School principal. Mom and Morgan deplored Charlotte's fighting, but they were no fools to the fact that Mitchell teased her at every turn. Charlotte's feelings had been overlooked in this equation because, of course, "Boys tease little girls, especially little girls with red hair, who do stand out," as Mrs. Abington said at the conference in the principal's office. This statement was repeated by Mom in the kitchen over and over again whenever Charlotte wasn't nearby. The teacher and principal made the judgment that Charlotte should just get used to it because her red hair would always attract attention. A judgment not accepted by our parents. Mom declared, "Rachel Abington just better get used to me calling her if Mitchell teases Charlotte again."

With the appearance of Hetty Carmichael on the playground, Charlotte had found an ally and a moral champion. She brought Hetty and Jesus into our lives. From what I understood, Harry Carmichael was chosen by St. Barnabas because they were open to a ministry of social justice and he was open to upholding their high church ways despite his low church preferences. He got out the incense and they signed the petitions that he produced month after month, trying to make Omaha a better and more just community. In Hetty, Reverend Carmichael produced a daughter who didn't fall very far from the tree.

Hetty's sense of the evils of discrimination were finely tuned to the mold of her father, but her faith was stoked not by the form and traditions of the Book of Common Prayer but by the Gospel of Jesus Christ as sweated and shouted by Sparkman's Baptist preachers, both black and white. Hetty taught Charlotte to sing the Negro spiritual "There Is a Balm in Gilead" and they sang it together in the attic as part of a pantomime directed by Sarah and James when they were seven. All six parents watched the two girls in their hand-smocked dresses as they sang in clear, childish voices, cadenced by Hetty's Arkansas gospel tones, of the hope for healing all souls seek from the balm of Gilead tree. Hetty with her dark blonde hair and brown cat-eyed glasses sang with the conviction of a true believer.

I would be a liar to say that there were not strained moments for me with Hetty Carmichael. Especially when she asked me, "But, Fred, don't you accept Jesus Christ as your personal savior?" and she asked me this question on a regular basis. My personal desire on hearing this question was to strangle her. Like Morgan, I liked my religion personal, private, and at a distance. But it could not be denied in our household that Hetty truly saved Charlotte from the worst part of herself—her temper—and that Charlotte offered Hetty, as Helen Carmichael told Mom, "her first real friend." The two girls were inseparable.

Hetty also brought something else into our home—Tiger, the orange-colored kitten that Morgan had told Charlotte "she was not to bring home or bring into the house. Do you hear me, Charlotte?" But Charlotte was so taken with the litter of kittens that Hetty's cat, Mrs. Gamp, had produced, she so desired the sweet little tomcat that she brought him home anyway, ignoring all of Morgan's warnings. Morgan did not find Charlotte with the kitten. He found the kitten curled up next to a sleeping Laurence, whose hand was curved around the small cat's body. Tiger held no affection for either Hetty or Charlotte, or the doll clothes they dressed him in, or the doll carriage that they pushed him in when he was all decked out in baby-doll drag. Morgan, of course, was livid at the unfairness of the universe on the evening when he and Mom argued in the rose garden over what to do about Laurence and Tiger.

"Goddammit, Eileen, I can't take the stupid cat away from the boy. He adores it, and he never asks for anything. But Charlotte flouts the rules she doesn't like. She only hears what she wants to hear. And lo and behold, she'll get her cat by hook or by crook."

"Charlotte is not getting the cat, Morgan. Laurence is. That's what we have to make clear to her. We are keeping the cat, but it's Laurence's cat."

In the end, Mom was right. To Charlotte's great dismay, Tiger ignored her, adopting Laurence, and living out his days between trolling the neighborhood for small indefensible prey and sleeping on Laurence's bed.

"But he's my cat," Charlotte would argue at night as she tried to take Tiger from Laurence while Mom unclenched her fingers from the poor creature's body, saying, "No, he's Laurence's cat, and you know that."

Even Hetty pointed out to her that she wasn't supposed to have taken the kitten home in the first place, but Charlotte was not much for details that disagreed with the memory she was creating.

"Oh, Charlotte," I overheard Hetty exclaim one day, after Tiger had been officially proclaimed Laurence's animal, "you are the stubbornest girl in the whole world."

"But I feel like I'm right about Tiger. And when I feel that way about something, sometimes, that's all that I can feel," Charlotte told her.

Charlotte felt with passion. She and Hetty shared a deep conviction about the primacy of passion and the truth in feelings. It was the glue and the salvation of their friendship.

NOT ALWAYS, BUT frequently, when I take a piss, I think of Charlotte then. My kidneys work. Even one kidney can make the human body function quite well; that is the miracle of transplants. The healthy human has the richness of two kidneys to cleanse the water content of the blood. Sometimes taking a leak seems a minor miracle to me. The grand luxury of this relief that I too often fail to remember.

As I stood that Friday morning, pissing into the toilet, Sarah pounded on the bathroom door.

"Fred, do me a favor. Call Hetty for me and tell her that Charlotte's in the hospital. Hetty should be home from school by three-thirty."

"Sarah, wait," I said, grabbing Morgan's robe before opening the bathroom door.

"What's wrong with Charlotte?" I asked her. Sarah was dressed in a lime green summer dress and a yellow cotton sweater. Her hair was in a long black braid down her back.

"Glomerulonephritis," Sarah said, stumbling through the many syllables of the word.

"What's that?" I asked.

"Dr. Jensen said, it's what Charlotte has. It's the kidneys' reaction against a particular kind of strep infection." Sarah said.

"But Charlotte hasn't had a strep infection."

"Yes, she has. She's had strep without symptoms for a couple of weeks. Dr. Jensen has seen it before. That's what he told Morgan."

"But Sarah, won't medicine make the strep go away?"

"Yeah, but the problem is that the kidneys don't necessarily get well when the strep goes away. They'll take longer."

"How long?"

"Well, Charlotte thinks she'll be back in school by Monday, and she wants to borrow Hetty's white go-go boots. So maybe that's the way it'll go. You know Charlotte, Fred. She likes things her way." And Sarah smiled.

The Studebaker's horn bleated up the side of the house and into the open bathroom window.

"Look, I gotta go. Call Hetty," Sarah said, running down the hallway, bumping into James, who had just stepped out of the bedroom with Tiger Cat weaving through his legs.

"Where's the fire?" James called out to her.

Children's Hospital

THE CHILDREN'S HOSPITAL, where Morgan drove Charlotte that Friday morning, is now gone. It was a white building with a columned entrance that reminded me of a Nebraskan twist on a Southern plantation home. It looked far more like a house than a hospital, and looking back, I would presume that was the point of the architecture, to make children feel safe and comfortable about going into the building.

I made a short stay there myself somewhere between my third and fourth years. The only memory I have of that stay was the sensation of the color of white. Everything there seemed to float in white cotton, including the dark-haired, antiseptic-smelling nurses. I never thought about the place again, until I started to visit Charlotte. I never thought much about the University of Nebraska Medical Center, which surrounded the Children's Hospital not three full miles from our house on Thirty-eighth Street. I never considered what patients did all day. Or why they were in hospitals, or all the things that can happen to a body. There are people in this world who spend every one of their workdays caring for the sick. In these buildings there are people who spend the better part of their lives ill. Many of them are children. None of these facts and concerns pierced my reality the morning Morgan drove Charlotte to the hospital. Even the fact that much of Morgan's daily work dealt with actuarial charts related to health-care insurance policies figured little in my life. The point of Morgan's work always seemed to me to be to make money to care for us, and to satiate Morgan's love of numbers and their problems.

I did not think about the Children's Hospital that morning when James came walking down the hall in my bathrobe.

"Where's Sarah running off to?"

"Children's Hospital," I told him.

"Who's sick?"

"Charlotte," I said, "something to do with strep and her kidneys. She wants to be home by Monday so that she can borrow Hetty's go-go boots to wear to school next week, and that's what I'm sure will happen. Charlotte has that force of personality. She can will herself well."

"Ah, fashion as the driving force of health," James said, and we both laughed.

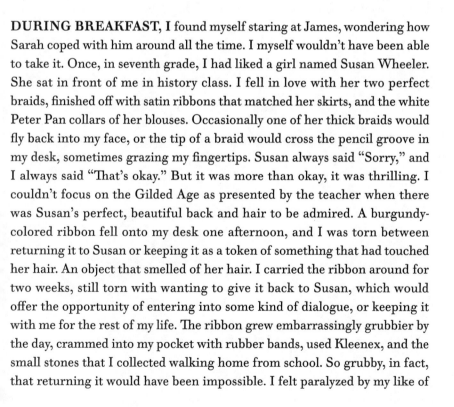

DURING BREAKFAST, I found myself staring at James, wondering how Sarah coped with him around all the time. I myself wouldn't have been able to take it. Once, in seventh grade, I had liked a girl named Susan Wheeler. She sat in front of me in history class. I fell in love with her two perfect braids, finished off with satin ribbons that matched her skirts, and the white Peter Pan collars of her blouses. Occasionally one of her thick braids would fly back into my face, or the tip of a braid would cross the pencil groove in my desk, sometimes grazing my fingertips. Susan always said "Sorry," and I always said "That's okay." But it was more than okay, it was thrilling. I couldn't focus on the Gilded Age as presented by the teacher when there was Susan's perfect, beautiful back and hair to be admired. A burgundy-colored ribbon fell onto my desk one afternoon, and I was torn between returning it to Susan or keeping it as a token of something that had touched her hair. An object that smelled of her hair. I carried the ribbon around for two weeks, still torn with wanting to give it back to Susan, which would offer the opportunity of entering into some kind of dialogue, or keeping it with me for the rest of my life. The ribbon grew embarrassingly grubbier by the day, crammed into my pocket with rubber bands, used Kleenex, and the small stones that I collected walking home from school. So grubby, in fact, that returning it would have been impossible. I felt paralyzed by my like of her. I didn't know what to do with the ribbon or even what to say to her. Finally, I asked the teacher if she would move me to the front of the class, explaining that I was suffering from a kind of eyestrain. Without Susan I felt rudderless, but I gave myself over to Teddy Roosevelt and the Rough Riders and then the trenches of World War I. When Susan looked at me on the first day of my seating change, I saw a hurt in her eyes, a flicker of betrayal. I felt fear and guilt, but I still could not imagine myself talking to Susan, so I threw myself even more into history and my homework, and avoided her in the hallways.

I STARED AT James eating a bowl full of Cheerios, sliced bananas, and milk, and considered how long Sarah had known him. How many times she had danced with him. The hundreds of days she had walked home from school with him. The thousands of hours Sarah had ridden around to dancing lessons in the backseat of a car with James Day, calculated to emotional infinity. Even our past summer of riding around in the backseat of his Galaxy 500 now seemed like miles and miles of agony for Sarah. I considered whether all love was unrequited as James poured more orange juice into his jelly glass, glancing up from his cereal to ask, "More, Fred?" It was frightening for me to consider that possibility. The belief I nurtured was that somewhere outside of Omaha was a girl who did not know it yet, but who was waiting to fall in love with me when it was the right time. She was going about her life in a parallel universe, but somehow, something would bend, forcing a rare intersection of our lives when it was time. When I was educated and traveled, and when I had found my museum.

I loved artifacts for their stasis. I returned to the Joslyn for the comfort of what I knew would be there. The Lipschitz sculpture, the Bougereaus, the Renoir, the Western paintings of buffalo and the Plains tribes—their lives once enacted on the very soil beneath the museum—played out in their unchanging tableaux. Only I changed in relation to the art. The museum's unvarying qualities settled me. Sadly, I would outgrow certain pieces, several paintings in particular, and grow into others, but the art itself was never unfaithful. It stayed there, mounted in the galleries, always waiting for my return. On each return, I was rewarded with what can happen to the eye and the brain when art is studied. The art changed on reflection—whether seen on rainy days, on sunny days, during a bad headache. After my heart was broken.

But even as a child I understood that the human was an active, ever-changing force. Humans grew and humans deteriorated. Humans held deep, seemingly immutable opinions that they could and sometimes would change without a moment's notice. What I felt was a responsibility to my dream, the mythical museum that waited for me somewhere outside of Omaha. The dream overpowered me. I did not give in to the possibilities that lurked all around me like mines in a battlefield. I kept girls at a distance.

In the autumn of 1969, as real as the Vietnam War to all of us was the reality that we sat between people in classrooms every day who would soon be married. Girls who would be pregnant within eighteen months of graduation and long into grandmotherhood by our twenty-fifth reunion. This was Omaha and this was America. When I think of those girls from my class of Central High School, 1970, I think of the words "kind," "delightful." When Sarah forces me to examine our yearbooks, I am always momentarily stunned by their beauty. Youth is beautiful. We were beautiful. But I did not want to stay in Omaha. These kind, delightful girls I saw as the trap. Far better to live the constant agony of the unrequited lover, I thought, than to wake up one morning next to a lover for life, a mortgage, pregnancies, and the always highly desirable season tickets to the University of Nebraska Cornhusker football games. It was not what I wanted, but I knew it wouldn't be that bad, and for many it would be wonderful. Knowing that life in Omaha would never be that bad was part of the minefield. Knowing that I was terrified of leaving my family was a hidden grief. Knowing that it would be very easy to stay in Nebraska was the greatest danger of all, because all around me were these delightful girls, and I loved them, each and every one, from my distance. And, of course, I have regrets about that time. Only an unfeeling slug would not. My regrets are as defining for me as my successes.

Looking at James Day that morning that was already almost early afternoon, as he read the funnies page of the *Omaha World-Herald* in my red woolen bathrobe, his sandy brown hair out of sorts with his face, I was stunned by Sarah's revelation. Even then I did not know how she could live with the knowledge that he did not love her the way she loved him. Even then, I understood the burden of Sarah's misplaced love. How long it takes, the months, then the years, for love to wear down, and how painfully it can reawaken over something silly. How many embarrassing moments I have logged in my years out of Omaha, sitting in cars weeping, tears triggered by a stupid song on the radio. The goddamn "Horse with No Name" spinning out its tune like an aching tinnitus, and me weeping for every lost lover. These were the clouds of my thoughts the day that Charlotte entered Children's Hospital.

Then I remembered how late I was for the museum.

"Look, James, you need to take me to Joslyn and then come back here and wait for Laurence. I promised the janitor I would tear down these crates today. Call your mom and tell her what's going on with Charlotte and stay here until Laurence gets home. I might be back in time. But remind me, I need to call Hetty."

James drove me to the Joslyn, wearing my red woolen bathrobe and singing "Oh, What a Beautiful Morning," all the way down Dodge Street, and leaving me at the museum's employee entrance with a big-armed wave. He waited for Laurence. Three hours later, after a slow bus ride home, I found them sitting in the kitchen, eating Oreo cookies with Tiger Cat drinking milk out of a bowl at the foot of the table. They were discussing taxicabs. Laurence loved yellow taxicabs almost as much as he loved Tiger Cat.

"I would like to take a yellow taxicab," Laurence told James "in a straight line all around the world."

"What about the oceans?" James asked, twisting apart an Oreo and handing its perfect white half and the other naked black wafer to Laurence.

"We can put it on a boat until we reach land," Laurence said. "Morgan told me the taxicab would have to go as cargo."

"What about the taxi driver?" James asked. "How will you find a taxi driver who wants to drive in a straight line all around the world?"

"Oh, I'll find him all right," Laurence said. "He'll be special, like me."

"And Tiger will go, too?" James asked.

"Probably, if we can take the litter box," Laurence said, licking the white cream fluff carefully off the wafer.

A SURGE OF feeling came over me as I walked into the kitchen and saw James breaking apart Oreos. Love was the one and certain feeling I could always identify. I loved James Day. I could not help but love him. At that moment, watching James and Laurence, I understood Sarah, how she could love having him so near, because her life, our lives, would have been far less without him. The phone rang. It was Hetty.

"May I speak with Charlotte, please?" Hetty asked.

"Hey, Hetty," I said, staring at James and Laurence, "Charlotte's in the hospital."

"What?" Hetty said to me, in a tone that sounded taken aback.

"Charlotte's in the hospital."

"Why didn't you call me?"

This was the thing about Hetty. She took great offense at anything related to Charlotte. She presumed that no one cared about Charlotte as much as she did.

"I was going to call you as soon as you got home from school," I told her. James was grinning from his seat at the kitchen table.

"I've been home fifteen minutes."

"Look, Hetty," I said, wanting to stave off a lecture, "I'm sorry, I just got in from the museum."

"Well, Charlotte's in the hospital and you never take her to the football games." Hetty said this with the voice of moral authority that she could always give to her own non sequiturs.

I felt her words like a stab. Charlotte was in the hospital and I never took her to football games. None of it made sense, but I understood what Hetty was saying, and how she wanted me to feel.

"Look, Hetty, we'll take her to homecoming. We'll take Charlotte to homecoming, and Laurence to homecoming, too." Laurence looked up at the sound of his name.

"You'll take me to homecoming. Charlotte won't want to go to homecoming without me."

"Sure," I said, "we'll take all of you to homecoming."

"I've got her homework," Hetty said.

"I'll come get it," I told her, glad that she was appeased.

"When?"

"After dinner, before we go to the hospital."

"I'll be waiting," she said and hung up. Without a good-bye.

Tiger Missing

AFTER DINNER THAT Friday night, we were all going to visit Charlotte at the hospital. As we were doing the day's dishes, Laurence came running into the kitchen crying, "I can't find Tiger." His moon face was blotched pink and his bottom lip quivered. Morgan, standing at the sink with his hands buried in soap bubbles, rolled his eyes and inhaled on the Marlboro that hung out of the corner of his mouth, muttering, "You two help him find that damn beast while I finish up these dishes."

"Tiger, Tiger," the three of us wailed as the moon rose nearly full and golden in the darkening sky.

We marched down Thirty-eighth Street and then back through the alley behind our house. Sucking his right thumb, Laurence held Sarah's hand while bleating out his small cries of "Tiger Cat, Tiger Cat, come home." The words were muffled by his thumb. Tiger did not come. When we returned to the top of driveway, Morgan was climbing into the Studebaker.

"You'll come tomorrow," he said as we walked up to the driver's window, "but tonight, I need to get there during visiting hours." Morgan looked at Laurence, who was whimpering, and motioned me closer to the car. I could smell bourbon and cigarette smoke on his breath and see the strain in his eyes. "Fred," he whispered, "please find the cat."

As Morgan backed out of the driveway, I saw Annie Little's Ford Fairlane pull up in front of our house. Joshua got out and waved at Morgan as he ran up the driveway. Micah was in the driver's seat.

"Fred, let's go. Micah needs a night out. Mom told him that he can't speak to Arianna Isaacs anymore. He's in a proper blue funk over it. Mom says that she doesn't want him spending time with white girls. She says they're a lynching proposition. Micah keeps telling her it's 1969."

"So will he stop talking to Arianna?" Sarah asked.

"Well, I wouldn't stop talking to her," Joshua said with emphasis, "but Micah doesn't like to disobey Mom. I told Micah he should stay Arianna's friend. I told him what is all this marching and protesting about, if not to talk. We need to talk. Everybody needs to talk."

"Arianna and Micah talk so well," I said, thinking of them in the parking lot at school.

Joshua laughed. "They do, don't they? They talk as well as any two people I know."

"It'll break Arianna's heart if he stops talking to her," Sarah said, looking toward the Fairlane. Laurence whimpered. Micah tooted the horn, three short blasts.

Joshua waved to the Fairlane and then asked me, "Ready?"

"I can't, Josh," I said, waving to Micah. "Charlotte's in the hospital and Laurence has lost his cat. And we have to find him. I'm sorry."

At that moment Neil Mahaffey's tan Volkswagen beetle pulled up behind the Fairlane and he tooted his horn twice. The Days' front door flew open. James came out in khakis and a sport coat. We watched as he skipped down the stairs that were cut into the hill of their terraced lawn. He looked jaunty in an earnest way. Serena stepped halfway out of the house with a confused look on her face to wave good-bye to him. James bowed to her and then waved to the Fairlane and to us up on the driveway. Everyone waved back as he grabbed the door handle and stepped into the Volkswagen. The bug gurgled, rumbled, and then roared down Thirty-eighth Street. Serena stared at the car as it disappeared from view before quietly slipping back into the house.

"I guess James isn't going out with us tonight, either," Joshua said. "Who's the guy? What's up?"

"Neil Mahaffey," Sarah said, looking at me. "He coached James at debate camp."

"Who would want to go out with a debate coach?" Joshua asked with a laugh.

"Someone who wants to win a debate," Sarah said.

Joshua smiled. "Well, it takes all kinds to make up this world. I'd better get going. Good luck with the cat." And then he started down the hill of the driveway, but as he reached the bottom, he turned around and ran back up. "Sorry to hear about Charlotte," he said. "Is it tonsils or something?"

"Kidney infection," I told him.

"Hope she's home soon."

"Tell Micah to hang in there. Your Mom might change her mind," I told him.

Laurence whimpered and tugged on Sarah's hand.

"We'll see. But you know my mom is not a woman of small opinion."

I nodded, knowing that I wouldn't want to cross Annie Little.

Sarah and I waved, and Laurence called out, "Tiger Cat, Tiger Cat."

Two hours later, I found Tiger in the rose garden, curled up behind Morgan's wheelbarrow next to the pile of leaves. Tiger's ear was scratched and he smelled of piss. I carried him into the kitchen, where Sarah washed the ear with soap and water while I held the squirming, scratching cat.

"Don't hurt him," Laurence yelled.

"I'm not hurting him. And if Tiger would stay out of fights, we wouldn't have to do this."

"Tiger doesn't fight," Laurence said, stamping his foot.

"Well he sure plays hard then," I said, handing him over to Laurence. "Don't let him out of the house this weekend."

"But he likes to go out."

"No, Laurence. Keep him inside. We have enough to do around here without chasing him all over the neighborhood."

"But he's my cat."

"Right now, you sound just like Charlotte."

"I do not." Laurence stamped his foot again.

"Exactly like her," I said, stamping my foot back at him.

"Fred, leave him alone," Sarah interjected.

As Laurence was about to stamp back at me the doorbell rang and he rushed away with Tiger in his arms when I moved to answer the door. I opened it to find Hetty Carmichael standing there.

"Hetty," I said, "it's after dark. What are you doing here?"

"I waited and waited for you to come to get Charlotte's homework."

"I forgot," I said, remembering with a stab of guilt. "Tiger Cat didn't come back for hours and we searched and searched for him." The words sounded inane as I said them.

Holding Charlotte's books against her chest, Hetty stared at me from behind her cat-eyed glasses.

"I'm sorry," I said, not knowing what else to say to Hetty, who I knew would judge me harshly for this breach.

"My dad said you would walk me home, because you are a gentleman."

"Sure, of course," I said, thinking that no one had ever described me as a gentleman. "But I need to tell Sarah."

Hetty handed me the books. "I wrote everything down for Charlotte. It's there in her math book," she said, pointing at a piece of paper with doubt in her eyes.

"Step in, step in," I said. "Just let me tell Sarah I'm walking you home." I ran to the kitchen with the books.

"Sarah," I said, "I'm walking Hetty home." Then I placed the books on the kitchen table as Sarah turned from the sink with her hands, encased in yellow rubber gloves, held up in the air, and her mouth opened, about to speak, and I was gone, hearing nothing.

My life as a gentleman began that night as I walked Hetty Carmichael home. I walked next to her on the street side, negotiating the tree-rooted humps in the sidewalk, so as to get her the four blocks to her house without incident. Reverend Carmichael named me a gentleman that evening, and I aimed to prove to the skeptical Hetty that I was neither a fop nor a fool. I sensed that the rector's intractable daughter thought me both. Looking at Hetty under the orange glow of the street lamps, I saw a slightly chubby girl in knee-high white socks that stuck out of her white go-go boots, faded Madras shorts, and a summer shirt hidden by a buttoned-up red cardigan. She was at least a foot shorter than me, with blonde braided hair at least a foot long. Hetty, like Charlotte, was a child on the cusp. At ten, she was chubby and childlike, entering into the quandary of fifth grade, knowing that something was about to end, wanting the growth that her body was about to begin and at the same time being terrified of it. I know this now because I have seen it in my own daughters, and even all those years ago, at seventeen, I had seen it in Sarah, and had a memory of it in myself. The hoary mysteries of fifth grade, built upon so much wanting and not wanting, stood before me in Hetty Carmichael, and in Charlotte, only few miles away in Children's Hospital.

Hetty did not say a word to me all the way home. When we reached the Carmichaels' front gate, she turned to me and reached out her hand as if to shake. I took it. Her small sweaty fingers held on to me with a fierceness that almost hurt.

"Thank you for walking me home."

"You're welcome," I said, wondering when Hetty would release my hand. Her father's imposing figure was an outline in their screen door not twenty feet away. The porch light glowed, beckoning Hetty, but she did not let go.

"Fred," she said, "Charlotte's my best friend in the whole world."

"Hetty," her father called gently through the screen.

"I know," I told her, looking down into her serious face and into those cat-eyed frames to feel her grip tighten even more. "Everyone in our family considers you the best thing that ever happened to Charlotte."

"That's the way I feel, too," she said, still not letting me go.

"Hetty," her father called, "it's late. Say good night to Fred."

"I have to go," she said, loosening her grip, then dropping my hand.

"Thank you for bringing Charlotte's homework," I said. "I'm sorry I forgot to pick it up." In the drop of my hand I was already missing hers. The feeling of its fierce innocence. As Hetty Carmichael ran to the figure of her father, I smelled autumn in the air. Summer was over. Walking home I felt sad, knowing that Hetty and Charlotte were about to become girls, a process I understood to be complicated and difficult. I would miss them. Our families' babies would be gone.

It was long after midnight when Morgan returned home without Mom. We were asleep and unknowing.

Homecoming

LAURENCE AND I visited Charlotte in Children's Hospital on Saturday night, the evening after her admission. Halfway down the hallway to Charlotte's room we saw Mom, who launched into a discussion about the catheter. "Charlotte screamed when they changed the catheter," Mom whispered to us as though we would understand. "She hates the catheter. The nurse kept saying, 'Sweetie, I'm sorry, if you could just relax a little bit, it might not be so bad.' I told the nurse, 'She's scared, Charlotte's just scared. She's never been in a hospital before, except when she was born.'" Mom said all this and then walked away from us and toward the door to Charlotte's room. Morgan trailed after her, holding Laurence's hand and leaving Sarah and me in the hallway.

"What's a catheter?" I asked Sarah, uncertain of why Charlotte would hate it, or why she would scream. I whispered the word as though it were an obscenity.

"It's a plastic tube they put up Charlotte to drain off her pee," Sarah told me as she held Charlotte's schoolbooks against her chest. "Mom was still on the bus when they tried to do it the first time and Morgan asked me to stay in the room with Charlotte while he called the office. I think it made Morgan sick to his stomach to think about it. The nurse explained it all to me and to Charlotte, but Charlotte kicked and screamed until Mom got there. And that's when they finally got it in her."

Immediately I visualized what the nurse had done to Charlotte and I blanched. About all those things related to private parts we were a prudish family, a family of euphemisms and embarrassments. We were not a family of vaginas and penises, or of menstrual cycles and of sex education. There was no "talk." We were a family of long silences between the ellipses that denoted explanations, of pamphlets left on bed pillows, and of indications of information that could be found in the *World Book Encyclopedia.* My parents were raised on a benevolent type of ignorance, something they were more than happy to pass on to us. They learned about their bodies through whispers and sneaked glances into library reference books. Even on that second night of Charlotte's hospital stay, it was apparent that we were all going into a world of accuracy and science, blunt talk, and specifics. Of things that were black and white, of things that we would have to do.

When we walked into her room, I was comforted to see Charlotte wearing her pink flannel pajamas with the white French poodles cancanning across the surface of the material. Bandaged to her left hand was an I.V. drip. Her cheeks were flushed and the skin beneath her eyes was bruised and puffy. She looked strained and scared and not a little relieved to see us walk through the doorway. Sarah and I sat down on the empty bed next to hers. Sarah rested the schoolbooks next to the pillow. Laurence stood at the side of her bed carefully examining the I.V. drip. Morgan and Mom stood on the other side of the empty bed, whispering, and then Morgan left the room.

"Hey, Charlotte," I said to her.

"Hey, Fred, hey, Sarah," she said to us. On a tray that rested on a swivel arm in front of her was a seemingly untouched dinner.

"What's for dinner?" I asked her.

"That," she said, pointing at the tray, which held a chicken breast, green beans, and applesauce.

"Aren't you going to eat it? It looks pretty good to me," I said. It did. Morgan had made tuna-fish sandwiches for our dinner that night without pickles or even Miracle Whip. The sandwiches, both dry and greasy, were still lying uncomfortably in my stomach.

"They won't give me salt. I want salt for the beans and chicken," she said, looking at Mom, who looked away.

"Why not?" I asked.

"It's because I can't pee. Because it's all bottling up inside me. The nurse said that salt will make me keep my pee. They have to get the pee out of me."

"Wow, I didn't know that about salt," I said. I'd never thought about salt or what a person could or could not eat. Ever.

Laurence pulled his white wrinkled thumb out of his mouth and dropped his hand to his crotch, touching his fly ever so gently with his thumb before returning it to his mouth.

"But I still want the salt. I want to pee and I want salt, too. And I want to go home." Charlotte sighed when she said this, and I noticed that her lips were chapped. Mom offered her some water. Charlotte shook her head. Sarah stood up and moved to the window.

"Hetty called and she brought over your homework," I told her, pointing at the books on the pillow. I understood that I could not make Charlotte pee or give her salt, but that I could tell her about something that would lead her thoughts elsewhere.

"Will she loan me her go-go boots for school on Monday?" Charlotte asked.

"Sure," I said, remembering that I hadn't even asked Hetty about the go-go boots. "But something better than that is going to happen."

"What?" Charlotte looked at me.

"You're going to the homecoming game with us. You and Laurence and Hetty are all going with us. Hetty said you can wear the go-go boots to the game. And James will drive." Everything I said was true, except for the go-go boots, but I was sure Hetty would lend her the boots.

Charlotte grinned and Mom's shoulders slumped in relief. Homecoming was two weeks away.

"But we all can't fit into James's car," Charlotte told me. "So you'll have to take Sarah and Laurence in the Studebaker." I could feel Charlotte moving into her planning mode.

"Mom, can I get a new skirt?"

"If we have time, Charlotte, if we have time. Please try some of the green beans." Charlotte picked up a green bean and nibbled. "I'll get a pleated skirt and a new turtleneck and so will Hetty. Can I get go-go boots, Mom?"

"Eat the green beans, dear," Mom told her, moving toward the bed and not responding to the go-go boots question. Morgan hated go-go boots and miniskirts almost as much as he hated the Beatles. Charlotte had gone round and round with him about white go-go boots in the weeks before school started.

"Fred, please turn on the TV," Mom said, as Charlotte nibbled on another green bean.

A color television sat on a small platform anchored to the wall, positioned so that it could be seen from both Charlotte's bed and the empty bed, which would presumably be filled by another patient. I stood up and turned the dial. Color filled the screen.

Saturday night television in Omaha was generally dull. That evening a local channel was covering the coronation of the king and queen of Quivera at the Ak-Sar-Ben Race Track field house. Quivera was the golden kingdom that Coronado sought in the sixteenth century, pushing his conquistadors north into what would become Oklahoma, Kansas, and Nebraska, to no avail. But for a handful of decades, every September Nebraskans have celebrated this never-found kingdom of Quivera with the crowning of a king and a queen, princesses, countesses, and pages at Ak-Sar-Ben. The king was always an important businessman with philanthropic interests, in his fifties, and the queen was always a beautiful twenty-year-old girl who was the daughter of an important businessman with philanthropic interests. Both the king and the queen were announced the evening of the Ak-Sar-Ben gala. For weeks ahead of time the *Omaha World-Herald* would do multipage photographic spreads on the various members of the court. Countesses came from rural Nebraska and western Iowa. Princesses were Omaha born and bred. The paper covered the parties that led up to the evening of the ball.

Serena Day often helped mothers redecorate homes the year their daughters were presented as princesses at Ak-Sar-Ben. Mothers spent fortunes on chintz, flocked wallpaper, and Oriental carpets. Serena held women's hands as they sat in her sunlit office and argued with their husbands over the phone about the costs of making their hovel into a palace. James told me that a husband once barked at Serena, "Coronado never found the damn gold, but you sure have," as he ripped the check out of his checkbook. As we watched the coronation that night from Charlotte's hospital room, Mom kept mumbling to herself, "I wonder if Serena knows that girl."

The five of us sat with our eyes riveted to the screen, watching the procession of countesses and princesses in the grainy color of the hospital's television set. Used as we were to our old black-and-white RCA, the color TV seemed both brilliant and magical to us in 1969. The Quivera coronation was perfect television for a hospital room. Everything about the event was beautiful. In procession, the girls moved with the assurance of privilege through the flower-bedecked field house, and the throaty-voiced announcers gave hushed depictions of each sequin and bugle bead. Every dress, every satin dance shoe had been made or purchased in New York, they told us. Silently, Charlotte ate her cold, sodium-free dinner with her right hand as the drip pulsed its medicine into the vein of her left hand.

In years past the coronation had seemed a hokey, slightly rigged event like homecoming and prom. But that night Quivera seemed lovely to me. Perfect, hopeful, and slightly miraculous, as the tanned, white-toothed girls paraded into the beige setting of Charlotte's room. Dreams and ordinary life merged into possibility. In the presence of Quivera, it seemed right that Charlotte would be well and home by Monday, wearing Hetty's go-go boots—once again the nagging, persistent child I knew her to be.

Television would always have that soporific effect on me in Charlotte's hospital rooms. I relished *That Girl* and *Family Affair* and *Get Smart* on those evenings during visiting hours. Marlo Thomas was always elegantly dressed and unemployed in her nifty New York apartment. Agent 99 swooned over the bumbling, stumbling Agent 86. Uncle Bill and Mr. French loved their perfect little family. On color TV, the clothes looked beautiful and the apartments, smartly appointed, and the endings were always happy. Even on Charlotte's worst days she could be comforted in the evening by situation comedies. She demanded that we watch them with her in silence. The television box settled us all through the evenings as we waited for

Charlotte to get well. It promised us a land of happy endings.

The nurse's voice on the loudspeaker signaled that visiting hours were over halfway through the coronation procession. As we stood up to leave, Charlotte asked, "Sarah, would they let me go to homecoming dance? I mean, could I just go and see it?"

"I don't see why not. We could take you over so you could take a look," I said, answering for Sarah, whose eyebrows arched, but she didn't say anything as I continued. "Yeah, Charlotte, you could be my date. I mean, who would care?"

"I'd rather be James's date," Charlotte said. "Could Hetty come?"

"Charlotte," Mom said, standing by her bed, "let them go home now. We'll discuss homecoming later." Morgan was at the door. Sarah and I walked toward him. Laurence pulled his thumb out of his mouth, kissed his hand, and patted Charlotte's leg. It was what he could reach. Laurence was short for a twelve-year-old.

"Fred," Sarah said to me as we walked across the parking lot underneath the moon to the Studebaker, "you understand that Charlotte's really sick. She won't be coming home on Monday."

The gulf between yesterday and today loomed beneath the moon. A gulf that has revisited me throughout my life. Sarah stood ten feet from the car as Morgan and Laurence sat in the Studebaker, listening to the radio and waiting for us to get in.

"Do you understand?"

"What, about homecoming? Will she be well by homecoming? Two weeks is a long time." I didn't want to understand and I wasn't ready to understand.

"Possibly. But it could be longer than that. So be prepared to help Charlotte understand if she can't be out by homecoming."

"But if she is, she'll be my date."

"Fred..."

Sarah looked at Morgan and Laurence in the Studebaker and then looked up at the moon.

"What?" I said.

"Someone's asked me to homecoming."

"Great," I said, looking at her profile in the moonlight.

"But it isn't James."

"Let James go, Sarah. There's nothing there."

"There's Neil Mahaffey."

"Do you think that James would have asked you to homecoming if he didn't know Neil Mahaffey?"

"Well," she said, "before Neil, I had hope. And now my hope is gone."

"He's a good friend to us. James is a good friend."

"Don't be so fair. I want you to side with me."

"I can't."

"I know."

I watched a tear slide down the side of Sarah's face, and my stomach clenched so fiercely that a small spasm shot through my gut. Tuna fish mixed with bile surged up my esophagus and into my throat, and for a second I thought I might retch.

"I'm sorry."

It was the truest thing I could think to say and it sounded so limp and hollow as I said it. Another tear slid down the curve of Sarah's face. So many times in my years of observing art, I think of my sister crying in the moonlight, and know that is the place where so much art comes from.

We walked to the Studebaker and sat in the back, listening to Laurence in the front singing along to Nancy Sinatra's "These Boots Are Made for Walking." Morgan was silent all the way home. He went straight to the rose garden after he climbed out of the car and stood there smoking for an hour. From the window of our bedroom I could see the burned ember of the ash of his Marlboro in the darkness. I wanted to go to him, but did not know how.

Two Weeks

TWO WEEKS IN the life of an illness can mean miraculous things. People who have been near death are up and about again. They are free of fever and the pain has already become memory. In two weeks, an acute illness can already have migrated into the province of story and personal history. Something spoken of in the past tense and relegated to the ordinary.

But after Charlotte had been in Children's Hospital for two weeks, things were much worse. The kidneys were not responding to the medication. Fluid was found in her left lung. She was constantly feverish. She couldn't pee. Worst of all, Hetty could not visit because she was only ten years old. During evening visiting hours, I found it oddly disconcerting listening to their telephone conversations. By the end of the first week, it had become apparent even to Charlotte she was too sick to attend homecoming, but Hetty's calls were filled with plans for the game and what they would wear. Charlotte would listen to Hetty, but rarely respond. When Hetty would change the discussion to the topic of school, Charlotte would abruptly interrupt.

"I've got to go now, Hetty," she would say officiously in a grown-up voice. "The nurse is here with my medication." There would be no nurse, just us in the solarium next to the telephone. What the diligent Hetty could not know is that Charlotte had barely opened a book since entering the hospital. Mom would work with Charlotte in the afternoon and Morgan would walk her through a page of arithmetic problems in the evening, but Charlotte did not pay attention to them.

I watched in those first fourteen days as Charlotte's illness reached into her soul, chipping away at her hope. She stopped asking questions about home and she stopped wanting Hetty to visit. Charlotte slipped into a flickering world dominated by afternoon soap operas and evening situation comedies. The stories of the hospital staff's lives became the stories she told us when we visited her. Their world and worries became hers. A pharmacist taught her hand knitting and a candy striper taught her origami. By her third week, Charlotte had moved on to knitting needles, and was folding a paper village to live under the dozens of origami birds that were flying, held up by yarn, across the ceiling of her room.

ON THE FIFTH afternoon of Charlotte's hospitalization, Sarah, Laurence, and I returned from school to find chocolate chip cookies and Parker House rolls waiting for us on the kitchen counter with a note from Serena Day: She'd left a chicken casserole and green salad in the refrigerator. It was our first meal from a neighbor. It was the best meal we'd had in days. Even Morgan perked up when he walked into the kitchen and smelled the casserole baking. After dinner that night, as we were washing dishes, Sarah announced that she was walking over to the Days' house.

"I'll be back in a minute," she told Morgan and me, handing me the dish towel.

Laurence looked up from the red and green tiles of the linoleum floor that he was supposed to be sweeping but where instead he was sitting and playing tug of war with Tiger Cat over one of Charlotte's old hair ribbons.

"I wanna go to Serena's too, Sarah," he called to her from his position on the floor.

"Not tonight, Laurence," she said, dropping her apron on the oak slats of a chair back as she marched out the door.

"What do you think that's all about?" Morgan asked me.

I almost said "homecoming," but I stopped, realizing that it was Sarah's job to tell him about her invitation, not mine. Part of me wondered if Sarah only wanted to see James. For two days after school, I'd seen Neil Mahaffey's tan Volkswagen in the Joslyn Art Museum parking lot at the edge of the Central High School campus. Each of those days, James had tossed me the keys to the Galaxy 500, promising that he would meet Sarah and me at home.

"Tell my mom I'll be home for dinner," he would say as the keys sailed through the air. "Tell her not to worry. It's only a little extra coaching."

Sarah's eyes would follow the arc of the keys from James to me, and then turned to glance as James loped across the parking lot toward Neil. Each day James passed the empty patch of chipped white rock where Arianna Isaacs and Micah Little no longer met.

The silence between Arianna and Micah was so loud that it might be called booming. The first day that James's keys sailed toward the sky and I twisted to catch them, I watched as Micah walked past Arianna without a word.

"Micah," Arianna called out to him, but he did not stop.

I did not see Micah's face, but I saw Joshua's as he ran to catch up with his brother. It was constricted with anger. "Say hello," I heard him hiss, but Micah looked away and began to run to the Fairlane.

The light drained out of Arianna's eyes. Arianna's ninth-grade brother, Gus, walked up to her, as did her best friend, Sally, who tugged on her arm to make her leave, but she stood still and unmoving until the Fairlane pulled out of the parking lot. For three days Arianna waited after school for Micah, wearing fishnet pantyhose and black patent leather shoes, and a series of almost-short dresses in the bold colors of orange and green and red, white, and blue, looking perplexingly sad and modern in those outrageously happy colors. Each day she called out to him, "Micah," and each day Micah ran. Everyone watched but James, who was running toward Neil Mahaffey.

The pain I witnessed in Arianna Isaacs those afternoons left me confused and fearful. All the romance of my crush on her washed out of me. As the light in her eyes died, my love for her slipped away. I felt an enormous shame for my infidelity, knowing that my love for Arianna came from the beauty that Micah heightened in her. The light in which she shimmered had come from him.

The bogey of the real world that Morgan and vice principals and the *Omaha World-Herald* and President Nixon always conjured up to use against the young, against us, slapped Arianna Isaacs as Micah Little's silence ran past her. It slapped Micah, too. The real world that Annie Little feared, of lynchings, mailboxes filled with dog shit, and crosses burned on lawns seeped into me that very first afternoon in the twist of my jump for those keys. The real world's seriousness was framed in the anger of Joshua's face. But James missed it as he ran toward Neil Mahaffey.

SARAH CAME HOME from the Days' house to announce to Morgan that she was going to homecoming with a boy named Mike Raven. He was a junior, like Sarah, and a boy I did not know. She and Serena Day spent an hour planning the event, from dress to shoes to hair. Serena threw herself into the dance like a madwoman. Neither set of parents asked why James and I were not going to our senior homecoming dance. Serena and Ronald Day clearly avoided the topic of Neil Mahaffey. Charlotte's illness left little room or energy for Morgan or Mom to think about the rest of us, although both of them were thrilled by the attention Serena gave Sarah.

At the end of the first two weeks of Charlotte's hospitalization, Mom resigned from her job as a receptionist in the Medical Arts Building. Morgan took out a loan from the Mutual of Omaha Credit Union to pay for Laurence's tuition at the Madonna School. They applied for an in-hospital tutor for Charlotte from the Omaha Public Schools. At breakfast that Monday of the third week of Charlotte's stay in Children's Hospital, while Laurence was searching for Tiger Cat, Morgan picked up the box of Cheerios and started talking.

"Christmas is going to be simple this year. Just presents for the little kids," he said.

Sarah and I looked up at him.

"There isn't going to be Santa Claus for you two," Morgan said, peering at the Cheerios box through the lenses of his thick bifocals.

"What?" Sarah asked.

"Sarah's present this year is her homecoming dress," Morgan said to the bright yellow cardboard of the box.

"What's my present?" I asked him. "I'm not going to homecoming."

"You're going to college," Morgan answered, putting down the box of Cheerios. "That's present enough."

BEFORE HE LEFT for work that morning, Morgan scooped up the dusty pile of college catalogs from the buffet in the dining room. As Sarah and I climbed into the Galaxy 500 with James, I could see Morgan holding Laurence's hand on the green hill of the front lawn, which was dusted with yellow and amber leaves. They were waiting for the Madonna School bus to arrive.

"What's Morgan got under his arm?" James asked.

"College catalogs," Sarah answered before I could speak.

"I'm going to college," I said, looking at Morgan in his business suit, holding my catalogs.

"Well, who didn't know that, Fred?" James said, laughing all the way down the driveway.

And for a moment I realized that despite all my dreams of museums and collections, I hadn't realized I would be going to college. I would be leaving Omaha.

The Laws of Probability

ACTUARIES APPLY THE laws of probability so that insurance companies, pension managers, and investment groups can price their products for a profit. They factor in whole sets of risks for either individuals or groups, spreading out the costs so that the money can be invested to cover claims, pay salaries, and allot bonuses. Investments and pensions are also priced out this way, as are property and casualty insurance plans. In the 1960s, when Morgan was a midlevel actuary for Mutual of Omaha, the company sold both group and individual major medical health insurance policies that made profits. It was a uniquely halcyon time for the health insurance industry. They made profits and the doctors loved them because they rarely questioned a claim or denied a referral. There were few miracle medicines, surgeries, or machines then; patients died, keeping costs down. Morgan was proud of the care and the safety net that insurance companies provided for families.

Morgan loved Mutual of Omaha. He loved walking to work every day, and he loved the actuaries with whom he worked. They were a peculiar lot, as was Morgan. Unlike the other employees—clerks, filers, telephone operators, lawyers, doctors, field operations people, and the flocks of department managers—actuaries rarely played in company-sponsored golf, softball, basketball, bowling, or tennis leagues. However, they dominated the bridge and poker groups and acted in an oblique way as pricing consultants to the employees who ran the football pools and delivered bets to the Ak-Sar-Ben Race Track on their lunch hours. And like all Mutual of Omaha employees, they were addicted to watching *Mutual of Omaha's Wild Kingdom* on Sunday nights and were thrilled when they sighted Marlin Perkins walking through the company headquarters. The actuaries were hobbyists—birders, orchid growers, motorcycle rebuilders, dog breeders, jazz club aficionados, investment club joiners—before there were even investment clubs, cross-country train travelers, and water colorists. Although their work lives were permeated with the science of predictable numerical outcomes, they tended to be phobic and rather ritually impaired. They were a superstitious group, repeating daily behaviors as though life depended on it, and were known for wearing peculiar suits and driving ancient cars. Moreover, they knew everything about everyone and everyone's family in their departments. Quite literally, they believed that God was in the details, and these men knew the details.

What Mom and Morgan referred to as "fluid in Charlotte's lung" Morgan's actuarial colleagues knew to be pneumonia. I did not know that fluid in the lung was pneumonia. I did not know that pneumonia in healthy people can have a devastating effect on the body. Nor did I know that pneumonia often creates a susceptibility to more pneumonia. Neither Morgan nor Mom discussed the meaning of fluid in the lung with us, nor how quickly the residents at Children's Hospital, and then the supervising physicians, changed Charlotte's medicines. How the kidneys momentarily fell to second place in relation to their concerns about fluid in the lung.

The actuaries at Mutual of Omaha understood all the code languages of the hospitals. Individually, they began to note the medicines that Charlotte was given and the therapies that Morgan mentioned when he returned from his lunch-time visits to the hospital. Surreptitiously they made notes from the *Merck Manual* and checked the *Physicians' Desk Reference*. They cross-checked the actuarial tables. And Morgan did the same. As the weeks passed into months, they knew that Charlotte's prognosis was not good. But like the doctors and the nurses, the actuaries understood the mysterious power that belief held over the statistics of an ill body. If Morgan believed and

Mom believed and Sarah believed and Laurence believed and I believed, and most of all, if Charlotte believed that she would get well, it increased the likelihood of Charlotte's getting well. Of Charlotte's coming home to us. So what Morgan and the actuaries never discussed in the eight hours they spent together five days a week all those months that Charlotte was ill were the predictions, the likelihood of Charlotte's regaining her health.

Instead, as good friends often do, Morgan's actuarial colleagues used their energies in another way to help our family. They studied the college catalogs that sat on Morgan's desk, calling friends and family members to find out what needed to be in the essays for application and what the individual universities and colleges were like. They knew from their lunchtime quizzing of Morgan that I wanted to work in museums and to study art history. They knew that I had a 1530 on my SATs and a 29 on my ACTs. Various actuaries filled out college applications for me. They collectively wrote essays, describing my family, Omaha, the Joslyn Art Museum, and my dreams. The Fred Holly they created during Mutual of Omaha's thirty-minute cafeteria lunch hours was a young man who later I would aspire to be, and a young man that I daily thank them for creating. It was not me, but it was the doppelganger that softened the hearts of the admissions committees who held the keys to the universities' doors. In the spirit of the numbers men they were, they set up betting pools that rode on the possibility of my acceptance to some of the big-name universities.

Decades later, Morgan told me that a man named Seymour Fineman filled out my application to Stanford, and that when Seymour stopped by Morgan's desk to get a check for my application fee, he told him, "Stanford's a happy place, Morgan. Students love it. My cousin Benjamin went there. He's the happiest guy in our family."

Morgan told me all he could think to say then was, "Thank you, Seymour, Fred could use a little happiness. We could all use a little happiness right now."

It was Seymour Fineman who also explained the intricacies of the financial aid system to Morgan, making sure that my loan and grant applications were completed in a timely manner.

What I know is that these men saved me from the war and they saved me from the worst parts of myself, which seemed to blossom and flourish my last few months in Nebraska. They saved my family from the likelihood of my not receiving a deferment if I was drafted. Drafts were almost monthly that year, as they needed more soldiers. I would be turning eighteen on February 27. But I knew nothing about Seymour Fineman then. I knew only that Morgan had taken the catalogs to work.

Most of all, I knew that Morgan and Ronald Day had stopped talking about the war. Morgan's perpetual quizzing of me about the war and the draft ended during those first few weeks of Charlotte's hospitalization. All that the fathers spoke about then was college, that James and I were going to college. The numbers men were on the job. They planned to send me safely to my land of dreams. The actuaries understood that the likelihood of saving me was far greater than of saving Charlotte.

The Game

I TOOK HETTY Carmichael and Laurence to the homecoming game while Sarah attended the game with Mike Raven, a shy boy with a slight stutter. Serena, Hetty, Laurence, and I stood in the foyer waiting for Mike Raven to arrive and for Morgan to answer the door and for Sarah to make her entrance down the stairs. As soon as Mike came in I knew from the first word out of his mouth that the whole evening would be a failure for her.

When Mike Raven said, "I am here for S-s-s-," he lingered so long on the first letter of Sarah's name that the five of us, including, Laurence, said "Sarah" for him. My stomach clenched in the anticipation of the evening's failure. At the end of this chorus, Morgan grabbed the boy's hand, pumping it up and down and saying three times, "So nice to meet you, Mike." Standing in the foyer, Mike looked tongue-tied to the point of helplessness as to what to do after the handshake. Morgan, who was so thoroughly happy to be shaking a boy's hand who did not look to be an ax murderer or a sex fiend, forgot to call upstairs for Sarah. After Morgan's pregnant pause sucked itself into the range of dead air, Serena jumped into the fray, trilling, "Sarah, Sarah, Mike is here." The minute Mike Raven saw Sarah at the top of the stairs, he blushed a red so scarlet that I thought he might have a heart attack.

Morgan posed them together outside at the foot of the steps for a photograph. It seemed to take him forever to get the two of them into focus, and each time he was close to being in focus, he would apologize to Mike about Mom not being there.

"Mrs. Holly is so sorry that she can't be here to meet you, Mike. Sarah's sister, Charlotte, is in the hospital, and she couldn't get away."

This would lead to Mike's apologizing to Morgan about Charlotte being in the hospital, and, of course, he drowned in the stuttered sound of the word "sorry."

In utter sympathy with him, Hetty barked out the word, "Sorry," making Mike blush an even deeper red. Laurence just stared openly at him and then at Sarah. Sarah looked chalky and scared, as if Mike were an alien from another planet. Lost in a kind of agony for Mike, Morgan would again lose the focus of his old black-and-white Brownie camera and begin mumbling about Charlotte and Mom. We went through this exchange four times before Mike and Sarah were photographed and out the door to the game.

Mom was spending the night at the hospital so I could drive Hetty and Laurence to the game in the Studebaker. It was a cool night and Hetty chattered all the way to the field, as if Laurence and I were Charlotte. Since she could not visit Charlotte in the hospital, Hetty had taken to visiting us after school. It became apparent during those visits that Charlotte was her dearest friend at Saunders Elementary School. Possibly Hetty's only friend. Not knowing what to do with Hetty, Sarah, Laurence, and I opened the door and invited her into our lives. She treated all of us as though we were an extension of Charlotte, telling us exactly what she thought, and what Charlotte thought about things. Hetty introduced us to a Charlotte we did not necessarily know.

Sitting next to me in the Studebaker, Hetty talked about Sarah's green-and-black plaid Pendleton skirt, and how Serena had "plaited Sarah's hair into the simple complication of a French braid." Hetty used terms like "plaited" and "simple complication" with competency. She sounded old when she spoke, but physically she had the chubby aura of a third grader. The white go-go boots, a red corduroy jumper with a brown-and-gold striped turtleneck, and the Yardley lip gloss on a chain that twisted around the sterling-silver chain of her cross could not overcome her awkward youthfulness. Laurence and I were mostly silent when she talked, slipping in an "Oh," or "Yeah," now and again. As we neared the field, she asked me a question.

"Do you think Sarah is in love with Mike Raven, Fred?"

"No," I said with a snort.

"Why not? Why don't you think she's in love with him? I mean she's going to homecoming with him." Hetty tossed one of her braids and looked at me through the brown frames of her cat-eyed glasses.

"It's just a date," I told her, signaling a left turn.

"But Sarah must at least like him, or she wouldn't be going on a date with him," Hetty countered.

"Well, maybe Sarah is going on a date with him to find out if she might like him. Dates aren't all love and romance, Hetty. Sometimes they're about curiosity. Sarah may want to find out if she might like Mike." My words sounded right to me.

"How would you know anything about dates? Or love? Charlotte told me you've never been on a date." Hetty said this earnestly, without a note of snottiness. Not with the complete derision that Charlotte would have employed in making this pronouncement.

I said, "Ouch." And I meant it.

"Did that hurt?" Hetty asked, pushing up on the frames of her glasses.

"Sure it hurt. Don't dateless people get to have opinions on dating? Couldn't I be in love without ever having gone on a date?" I could feel a kind of anger coming over me toward Charlotte and her opinions. The healthy Charlotte of the summer. The snoopy Charlotte who was always borrowing my albums.

"Fred," Laurence called out from the backseat, "are you mad?"

"I'm sorry," Hetty said, sliding away from me and toward the passenger door.

"Look, Hetty, if I had a date tonight, you and Laurence would be at home and not going to the football game. So do you know what I am?"

"No," she said in a very small voice.

"I'm your gift horse, so don't go peering into my mouth."

She didn't say another word for the rest of the ride.

It dawned on me as we pulled into the South High School parking lot that I could have had a date. I could have asked Arianna Isaacs and the worst thing that could have happened is that she might have said no. Or yes. And then I would have been like Mike in the foyer of Rabbi Isaacs's home, standing next to a girl who was in love with someone else. But it would have been a date, and possibly Arianna might have been curious enough to at least want to get to know me. Possibly, I would have found the words to make her laugh and would have seen that sparkle in the burnished gold that laced her brown eyes. She might have fallen in love with me. I might have fallen back in love with her. The stain of regret flooded over me as I climbed the bleachers with a silenced and blotchy-looking Hetty. Laurence began to suck his thumb, an anxious habit he'd nearly broken but had taken to again with a vengeance at the end of Charlotte's second week in the hospital.

As we sat down, Hetty whimpered, and Laurence looked at me over his thumb as if the sky was falling.

"Look, Hetty," I said.

The whimper burbled up again, sounding wet and soggy.

"I'm sorry."

Then tears ran down her face and she wiped her nose with her hand. Laurence sucked his thumb with loud, slobbery lips.

"I'm really, really sorry, Hetty," I said, reaching into my pocket for the handkerchief that Morgan always made me carry and handed it to her.

"Charlotte told me that you didn't want to date. Charlotte told me all you want to do is get out of Omaha. That's what Charlotte told me."

"Charlotte doesn't know everything about me, Hetty," I said, handing her the handkerchief. She wiped her eyes.

"But you're her brother," Hetty whispered, looking around trying to see how many people knew that she was crying.

"You're my date tonight, Hetty. Laurence is my brother, and you're my date tonight. That's all that matters right now."

I said it because in her sadness, Hetty had compacted. Everything about her had become smaller. Her face disappeared into a cloud of pink and white blotches behind what now seemed to be giant cat-eyed glasses. The tears and snot flowed out of a nose that seemed disconnected to a body. Her body seemed capable of slipping away from Laurence and me, of sliding through the bleachers to the mud and muck and the cigarette butts and beer cans of the land below. I said it because I did not want people looking at Hetty crying. I said it because it was true. Hetty Carmichael, not yet eleven years old, was as close as I was going to get to having a date to my senior-year homecoming game.

"Thank you," Hetty said, sniffling, rising up again.

"I'm sorry, Hetty. I didn't mean to hurt your feelings."

"I'm sorry, Fred, I didn't mean to hurt yours, either."

For a while we watched the game in silence. Out of the corner of my eye I saw Arianna with her friends and her brother, Gus. Annie Little and her husband, Abram, sitting in a section of football parents, cheered on their boys. But it was not until half-time that we saw Sarah and Mike walking together. Laurence ran to Sarah, throwing himself on her, nearly knocking her over.

"Hey," Sarah said to the three of us. Mike nodded. He stood about a foot away from Sarah.

"I want to get Hetty and Laurence something to eat. Could they stand with you two for a moment?" I asked.

Sarah looked relieved. "Sure," she said, and then added, "Is that okay with you, Mike?"

Mike nodded.

"I'll be right back." With a wave, I sprinted for the concessions stand.

The lines were long and people were milling around. Everyone I saw, I didn't know well, or didn't know at all. Splashes of regret began to lap at me as I stood in line, wishing that I was with a real date, wishing that I hadn't made Hetty cry, wishing at the very least that I was with James. It was then that I saw him. He was standing on the outskirts of a group of boys that surrounded Neil Mahaffey, who was laughing. Boys called out questions to him, cheering him on when they heard his answers. I did not know any of those boys. James looked isolated and miserable. For a moment, I felt joy, knowing that James was not enjoying this homecoming almost as much as Sarah and I were not enjoying ours. That sensation of joy at someone else's misery soon turned into a shitty, guilt-like feeling that merged into the pool of my regret. From the swamp of my feelings, I knew that I wanted James with me.

"James, James, over here," I yelled, waving both my arms. People in the concession lines started to laugh and then they began to yell "James, James over here" with me. So we were all yelling and waving together. James looked up at the sound of his name. By then, I was jumping up and down. James came running, and Neil Mahaffey's eyes followed him. They narrowed when they saw me. The crowd applauded when he reached us.

"Hey, James," I laughed, clapping him on the back.

"Hey, Fred," he said, punching me in the arm.

"Come sit with me and my date."

"I didn't know you had a date." James looked around startled.

"Hetty Carmichael." I told him.

"What?"

"Hetty Carmichael and Laurence are my dates. Come sit with us."

James smiled.

"Come sit with us."

"I can't. I'm with Neil."

"It's homecoming. Our last homecoming. You're my best friend."

"But Neil…"

I wanted to say, "He'll never notice you're gone," but instead I said, "It's something we can tell Charlotte. That we took Hetty and Laurence to homecoming for her. I mean, we can do it for Charlotte."

At the mention of Charlotte's name, James blinked twice. He looked back at Neil Mahaffey. "Just let me tell Neil," he said, and ran back.

I bought Cokes and popcorn for everyone. When James came back, he carried the popcorn.

"How's Sarah's date?" He asked as we walked back to Hetty and Laurence.

"I think it's hell. Living hell," I told him.

"I'm sorry."

"She wanted to go with you."

"I know, but I didn't want to hurt her. I don't feel that way about her.

She's like my sister."

"I know."

"You've known all along?" He asked, his eyes serious and somber.

I nodded. And I guess I had.

"I love Sarah. I always will. But I'll never feel that way about girls."

The new moon was a sliver above us. The Coke sloshed on my hands. I didn't care about the way James felt about girls or didn't feel about girls. Even then, I understood that each of us loved whom we loved. Like I loved art and James and Sarah loved dance. But I didn't trust Neil Mahaffey, and I was glad to have rescued James from his clutches. To have brought him home to us, at least for a little while.

Thanksgiving

CHARLOTTE DIDN'T COME home for Thanksgiving, because she had pneumonia. This time, Morgan and Mom called it pneumonia. Mom slept at the hospital night after night Thanksgiving week. Sarah, Laurence, and I visited her on Thanksgiving afternoon before we went to the Days' house for dinner. Charlotte was asleep. Oxygen tubes ran up her chest and into her nostrils. The ubiquitous I.V. catheter was bandaged to the yellow and purple bruises that were her swollen left hand. In silence, the three of us stood staring at her. Morgan was somewhere, talking to the resident on duty, while Mom was eating pressed turkey alone in the cafeteria. The hospital room was littered with plants and bouquets of flowers in varying stages of decay. Taped to the wall below the television set were the letters from Hetty and Charlotte's other classmates. Books, playing cards, boxed games, and her Chatty Cathy doll were piled on the window ledge. The bed next to Charlotte's was empty. Her roommate had been released to go home to Carroll, Iowa, for the holiday.

The hospital did not bustle on Thanksgiving Day. It was quiet and felt to me to be full of secrets and mysteries. The secrets of why some children could leave and others, like Charlotte, stayed. The mystery and miracle of health. The mystery of why Charlotte only seemed to worsen. The three of us witnessed Charlotte's labored breathing and the clumps of hair that were missing from her head because of a seizure caused by a new medication. "A medication," Morgan said at dinner the week before, "that they all thought would work."

In the middle of the seizure, Charlotte's free right hand had grabbed onto her drug-weakened strands and pulled out a handful of red hair by its roots from the crown of her head. The three of us had been forewarned by Morgan, who had been forewarned by Mom not to mention Charlotte's bald patch to her. Not to ask. Not to notice. But as Charlotte slept, we stood staring in a type of horror at the portion of her head that revealed a piece of scaly, white bald pate. Even thinking of the word "pate" made me think of Hetty. "Pate" was a Hetty kind of word.

On the way to the hospital in the Studebaker that Thanksgiving afternoon in 1969, Morgan told us that Charlotte was ashamed of her appearance. Of what people would think. She was afraid that she might have more seizures and that she was ashamed of the seizures. She did not want visitors.

Sarah said from her place on the front seat next to Morgan, "We're not visitors, Morgan. We're her family."

Morgan inhaled on his Marlboro, "That's right, Sarah. That's what we told her. But don't stare at her. Please don't stare at her. Talk to her like she hasn't changed a bit."

Now, the three of us stood and stared at her in the silence of the afternoon, taking in what was now Charlotte in her hospital bed, preparing ourselves not to stare, not to notice, not to mention what we saw. But she did not wake up. The room darkened as the weak November sun descended quickly into the west. Morgan whispered from the doorway, "It's time to go." But we did not move.

"Children, we need to go. Serena is holding dinner for you."

Finally Laurence walked up and touched the part of Charlotte's blanket that covered her feet. Sarah and I and did the same. None of us said a word.

Morgan dropped the three of us off in front of the Days' blond-brick house, and then drove south down Thirty-eighth Street to return to the hospital. We walked up the steps in the cut of the hill of their front lawn. A chill wind blew through the wool of my pea jacket. Silently we pushed the front door open as we always did. Warmth and the smell of roast turkey and sage wafted over us from the house's interior. Standing in the foyer we heard the loud voices of the three Days arguing in the kitchen and we could see the dining room table covered in white linen and set with lemon-colored bone china, etched crystal glassware, and gleaming sterling silver. The lights were dimmed and candles glowed on the table.

"You cannot go to Mexico with Neil Mahaffey over Christmas break, young man," Serena said in high-pitched voice. "It is utterly inappropriate."

"I am not going to Mexico with Neil, Mother. I have been invited by Neil's family to spend Christmas with them in Mexico."

"James, we have not met this young man. He has never stepped inside of our house. We do not know his family," Ronald said with gravity.

"He does not have manners," Serena said. "He honks that damn horn anytime he wants you, and you go running to him without a goodbye to your father or me."

"I'll bring him in. You can meet him." James's voice sounded desperate.

"It's not just that," Ronald said. "It's the Hollys. James, you must understand that Charlotte is gravely ill. We will need you here at Christmas. They will need you here at Christmas."

Sarah then walked quietly back out the glass-paneled front door. Laurence and I followed her and I gently tugged the door shut. The three of us stood on the steps outside the oak door and its leaded panels in our silence and in the chill of the now-dark afternoon. Laurence began to suck his thumb. Finally I rang the doorbell. Serena came running to the door, throwing it open and grabbing all three us into the circle of her arms. Wool, the chill of reddened faces, the smells of turkey, sage, onions, and Serena's Chanel No. 5 all came together in her hug.

"I was so worried," she said to us. "Where have you children been?"

"On the porch," Laurence said. "We have been on the porch."

Dinner was formal and filled with the noises of eating. The crystal sang in pure notes as our teeth clinked against it, and the porcelain whistled with each scrape of a sterling-silver fork tine or the cut of a knife blade. The food was perfect. The roasted turkey was golden and the mashed potatoes were piled high like clouds, dripping with butter. I could smell it all, but when it reached my mouth there was no taste. The tasteless food hurt as it passed down into my stomach. For the longest time, no one spoke. But finally, deep into the dinner, on his third glass of red wine, Ronald Day looked up from his plate, startled, and said: "How is Charlotte? I'm so sorry, we forgot to ask about Charlotte."

Serena looked up from the dinner that she had been pecking at like a bird, having eaten almost invisible bites, leaving her plate looking untouched.

"Oh, no. I'm so sorry," Serena said. "She's on my mind all the time. And we've forgotten to ask."

It was then that James looked at me for the first time during the dinner. He looked at me with miserable eyes. Little-boy eyes that could not wipe away their sadness or disappointment.

Looking down at her plate, Sarah spoke: "Charlotte didn't wake up."

Laurence, who was eating mashed potatoes, swallowed and said, "She sleeps under a blanket. It's a blue blanket and it's not from our house. The sheets are white and they aren't from our house either."

Ronald nodded at this information.

"But the pajamas are," Laurence added. "Charlotte was in her French poodle pajamas. They're pink."

I didn't say anything, but I felt shame for Charlotte, lying in her Children's Hospital bed, seemingly unable to get well. And I felt shame for Morgan and Mom, for Sarah, Laurence, and me for not being able to help her get well. Most of all, I felt shame for not being able to tell the Days the truth–that Charlotte looked horrible–swollen, bruised, and bald on one side of her head. That she could not take a piss and her body seemed to be brimming over with unspilled fluids. Sitting at that graceful dining room table, it seemed wrong to mention the truth. Part of believing that Charlotte would get well was remembering her in our daily lives not as she was in the hospital, but as the Charlotte before the hospital. The little redheaded girl who borrowed my records without asking and ran through the neighborhood in the darkness of summer evenings, playing night games with Hetty Carmichael.

Christmas

NURSES AND DOCTORS will tell you that the thought of Christmas can revive a dying soul. An impending birthday, an awaited telephone conversation, a holiday, the thought of holding a loved one's hand, or hearing a friend's voice can be the impetus for hanging on and fighting the good fight. This was true for Charlotte. Charlotte loved Christmas in a big way. She loved choosing the tree and unwrapping the decorations one by one on the floor of the sunroom. Year after year, she and Mom managed our Christmases like dictators. Charlotte aided Mom in every aspect of decoration and helped Morgan choose the Scotch pine tree that would be secured by cords in the trunk of the Studebaker. Charlotte liked the details of Christmas to be immutable. Beef tenderloin for a late dinner on Christmas Eve, with midnight Mass following the meal. She loved sleeping through Mass at St. Cecilia's, and jumping out of bed bright and early on Christmas morning, to awaken the rest of us to the shouts of "It's Christmas, it's Christmas." As if we didn't know. As if it were her responsibility to remind us forever and ever that it was Christmas morning, and it was time to get up. In case we might have forgotten.

During the dusk of Christmas afternoon, Charlotte would walk up and down Thirty-eighth Street with Laurence, bringing the neighbors boxes of Bauer's chocolate mints. In the darkness of Christmas evening, we would eat the Mutual of Omaha ham that Morgan was given annually as a holiday gift. The ham was served in the kitchen with Mom's baked beans, a Waldorf salad, and Parker House rolls. The menu was unwavering. These were our Christmas traditions, to which Charlotte applied unyielding standards.

What Charlotte loved most about Christmas was Santa Claus. Charlotte visited Santa Claus every December in the Mutual of Omaha cafeteria, where she stood by his knee and gave an embarrassingly detailed list of her wants, holding the bearded man's attention for nearly ten minutes, leaving the other dressed-up company progeny fussing and complaining. In truth, Charlotte loved presents. She loved the Sears & Roebuck catalog and wandering through the toy floor of the Brandeis Department Store in downtown Omaha to dream of all that she wanted from Santa Claus. Her deep faith in Christianity had to do with her deep faith in a Christmas thoroughly sopping with gifts. The more, the better, in Charlotte's estimation, because in believing in Santa Claus, Charlotte could believe in the infinite nature of his power. Charlotte believed that she was always a very good girl, and that her few faults were forgivable, and probably, in the end, someone else's fault anyway. Like my fault, as she often pointed out to me in our arguments over her snooping and borrowing habits.

Charlotte believed in Santa Claus the way Hetty believed in Jesus Christ, thoroughly and without question. Unlike other children, she had no desire to find out the truth about Santa Claus, and she avoided any steps toward growing up that might have forced her to face the facts. She believed that Santa Claus loved her and that she deserved to be loved by Santa Claus. She paid scant attention to the Father, the Son, or the Holy Ghost. Or the Virgin Mary, for that matter. Charlotte liked the magic of Christmas, and she held enormous affection for Santa's underlings–the Easter Bunny and the Tooth Fairy. Charlotte was never ever enamored with the idea of giving up something for Advent or Lent. But Mom emphasized the point to her that Santa Claus and the Easter Bunny paid attention to little girls who made sacrifices. Very much against her will, Charlotte gave up chocolate or desserts for the duration of the Church's religious seasons to make sure that she held Santa's attention.

It was apparent to me that she continued to make these sacrifices so that no one would ever tell her the truth about Santa Claus. Mom made sure that we were all co-conspirators in Charlotte's continuing belief in the magic bearded man. I chafed at the foolishness of it all, but I never challenged my mother. She seemed as unwilling to give up Charlotte the child as Charlotte was unwilling to give up Santa Claus.

Around the middle of December, Charlotte began to rally. Her lungs cleared and her color was better, though she was still swollen and had to be catheterized each day. Sarah, Laurence, and I began to take our homework to the hospital where we would study while Charlotte and her six-year-old roommate, Beth, from Carroll, Iowa, watched Christmas television specials until the end of visiting hours. Their favorites were *The Grinch Who Stole Christmas, The Charlie Brown Christmas Special,* and the movie *White Christmas* with Bing Crosby, Danny Kaye, Rosemary Clooney, and Vera-Ellen.

Sitting in her hospital room we grew used to her appearance. Each visit lessened the surprise we felt at her physical changes. The grotesque nature of the disease grew to seem normal. What she looked like in the summer was what I thought she looked like when I left the hospital. When I was home and thinking of Charlotte, she always appeared in my imagination like the fifth-grader she had been on Labor Day. But as I stepped into Children's Hospital, I expected to see the bloated and bruised Charlotte.

"I want Santa Claus to bring me go-go boots," she told us a week before Christmas. "And I want Yardley lip gloss on a whistle chain, Twister, and another Easy Bake oven, because I broke last year's."

Charlotte was rough on her toys. For years Morgan and Mom squabbled over replacing the Christmas toys that Charlotte had lost or broken. Mom would argue for replacement, and Morgan would argue against it. All replacements were negotiated, but the Christmas of 1969 was especially difficult because Charlotte was pushing for a pair of white go-go boots just like Hetty's.

Morgan did not want Mom to buy Charlotte white go-go boots for Christmas. In the face of all that Charlotte had gone through in October and November, I have never fathomed why Morgan fought the go-go boots fight, but he did.

Even his unspoken fear that Charlotte might die could not make him stop his war against go-go boots. It came to a head one Thursday evening when he and Mom were home together for dinner with us. Mom said, "Serena found a pair of go-go boots in Charlotte's size and bought them for me. I'll need a check for twenty dollars to pay her back."

"You won't be getting a twenty-dollar check from me," Morgan replied, pointing a spoonful of corn at Mom. "You know what I told you about go-go boots."

"Don't you point that spoon at me, Morgan Holly. I'm not your daughter."

"My money will not be going to go-go boots."

"Your money? Your money?" Mom said, looking straight at him. "So now it's your money, is it?"

"I told you, Eileen, that our girls would never dress like hippies. I won't have Charlotte in go-go boots."

"Don't you ever say 'my money' to me again, Morgan Holly. It is not your money. It is our money. I am not your child. And Charlotte will be getting go-go boots from Santa Claus, even if I have to tell Serena Day that you have refused a very ill child her Christmas wish. If I have to ask Serena to pay for these go-go boots, I will, but Charlotte is getting go-go boots."

Sarah, Laurence, and I sat staring at our parents. They were fighting, not squabbling or bickering.

"What is this world coming to anyway, Eileen Holly? Girls running around without enough clothes on to stop them from freezing to death and dancing around in boots that are bad for their feet? Marching around against wars that no one understands and taking drugs that hurt them? Why would anyone take a drug they didn't need? You answer me that. Tell me why, Eileen, tell me why?"

Morgan looked old then. His thin, veined cheeks were flaming beneath the yellow bags under his eyes, which were not quite hidden by his glasses. In the kitchen light, Morgan's hair looked white rather than gray. The spoon pointing at Mom shook, spilling the corn onto a meatloaf prepared by Mrs. Finnegan from down the street.

"It's Christmas time, Morgan. All the child wants is a pair of leather go-go boots. White leather go-go boots. Pretend they're cowboy boots. Pretend she wants to grow up to be a cowgirl, but at least pretend some happiness. Don't piss away what happiness we can bring her by spoiling Christmas. I can't do a damn thing about the war and hippies and drugs, but I can make Charlotte happy at Christmas. For God sakes, Morgan, if we can't make her well, we should at least try to make her happy."

They stared each other down, neither giving the other ground. It was as if their three other children were not around the table with them. The open wound of tension between them was new to us. Sarah looked white and shocked, while Laurence looked miserable and shaken, sucking on a thumb that could bring him no consolation. I wanted to flee. Their anger was palpable, intimate, and something I did not want to witness. I wanted to be excused from dinner, from high school, and from Omaha, to disappear, returning only when Charlotte came home well.

AT SCHOOL WE didn't focus on Christmas or Hanukkah, we focused on the change in the decade. The teachers were riveted to the discussion of what the new year would bring. The sixties were going to end. It was a defining decade for America. Camelot's reign had died on a sunny Dallas day in gunshots, Vietnam had escalated, another brother had been shot, and a minister had been murdered on a Memphis motel balcony. And there were riots. Plenty of riots, too many riots. Protests. Peaceful civil disobedience. Nixon was elected, and all the while men were being blasted toward the moon. The decade shook, it rattled, it rolled, and it roared, and like high school and my childhood, it was ending, whether I wanted it to end or not.

The sun had sunk deep into the western sky when we walked into the Central High School parking lot those cold, snowless December afternoons. Micah Little had begun to linger there, staring at Arianna Isaacs, who was always flanked by her friend Sally, and her brother, Gus. In the half darkness, I would wait for Sarah and James and study Micah's stare and Arianna's determined looking away. Even then, I wondered how lovers learned to forgive one another. There was no light in Arianna's brown eyes.

The look, the fire in the belly that Annie Little had fed her son was gone. Micah's face drooped with longing for acknowledgment from Arianna–the acquiescence that is the beginning of forgiveness. For three days, she did not give it. On the fourth day, she did. The glance between them was furtive and was missed by both Sally and Gus, but not by me, nor by James, who came up behind me in my snooping.

"Christmas break ought to be interesting for those two," he said, jangling his car keys.

"Don't tell anyone," I said.

"Fred, you sound like Juliet's nurse. You sound like a conspirator."

"Why shouldn't they?" I asked James. "Why shouldn't they be together? Why shouldn't two people who love each other be able to love each other? To be together?"

"You're a romantic. It's never that simple, especially for them."

"Why?" I asked him.

"He's black, she's white, for one thing. They can't walk down a street in Omaha without being noticed. They stand out. Together they're the antithesis of a secret."

"But don't you believe that they have the right to love one another, James? Don't you inherently believe that they, you, or I have the right to love who we love?"

He stared at me for a moment before answering: "Fred, you're all theory in the world of love. You've never taken a risk, or upset your own personal apple cart for one moment. Next June, you'll be out of here like a shot. I can name six girls who say they love you. Six girls you have never noticed. Their love for you means nothing. It floats all around you, and you've never noticed it."

James's words were laced with a bitterness that slapped me.

"I haven't meant to hurt any girl's feelings. Or ignore anyone. But I don't have those feelings for anyone right now. I just want to graduate and leave. What I can feel is that there is something out there, waiting for me. And it's not here in Omaha."

"You're in love with your dream museum. You always have been."

James looked so sad as he said this that I reached out to touch his shoulder, bringing my hand down his arm like it was a piece of bronze. Through his jacket I could feel his dancer's arm, its balanced and tensile weight. I pulled on his muffler, arranging the black thread of its fringes.

"If you were a statue, James, I would call you *Adonis in Blue Pea Jacket*."

"I wish you liked Neil."

"Who said I didn't like Neil?"

"You think he's a prick. Your eyes never lie. The whole world can tell you hate Neil Mahaffey."

"I don't hate Neil Mahaffey."

"You're lying right now. It's in your eyes, it's in your voice. You hate, no, you despise Neil Mahaffey."

"How can I have so much feeling for someone who's never greeted me? How can I have so much feeling for someone who has never acknowledged me? Or acknowledged our friendship?" With each uttered syllable my voice grew painfully agitated.

"Sarah's coming," James said.

I could see Sarah's coat swinging open around the pile of books that she clasped against her chest. She came out the school door in a hurry. Mike Raven was following her and she seemed to be rushing from him.

"You're it for me, James. You're it. You're my best friend. No matter what. No matter how far I go from Omaha. No matter how big the world gets, you're it. It's never changed for me. It never will."

Sarah was running from Mike Raven.

"You think Neil Mahaffey is a prick."

"He is," I said, looking directly into James's blue eyes. "But that doesn't change the way I feel about you."

James began to laugh. "It's going to be a crazy Christmas. Sarah's running away from Mike Raven and I want to run away with Neil Mahaffey. We'd better get the getaway car going so that Sarah can make her great escape."

I ran to meet Sarah. "What's going on?" I asked her.

"Talk to him. Tell him to leave me alone." She ran past me as I stepped in front of Mike Raven.

"Mike," I said, blocking him, "could I speak with you for a moment?"

"No," he said without a stutter.

"This is hard for Sarah. She's not ready to date anyone right now."

"Mind your own business." He shoved me.

"Sarah is my business. Stay away from her." I wanted to add, "you little prick." I wanted to shove him back and possibly take a swing at him. But I didn't. There was something about hitting someone who stuttered, even if he didn't stutter all the time, that seemed cruel to me.

"You're a faggot, Fred Holly. A fucking faggot."

"Stay away from Sarah," was all I could think to say, shocked at the vehemence of his words. As if he actually knew me. A me that I did not know myself. Mike Raven wasn't stuttering, and he felt dangerous to me, and foolish. After all, he'd had only a couple of dates with Sarah, hardly an engagement. She was barely sixteen.

He began to walk away, but then he took the time to turn around and flip me the bird. It stunned me. All I could think was, where did his stutter go? Who is this guy? What a creep. And what was the faggot stuff all about? I knew then that I could learn to hate a guy like Mike Raven. Neil Mahaffey was a prick, but I didn't hate him. In the growing dusk, I could see the lights of the Galaxy 500. It looked like a rescue ship circling the perimeter of the parking lot.

WHEN IT FINALLY happened, when Charlotte finally came home, it was for a twenty-four-hour leave from Children's Hospital. But we began to clean four days before she arrived. The house was floating in dust, and piles of unread *Omaha World-Herald* newspapers lined the foyer. The bathroom was grimy and the refrigerator was filled with covered dishes in varying stages of green and gray mold. For three nights, we took pile after pile of papers, fliers, and Christmas catalogs past Morgan's now leaf-buried rose garden to the alley, where we burned them in the barrel. Laurence loved to ignite the papers and watch the flames leap up into the darkness.

"Look," Laurence said, and he laughed as he tossed a match into the blackness of the barrel and the fire crackled and then roared toward the clear night sky. Tiger Cat stood between us, watching the flames. Laurence picked up the cat, petting the purring animal, and saying, "Look Tiger Cat, it's fire. We made fire."

That night, Morgan, Sarah, and I had driven to Shaver's Grocery Store to pick up the beef tenderloin and buy a tree at the lot next door. There was no snow on the ground. The boulevard trees were leafless in the December chill, and bunches of browned leaves scattered in the cold night wind. Bare and gray, Omaha looked rough and disheveled. Without the softness of snow, the Christmas lights looked exposed and garish. Sitting in the back of the Studebaker on the way to Shaver's, I was momentarily overwhelmed by an unspecific sadness. When Morgan paid for the tenderloin, I saw him wince at the price. Every tree on the lot was crooked, too tall, or too short. The Scotch pine we finally bought was both crooked and already dropping needles, but Sarah reminded us that it had to be a Scotch pine, "or we would never hear the end of it from Charlotte."

AFTER SHE WAS released from school for the Christmas holidays, Hetty called or stopped every day by to see if we were certain that Charlotte was coming home on Christmas Eve. Reverend and Mrs. Carmichael had arranged for Hetty to spend the holiday with Charlotte. With us. They told Mom it was the only Christmas gift Hetty had asked for.

"You see," Hetty told me that first evening of the holidays by telephone, "Christmas is a big season for an Episcopal rector."

"I can understand that, Hetty," I told her.

"And generally I have to be at St. Barnabas for everything. That's the rule."

"Well, sure," I said.

"But my dad understands. And he says that I can spend the whole time with Charlotte. That he will explain to the congregation why I am not at church." Hetty's voice sounded torn. It was obvious to me that by spending Christmas Day with Charlotte, Hetty was forfeiting the joy of Christmas services. For Hetty did find the Christ in Christmas.

It dawned on me as we all waited for Charlotte to come home how much Hetty missed Charlotte, and that Charlotte's affection for Hetty had not been felt by all of their fifth-grade classmates. So often when Sarah and I walked in the back door, we could hear Laurence and Hetty playing "Heart and Soul" on the used upright in the living room. Laurence had never mastered reading music, but Annie Little had taught him from the John Thompson piano instruction books by playing pieces with him over and over again until his ears and hands had learned them. But when Hetty came over after school, they would play raucous duets, pounding out their frustrations on the old upright. Hetty's frustrations had to be substantial because it was apparent that Laurence, our dear Laurence, was Hetty's best-friend-in-waiting. She loved him, while Laurence adored her. All through December, he declared, "I'm going to marry Hetty someday," making Sarah and me smile. The smiles were furtive and reflexive. Laurence wouldn't always catch them, but when he did, he would angrily retort, "I am, I am going to marry Hetty someday," leaving Morgan to soothe him. "Laurence," he would say, "Hetty's a fine girl. You have chosen a good friend."

ON DECEMBER 23, Mom taped a sheet of paper with Charlotte's diet to the refrigerator. It was a low-sodium, low-potassium, low-magnesium, and low-protein diet. Very little of what we would be eating would be on Charlotte's plate. The ham, the tenderloin, the baked beans, the Waldorf salad, even the celebratory glasses of Coke and 7-Up, would be forbidden to Charlotte.

Sarah and I stood at the refrigerator and stared at the menu while Mom watched us.

Finally Sarah said, "Mom, it won't be Charlotte's Christmas."

And I said, "Can't she break the rules for one day?"

"No," Mom said, her lips pressed into a thin line. "The doctors are very strict about this diet."

"But," I said, searching for an argument, "what's the use of coming home from the hospital, if it's going to be just as bad as being at the hospital? I mean, Charlotte's going to be really, really mad about this food. This isn't what Charlotte eats for Christmas."

Mom turned away from us. Sadness oozed down my chest, lodging somewhere in my diaphragm. I looked at Sarah and we walked upstairs to the attic, where Sarah stood at her barre and began to do nervous pliés. Tiger Cat looked up from a pile of afghans where he was sleeping to stare at Sarah while I rummaged through a pile of forty-fives to play a song on the small record player. The attic was cold and the doors to the cedar-lined closets were opened. Boxes emptied of Christmas decorations were scattered across the ballroom. Six red and green hand-knit stockings were draped over the two largest boxes. Our names were knitted into the stockings in a white woolen yarn. In one of the closets I could see our christening gown, swaddled in tissue paper and hanging from a hook in the wall. Resting against the wall was the frame of one our cribs and the backdrop for Sarah's seventh-grade science project on photosynthesis in roses. The red ribbon of second place was still attached to it.

"It feels wrong, Fred," Sarah said to me as she raised her hand above her head. Each of her fingers curved in an elegant relaxation. "Why are we making all this food that Charlotte can't eat?"

"Because Charlotte expects it. It's her Christmas. It's Mom's Christmas. It's the Christmas we've always done," I told her, adding, "and I don't think Mom knows how to do it any other way. But you heard what she said. Charlotte has to stick to the diet." I fished out a forty-five of Simon and Garfunkel's "Bridge over Troubled Water" and put it on the player. It was sad and soothing. I grabbed an afghan from Tiger Cat's pile, only slightly disturbing him. Curling up near the window, I whispered the words of the song, watching Sarah in her bare feet and blue jeans bend, extend, and stretch to a rhythm all her own. I wanted a cigarette, but I never smoked in the house. For so long, cigarettes had been my secret nightcap; now I longed for them more and more. Even the idea of smoking a cigarette appeased my anxiety. Imagining the smoke swirling down into my lungs curbed my fears and settled me.

"Hey, Sarah," I said, "what's with this Mike Raven guy? He was really a creep in the parking lot. A first-class prick. I mean, why did you go out with him in the first place? I don't get it."

"Because, I'm stupid. Because a girl I know said, 'Oh, Mike Raven really likes you. You should give him a chance,' and I wanted to try going out with him to see what it was like. I was flattered to be noticed. I wanted to get all dressed up for homecoming. You know what? When he's nervous, Mike stutters, but when he's mad he yells. He thinks that I should like him because he likes me. As if human feelings were an equation. I like you, so you like me. Well, I don't like him, and now he's bothering me at school. He's a jerk."

"Don't you think it's mysterious that Mike Raven likes you, but you don't like him? One person can have all this feeling for another, and the object of their affections doesn't have any of it in return for them. Our affections aren't necessarily parallel. True love must mean that affections are parallel." Then I added, "Or do I mean affections must intersect? Maybe there are people who would fall in love with one another, but they are living parallel lives, meaning they haven't intersected."

"But I have no affections for Mike," Sarah said, bending all the way to the cold floor, "and his affections for me mean nothing to me. We have nothing in common. He's only nice when he gets everything his way, and he's mean when he doesn't. He's a jerk. I never want to intersect with him. Ever."

"Yes, he is a jerk," I said, listening for a moment to the part of the lyric that goes, "Like a bridge over troubled water, I will lay me down," and then added, "Mike Raven called me a faggot. He also called me a fucking faggot. What's with him? The guy shoved me."

Sarah's head shot up from her bend to look across the room at me.

"Mike Raven called you what?

"He called me a faggot."

"That little shit. I told him that I really loved James and that I couldn't keep going out with him when I really loved James. Then he said to me, 'Everybody know that James Day is a faggot, and he's going to burn in hell.' Mike's a Baptist, or some religion like that. Some heartless religion. So, of course, you're James's friend, so you must be a faggot, too."

"You said you were in love with James and then he called James a faggot?" I asked her as Art Garfunkel crooned to some atmospheric high. "Aren't you supposed to break up with guys by telling them you want to be their friends, but that you just don't feel that way about them?" I made quotation marks in the air when I said "that way." "Isn't the truth what you're supposed to avoid telling them?"

"I tried that. I told him I didn't feel that way about him." Sarah said as she spread her arms out into something like wings from her bend at the waist position. "But he said he wanted to keep seeing me, even as a friend. And then I told him that Charlotte was so sick that I couldn't see him, and I felt horrible for using Charlotte that way. Mike tells me he'll go to the hospital with me. We can do our dates at the hospital. He tells me he doesn't mind being around sick people. So I told him the truth. I said that I was in love with James Day and that I didn't want to see him anymore. And then he called James a faggot, and I thought he was going to hit me on top of it." Sarah shuddered as her arms floated through the air.

"Why the hell did you go out with him?" I asked her.

"I told you, a girl said he liked me. I wanted to go to homecoming. Don't be such a pain. I made a mistake."

"Well, next time wait to go out with a guy who hates you," I said. "He'd be a step up from this creep."

Sarah started to laugh and then threw a ballet slipper across the room at my head. I caught it.

"So what do you think about my affections theory of love? Do you think that lovers live these parallel lives until something shakes up their personal universes, forcing them to intersect? At this very moment, living a parallel life is your great love, and there will be some great rupture in your life that will allow you to meet him? A tear in your heavens that will bring you together?"

"How long have you been working on this new theory?" Sarah asked, slowly slipping into a scissors split.

I thought for a moment and then said, "About ten minutes, but I like it. It works for me."

"Well, in between concocting this highly unusual approach to understanding romance and love, have you bought a single Christmas present yet?"

"The presents are in the bag," I told her.

CHARLOTTE WAS RELEASED from the hospital at seven minutes past eleven on the morning of Christmas Eve. Sarah, Laurence, and I were waiting at home with Hetty. We knew, but Hetty did not know, that Charlotte didn't want Hetty to see her. She was afraid of Hetty's seeing her. Twice that week at the hospital, she had thrown tantrums, protesting Hetty's spending Christmas with us. But Mom and Morgan were unyielding. They both liked Hetty, and they thought that Hetty would feel better if she could spend some time with Charlotte. And they knew that Charlotte would be better off if she would let someone outside the family and the hospital look at her.

Morgan drove the Studebaker into the garage and helped Mom and Charlotte get out. When Hetty saw Charlotte step out onto the driveway, she gasped. Charlotte was too swollen to wear her princess-style winter coat. Instead she wore a second-hand fake fur coat that Mom had found for her at the Goodwill. It was gray and hung loosely around her body, brushing the tops of her fuzzy pink slippers. Tied around Charlotte's head was a red scarf of Sarah's that hid her bald spot. Charlotte held Mom's hand while Morgan carried her overnight case and hospital supplies. Hetty inhaled deeply in a shocked amazement before she stepped out of the doorway to greet her.

"Charlotte, Charlotte," she cried, running down the stairs and out onto the frozen, snowless backyard.

"You're wearing your go-go boots," Charlotte called out in response.

"Merry Christmas," Hetty said.

"Santa Claus is bringing me go-go boots for Christmas just like yours, right, Mom?" Charlotte tugged on Mom's gloved hand.

"I have no idea what Santa is bringing you for Christmas, Charlotte Anne Holly," Mom said, smiling. "I am not Mrs. Santa Claus. Nor am I an elf. You will just have to wait and see like you do every year. Merry Christmas, Hetty."

"Merry Christmas, Mrs. Holly," Hetty said, taking Charlotte's other hand.

Mom settled Charlotte under a pile of blankets on the couch in the sunroom, across from the Christmas tree. Hetty sat next to her, still holding her hand. Sitting in her new set of yellow flannel pajamas with the red scarf around her head, Charlotte ordered everyone around, including me. "Fred," she said pointing, "move that gold ball farther up on the tree. We always have it higher. And straighten out the angel's skirt. She looks sloppy."

Numbly, I followed Charlotte's orders. The two Charlottes of my mind were merging into the one before me. I realized as I reached to straighten the angel's lace skirt that I was forgetting what Charlotte looked like before the hospital. Now that she sat in the sunroom, holding Hetty's hand, the old healthy Charlotte was beginning to fade from my memory. All my imagination could hold on to was the present Charlotte, sitting like a troll, swollen and feverish in her red scarf. The blue eyes were the same, as was the sound of her voice, but the ten-year-old girl of curly red hair on the chubby cusp of a growth spurt was gone.

As Mom worked in the kitchen and Morgan crawled around the Christmas tree adjusting the strings of lights, Charlotte talked to Hetty about the hospital and Hetty listened. Charlotte explained the routine of her days, described the blandness of hospital meals, the pain of the catheter, and how she dreaded each new medication. She said, "One time, I had a seizure. Like an epileptic." Hetty looked genuinely shocked at this news.

Charlotte talked to Hetty as if the rest of us were not there. She talked to Hetty in a way that she talked to no one else. The rest of us moved around the house in a kind of dazed shock, listening to Charlotte talk and Hetty ask questions.

"Is your tutor nice, Charlotte?" Hetty asked when Charlotte complained about the tutor who visited her twice a week.

"She's nice, but she wants me to do my homework."

"Of course, she wants you to do your homework, Charlotte. So that you can come back to fifth grade."

"But I'm sick. And I don't want to do it."

"Well, what do you want to do?" Hetty asked.

"I want to watch soap operas," Charlotte said.

I could see Morgan's shoulders stiffen beside the Christmas tree, where he was replacing a blue bulb on a strand of lights. Laurence picked up Tiger Cat, put his thumb in his mouth, and left the room. "Sarah," Mom called from the kitchen, "I need your help."

"You get to watch soap operas?" Hetty said with a look of serious amazement. "My parents won't let me watch soap operas, even on summer vacation."

"As long as I do something like finger knitting, or work on my hand loom or finger-paint, I get to watch soap operas. And I love them."

Then Charlotte said the worst thing of all. The thing that I knew would drive Morgan crazy. "And all afternoon, people eat their lunch with me and Beth, my roommate. The pharmacists, the med techs, the nurses, and the orderlies." Charlotte raised a finger for each variety of profession that happened to drop in to watch soap operas with them as the two girls did their occupational therapy. "Even the residents sometimes."

Morgan groaned as he straightened the Christmas tree skirt and stood up.

"I think I left something in the car," he said to the two girls and he walked past me and into the foyer, grabbing his jacket before slipping out the front door.

The reports from the tutor were a constant tension between Mom and

Morgan. They discussed them and argued about them after they returned home late at night from the hospital, when they assumed we were all asleep.

"She needs to study." Morgan would say. "Charlotte needs to get ready to go back to school."

"Morgan, the child's sick. These people are her friends and her world."

"Eileen, she needs to study. She's falling behind, and she doesn't care. The hospital's becoming her world. The damn soap operas are becoming her reality. Charlotte needs to know that she's going to get well, and that she will be going back to school. You have to make her study."

"I try, Morgan. But you're not there every morning when I pull out her schoolbooks. At this point, Charlotte can't imagine not being in the hospital. It's as if she can't believe she'll get well. So all she wants to do is escape into the television."

"Or those damn comic books. Don't forget those." To Morgan's chagrin, Charlotte read piles of comic books. I saw them all over her hospital room. And she read them aloud to Beth, who was growing to love them as much as Charlotte.

"She'll have to repeat fifth grade at this rate."

"Well, I'll just be glad to have her in school next year, Morgan Holly, I don't care what grade Charlotte's in."

"So we're saving her kidneys," Morgan would say, "but tell me, what will be left of her brain?" Mom never responded. All I would hear was the sound of the bed lamp clicking off.

CHARLOTTE AND HETTY ate Christmas Eve dinner in the sunroom, with Hetty eating exactly what Charlotte ate—a small piece of broiled chicken, dry white bread toast, peeled apple slices, and steamed frozen green beans with pepper and lemon juice—while they watched television. Charlotte did not look at the dining room table decorations, nor did she ask anything about what the rest of us were having for dinner. She showed no interest in anything but Hetty and the television.

Mom, Sarah, Laurence, and I went to midnight Mass. The cathedral was packed. I was not, nor am I now, a great believer, but I prayed that night for a happy Christmas for Hetty and Charlotte. When we returned, the two girls were asleep on the couch as the CBS test pattern flickered across the screen of the television. While we were away, Morgan had lined the tree with Santa's presents and set out the six stockings filled with navel oranges and Hershey's chocolate bars. The name on Morgan's stocking was covered in white paper and the name "HETTY" was lettered in bold black down the length of it. There was no chocolate in Charlotte's stocking.

<hr />

IN THE MORNING, it was Morgan who woke us, and it was Morgan who handed out each of the gifts.

Laurence and I always bought our gifts together. We gave Sarah a hand-sized replica of the Joslyn's plaster cast of Edgar Degas' *La Petite Danseuse de quatorze ans–Little Dancer, Fourteen Years Old.* To Charlotte and Hetty we gave sterling-silver friendship necklaces. Each necklace was a broken heart that could only be made whole by the two girls' joining them. They, of course, loved the brokenhearted necklaces. Every year since Laurence was born, he and I had given Ice Blue Aqua Velva to Morgan and lavender-scent talcum powder to Mom. We did the same in 1969 and listened to the appreciative murmurs of our parents. Laurence gave me a belt he had beaded at the Madonna School, and I gave Laurence a brass kaleidoscope. Laurence spent the whole morning looking into the weak December sun, bedazzled with each twist on the kaleidoscope's body.

The most beautifully wrapped box of all held the go-go boots. Santa's elves had outdone themselves with red and gold paper and a white satin bow. Charlotte squealed when she pulled out the first boot.

"Thank you, thank you, Santa," she shrieked, true believer that she was.

She kicked off her blankets, pushed up the loose yellow flannel of her pajama legs, and tried to put on the right boot. It dangled from her swollen foot.

"Mom," she wailed, "fix it."

We all looked silently at Charlotte's swollen legs and at the stiff leather of the white go-go boots. Her legs were purple with bruises and feverishly red looking with fluid visible under the skin, as were her feet.

"Charlotte," Morgan said, "we will have the boots softened and stretched, and they will be fine for summer. Then you will be well and they'll be perfect. You can wear them all summer and every day next year to school."

"Are you sure, Morgan?" she asked him with a note of trepidation in her voice.

"I'm certain. You will be well by summer, and with a little help from the cobbler, they'll be perfect."

Charlotte looked at Mom while a shocked Mom looked at Morgan and then nodded to Charlotte.

Charlotte hugged the go-go boots.

I kept comparing Charlotte's swollen feet to the go-go boots in wonder that we had not considered what her illness might have done to her feet. Her feet existed for all of us in some wellness dimension, in a universe of shapely little-girl feet. Only the go-go boots of a troll child would fit Charlotte's feet now. Staring at her feet, I couldn't imagine them well by summer, but I wanted to believe that she would be in the white boots by June.

I did not expect anything for Christmas, because I understood that I was going to college. But Morgan and Mom brought out a large gift that they'd hidden in the coat closet in the foyer.

"This, Fred," Morgan announced, "is not from Santa Claus."

"No, it's from us," Mom said.

"It's not new," Morgan then said.

"But it's in great condition," Mom hurried to add.

"Hurry up and open it," Charlotte called from her place on the couch, where she still held the go-go boots in her arms.

I did. It was a large honey-colored leather suitcase with brass fittings and a few scratches from travel. It was indeed beautiful.

"Do you like it?" Morgan asked, lighting a Marlboro and then inhaling.

"I, I, I...love it," I whispered to them, remembering finally to say, "Thank you. I love it."

"Oh, honey," Mom said, "we found it at the Goodwill. And we thought you could use it for college."

"What's college?" Laurence asked.

"It's going-away school," Charlotte said with the knowledge of someone who watched soap operas.

"Will I go, too?" Laurence asked, putting down the kaleidoscope.

"No," Charlotte said, "you'll always live with Morgan and Mom. You'll never go to college."

"Good," Laurence said, looking relieved.

TWO HOURS LATER it was time to take Charlotte back to the hospital and that's when she began to cry. At first it was a little whimper and then it became a wail. Looking frightened, Hetty put her hand on Charlotte's shoulder.

"I don't wanna go," she told Mom, who was packing her overnight bag.

"Charlotte," Mom said, "we talked about this at the hospital. You have to go back. You need to be catheterized. You need to go back on your drip. We can't do this at home."

Big tears ran down Charlotte's face and as she fiercely wiped them away, her head scarf began to loosen. The red cloth slid onto Charlotte's shoulder, covering Hetty's hand. It was then that Hetty saw the thin wisps of Charlotte's remaining hair and the few carrot-colored strands that had sprouted in her still bald spot. Then, brave Hetty, not yet eleven-year-old Hetty, began to cry, too.

"I'm so sorry," Hetty said in front of all of us. "I am so sorry."

"Me, too," Charlotte told her.

I felt helpless, then, and constricted in my chest, as though I might not ever breathe again.

SARAH, LAURENCE, HETTY, and I stood across the front lawn in coats, hats, and mittens, waving as Morgan backed the Studebaker down the drive. One by one, the neighbors opened their front doors and stepped onto their porches in Christmas sweaters and aprons, high heels and red velvet dresses, and in the plush bathrobes of the season. The parents held newspapers, coffee mugs, and cigarettes, while the children dangled dolls and dragged toy dump trucks behind them. They waved along with us. The three Days were the first to call out to the passing Studebaker, "Merry Christmas, Charlotte Anne Holly, Merry Christmas." The words echoed down the block.

THE THREE OF us walked Hetty home.

"I'm sorry," she said as we neared the St. Barnabas parsonage.

"For what?" Sarah asked.

"For crying," Hetty said, her lower lip trembling.

"You have nothing to be sorry for," Laurence said to Hetty. It was what Morgan was always saying to Laurence.

"That's right," Sarah said, tugging on one of Hetty's braids and hugging her.

"You are a brave girl, Hetty Carmichael. I admire you." I said those words, meaning something bigger and better and greater, but all I had to offer Hetty were my words. She hugged me, pushed the gate open, and ran to her father, who was still dressed in his rector's collar and suit. Hetty wept every step of the way.

Epiphany, 1970

EARLY ON THE morning of Epiphany, it began to snow heavy wet flakes, blanketing the city and softening the harsh colors of the holidays. James Day turned eighteen on that final day of Christmas, six days into the cusp year that latched us between two decades. Serena invited Sarah, Laurence, and me to celebrate James's birthday dinner, knowing that Mom and Morgan would eat at the hospital with Charlotte.

"Fred," Serena said on the phone, "I am so embarrassed at how frightened I am of the draft. I keep wanting James to move to England and declare himself a citizen of the United Kingdom, but I am afraid that Ronald would die of shame. He would want James to face the music, to be a man. And all I want is for you and James to live."

"James will be okay," I told her, believing that. I couldn't imagine James being unlucky enough to be drafted. "He's more a Peace Corps guy or a USO show director," I added, imagining James building a school or setting up a stage. I could hear Serena sigh.

They'd invited Neil Mahaffey to this dinner, and Serena was nervous about it.

"James is crazy about this debating coach," she told me over the phone. "I couldn't see any way of getting out of inviting him, James wanted him so badly to be here. All I really wanted was family. All I really want are you three Hollys."

"It'll be fine," I said, lying through my teeth, because I was just as nervous about the evening, of things going wrong, of saying the wrong thing. Sarah balked at going to the dinner.

"Oh God, not Neil Mahaffey," she wailed to me in the attic when I told her what Serena had said. "I can't stand the idea of eating across a table from him. I won't go."

"You have to go," I said. "Serena wants us all there. She made me promise that you, Laurence, and I would be there. That she and Ronald wouldn't have to face him alone."

"I'll have to be nice to him. I'll have to be polite to him. I can't stand it."

"Well, it could be worse," I told her.

"How could it be worse?"

Then, of course, I had to think of some way it could be worse. "Well with Serena and Ronald there, Neil Mahaffey has to be on his best behavior. He can't get away with the stuff he does to you at debate matches. And I'll be there. Stay near me. Worse would be a party without Serena and Ronald and me."

It was all I could think to tell her. Sarah wilted down into a scissors split, her face against her kneecap, her hands grasping the bare arch of her right foot. Tiger Cat unwound himself from his pile of afghans, gingerly making his way to Sarah to brush against the side of her ribcage.

"Oh, Tiger," she murmured, "first Mike Raven, and now this. Boys are such bastards."

"Well, I'm not a bastard," I told her, gently placing the phonograph needle into the vinyl groove of "Eleanor Rigby" on the record player, and entering into the melancholy pop sound of the song. "And neither is James or Ronald or Morgan or Laurence or Micah or Joshua, or Tiger Cat." Then I lit a Marlboro from a pack I had stolen from Morgan.

"Oh, Fred, don't smoke up here, Morgan hates it," Sarah said from her position on the floor.

"He doesn't notice anymore," I said, inhaling deeply.

"God, I hate it when he doesn't notice. It's a like a part of him is gone," Sarah said. "Give me a drag."

I crawled over to hand her my cigarette, grabbing one of the afghans along the way.

"I guess this makes me almost a real dancer," she said, as she came up from her bend to take the cigarette. "That's probably my most bizarre memory from my days in *The Nutcracker* was how much the grown-up dancers smoked. It almost seemed liked the only time they weren't smoking was when they were dancing. I hated it. The practice stage was like a chimney." Sarah took a puff. "God, I hate it that I enjoy cigarettes so much. We shouldn't smoke inside, Fred. We need to contain our vices."

"Well, I have something more important for us to worry about than our vices. What should we do about Charlotte's birthday?" I asked her as I pulled the afghan around my shoulders. "How can you practice up here when it's so cold?" The Beatles crooned on about Eleanor Rigby.

Charlotte's birthday was January 21, technically a pretty lousy time for someone who loved presents as much as Charlotte. For years, it had created consternation between Mom and Morgan, because Morgan always felt that Charlotte had gotten more than enough presents at Christmas time and that her birthday could be celebrated with less.

Sarah inhaled deeply, handed me the cigarette, and returned to her extended bend.

"All the great dancers practiced in the cold. Central heating is a relatively new invention, you know. Anyway, it keeps my mind off things. Getting back to Charlotte's birthday. We know that clothes are a bust. She can't fit into anything. But there's makeup, jewelry, and albums."

"There's Hetty."

"What about Hetty?" Sarah asked, not moving.

"I think we should sneak her into the hospital for Charlotte's birthday."

"The staff would be major, big-time pissed off if we brought Hetty and her germs into the hospital," Sarah said, her face popping up from her kneecap to look me straight in the eyes.

"I think we should do it."

"Well, I'll think about it. Have you gotten James's birthday present yet?"

"It's done, it's taken care of," I told her. "Think about Hetty."

SNOW WAS FALLING as the three of us walked to the Days' house with Sarah carrying a stack of presents. Laurence stopped every step of the way to make snowballs that he promptly threw at one of us. Sarah and I left him in the front yard working on a snowman, knowing that there would be drinks before dinner, and glad for the few minutes that we would have with the Days before Neil Mahaffey arrived.

Stepping in from the snow-white darkness of the outside into the foyer of Serena's house felt like walking into the prism of a jewel. The house gleamed with the polish of spotless surfaces, candlelight, and the brilliance of yellow light breaking through the crystals of her chandeliers. Everything about Christmas was gone. The linens in the dining room were cream-colored, and Serena had set the table with a Jensen sterling-silver pattern that she had been collecting for years. Peach-colored rosebuds were massed in a low Waterford vase at the table's center. At James's plate was his engraved baby cup, marking his space as the birthday boy. Serena was in a perfect black dress with pearls at her neck and a pink cashmere sweater to ward off the night's chill. She was lighting more candles at the buffet as we walked into the dining room. And she was crying.

"Serena," Sarah said, holding out the presents.

"I'm having a good old-fashioned weep as I light these candles, children. What else is a mother to do on her son's eighteenth birthday?" Serena said this as she blew out the match, and then grabbed Sarah into her arms. "Come here, Fred Holly," she called to me, "and give an old woman a hug."

I put my arms around the two of them, looking down into her blonde hair, now slightly faded with white strands, startled by my own size and the feel of Serena's birdlike bones next to the heft of Sarah's muscle and ligaments.

"That boy of mine wants to grow up and I'm just not quite ready for it."

When she said this, I tightened my hug, wanting to protect her and Sarah and the world that our parents had made for us there on Thirty-eighth Street in Omaha, Nebraska. For one moment in my life, I was wanting something within my grasp.

"Where is this Mr. Neil Mahaffey?" Serena asked as she gently pushed away from us. "This goddamn Neil Mahaffey that we all hear so much about? I'll tell you where he is, children. I'll tell you where he is. Not here. He's late. This young man is late. Making the bloody world wait for him, just as he always makes James wait for him."

"Serena," Ronald called from the kitchen, "is that the Hollys? What do they want to drink?"

"Oh, Ronald, goodness knows the world wouldn't spin if we didn't start drinks on time." Serena laughed, wiping her eyes with a crumpled handkerchief. "I need to stop this crying. James won't have it."

"Serena, where are the cherries?"

"I'm coming," she said moving toward the swinging door that led to the kitchen. "Sarah, call James down. Where's Laurence? He'll have his usual Roy Rogers, won't he?"

Sarah climbed the stairs to the landing to call for James and I went to the front door to get Laurence, and that's when I saw them: Laurence and Neil Mahaffey, building the snowman. Laurence was laughing as he and Neil lifted the second ball onto the snowman's trunk. I stood there for a few minutes watching them roll the snowman's head, Laurence chattering away at the questions Neil Mahaffey put to him.

I was and am a sucker for any kindnesses that the world has shown Laurence. Any relative of a disabled person can tell you of the host of cruelties that are perpetrated on these people, from name-calling to sexual abuse. Rare is the family that has not experienced both of these, and everything in between. Watching Neil Mahaffey in the snow with Laurence, I witnessed an extravagance of kindness. Years later, Morgan and Mom telephoned me to tell me that a group of teenage boys had jumped Laurence and stolen his wallet as he walked home from the bus stop on Dodge Street. "But worse than that," Mom said, tears spilling into her voice, "they took Laurence's socks, his shoes, and his galoshes, making him walk home barefoot through the snow." Later in anger, I cried, too, but then I remembered Neil Mahaffey with Laurence on the night of James's eighteenth birthday. A memory of kindness in the snow, and Laurence laughing. Something to hold on to.

As I watched Laurence and Neil Mahaffey build the snowman, my opinion of the debate coach altered. A lens shifted. Bleeding into my black-and-white version of Neil was a grayness, an uncertainty in my point of view. Looking out onto them in the swirling snow, I understood what I had kept at the periphery of my vision. For James it was more than being the "fucking faggot" of Mike Raven's estimation, it was that he loved Neil Mahaffey. He loved Neil Mahaffey so much that it was breaking Serena's heart. At that moment, I thought, Neil was worthy, at least, of some of this love.

JAMES CAME TO the dinner table dressed in a blue sport coat, gray trousers, and a striped tie. His sandy brown hair was brushed back off of his face and he had shaven. I felt shabby next to him, wearing the same blue trousers that I had worn for three days and an old work shirt of Morgan's that I had borrowed because I knew it to be clean. I felt like something, as Mom would say, "that the cat had dragged in." James looked collegiate and older and not like me.

Unlike James, Sarah, and me, Neil Mahaffey was accorded the privileges of the twenty-seven-year-old man that he was, in that he both drank and smoked along with Serena and Ronald while we nursed Cokes throughout the meal. Neil was too much of a debater to be described as garrulous, but the scotch and water and the two glasses of burgundy did seem to loosen his tongue. Like James, he looked handsome and collegiate, in khaki pants and a V-necked blue sweater over a button-down shirt and tie. Neil looked to be James's counterpart, while I felt myself to be the boy next door, outside their circle. James drew out his parents and Neil, encouraging him to talk, while Sarah and I listened and Laurence observed.

We found out that Neil's father owned a large industrial real estate company in Omaha and that Neil was asked to leave Creighton Prep after his sophomore year there. Why he was asked to leave was not mentioned. After a miserable year at Westside, "I begged my way back into the Jesuits' good graces," He was allowed to return to Creighton Prep for his senior year. Neil did mention that he was a "Phi Beta Kappa graduate of Northwestern University," and that he had been "thrilled to write a letter or recommendation for James" to the Northwestern admissions office. James blushed when he said this, smiling through his blush.

Dinner was roast beef, Yorkshire pudding, green beans, and mashed potatoes and gravy. Serena and Sarah kept running to the kitchen to replenish the food. The three of us Hollys ate as though we hadn't eaten in months. Serena completed the dinner with a three-layer chocolate cake iced with a heavy buttercream frosting. Eighteen candles burned in six tightly compacted rows of three.

Neither Sarah nor I had to say much because Neil didn't really pay any attention to us. Things were going swimmingly. We all sang "Happy Birthday" to James, applauding when he blew out the eighteen blue candles. As Serena began to cut the cake, Neil Mahaffey made an announcement.

"Today," he said, "I learned that I was accepted into the Jesuit seminary."

The voices around the table grew silent and Serena stopped cutting in mid-slice.

"What's that?" Laurence finally said in the middle of the awkward silence.

"It's a place where men go to study to become priests." Sarah whispered.

"Will I go there?" Laurence asked.

"No," Sarah whispered.

"Will Fred?" Laurence persisted in his questioning.

"No," I said.

We all looked at James, who had gone white, and then Ronald said, "Well, congratulations are in order. Your family must be very proud of you."

While the rest of us murmured our congratulations, James pushed back his chair, tipping it over, and ran out of the dining room. We heard a series of doors slam and felt the cold snow air slip around our ankles.

Without a word Neil Mahaffey jumped up to follow him. Serena sat down, putting her face into her hands. We listened as one car's engine started and then another. Ronald lit a cigarette and moved around the table to Serena, and sat next to her, rubbing the pink cashmere that covered her back with his free hand. Sarah began picking up the plates and I took the cake to the kitchen, the knife still wedged into the first slice. Laurence followed me into the kitchen to eat cake as Sarah and I washed the dishes. From the dining room we could hear Serena sob and the muffled sounds of Ronald's words.

LATER WE TRUDGED the short walk home past Laurence's still faceless snowman, through an even denser wall of snow.

"What were our presents, Fred?" Sarah asked.

"All his favorite books in hardcover, *The Catcher in the Rye, Franny and Zooey, Nine Stories, Raise High the Roof Beam, Carpenters and Seymour: An Introduction,* and *A Separate Peace.* I've been hunting them down at the secondhand stores for the past year. James loves all that coming of age, break-your-heart, friendship stuff."

"And now it's all happening to him," Sarah said, looking toward our dark house.

"Why did James leave, Fred?" Laurence asked.

"He left because he was sad that Neil Mahaffey is going to go away."

"Like going to college?"

"Well, when you become a priest you can't ever really come home to live again and you can't get married," Sarah told him.

"Their friendship will have to change, Laurence, and James is sad about that," I said.

"And Neil Mahaffey shouldn't have announced it that way. It wasn't fair to James. It was too public," Sarah said. "It was thoughtless."

"I like Neil Mahaffey," Laurence said, bending over to make a snowball. "He helped me build my snowman."

Sarah looked away to a point far down Thirty-eighth Street, stopping herself from saying anything more about Neil Mahaffey.

"We have school tomorrow, Laurence. Put the snow down. We all have to get to bed," I called to him as I pushed open the back door.

Our house was dark and it felt empty to me, like it always did whenever Morgan and Mom were gone. They were still not home from the hospital.

For a long time in bed, I listened for the rumble of the Galaxy 500 or the hum of the Studebaker, but all I heard was the whisper of Laurence's breathing, water as it gurgled through the radiators, and the soft thuds of heavy snow falling off tree branches. Tiger Cat jumped up next to Laurence, turning himself in three full circles before he settled down for the night.

A desperate loneliness crept into my chest as Tiger Cat began to purr in his sleep. I wanted, I hoped, that James would come home and up the stairs to sprawl out on the floor between Laurence and me. In the months since Charlotte had entered Children's Hospital, James had ripped himself out of the book of our lives. He was away in some foreign land to which there were no maps, at least none that I could find. I needed to tell him I was afraid. About losing Charlotte, about losing him. I felt that James no longer remembered me. He'd forgotten our language and there were no dictionaries for the language in his new country. The vast arctic wilderness that was Mahaffeyland. The snow muffled everything. I buried my face in the pillow to stop the tears. Then I slept.

Hetty Visits the Hospital

IN 1970, THERE were strict rules about visitors at Children's Hospital. Exceptions were frowned upon and were rarely granted. Young children were seen as the incubators of the most dangerous kinds of germs and viruses, and they were not allowed to visit their siblings if they were under fourteen. I am certain that Morgan and Mom would have lied about Laurence's age if asked, because he was thirteen, not fourteen. But the nurses probably had not asked them about Laurence because he was a Down syndrome child, and not all of them were altogether comfortable with his disability. In 1970, Laurence was considered retarded, not disabled, and there was a spookiness about that to many people. It was not as common then for families to keep disabled children at home, and there were strong opinions among medical personnel and educators about these types of things. Some of the staff gave Laurence a wide berth, but most of them only ignored him, the way they ignored Sarah and me. The staff cared for the patients, but had little energy left over to care for the families that wandered down their corridors. Our job was to care for one another.

I must admit that I cannot remember a single doctor's or nurse's name, but I do have the distinct memory of a pharmacist who would on occasion wave to us as we walked down the hallway to Charlotte's room. It was the pharmacist's smile that stood out, like that of the Cheshire Cat, not the sex or the name of the person in the white jacket. At one time I knew the names of the doctors and nurses, because they were Charlotte's world for those months. But I cannot recall these people, no matter how many times Sarah, or Morgan, or Mom, has told me. I do remember Beth Sullivan, Charlotte's five-year-old roommate for four-and-a-half weeks.

What I will not admit to my remaining family is that I grew to hate the hospital, to loathe its smells and efficiencies. My loathing began sometime after Christmas, and I believe now that its genesis was my own fatigue, and the fact that Beth grew well. Beth, whose diagnosis was nearly the same as Charlotte's, began to resurrect her kidney function.

During the evenings of the first week in January, Sarah and I would sit in Charlotte's hospital room with our textbooks spread across our laps while Laurence leaned against the chrome rail of Charlotte's bed to watch television. It was then that Beth's mother would walk her small daughter to the girls' shared bathroom. We could hear real pee dribbling out of Beth and into the water of the porcelain toilet bowl. Pee that Beth's kidneys and bladder and muscles pushed out of her without a catheter. The first evening's slightest dribble beckoned to our ears, fluid hitting fluid, like music, the sound of healing. Gray-haired and older than her years, Mrs. Sullivan, mother of eight and a farm wife, came out of the bathroom, holding Beth in her pink elephant nightgown, to cry more tears than Beth could have peed.

As the small girl's color improved, her swelling subsided, and her visits to the bathroom became regular, it became apparent that Beth would be returning to the farm in Carroll, Iowa, and her life as a kindergarten student and sibling. The medicines worked for Beth. Beth demonstrated the possibilities of science.

Beth's ongoing recovery led to the painful and private examination on the part of Mom and Morgan as to what we, the Hollys, had done wrong in relation to Charlotte. Where Mom looked to God, the Virgin Mary, and the saints, Morgan looked to hospitals and research facilities. Mom kept a rosary in her pocket, fingering its crystal beads in silent prayer, while Morgan made lists and wrote letters. New doctors, experimental medicines, and inquiries to researchers were Morgan's way of setting the balance right as the doctors prepared to send Beth home.

Charlotte did not respond well to the notion that Beth was leaving, that the world they shared, no matter their age difference, would now be her world alone. Three days before Beth was to leave, Charlotte quit speaking to her. The night before Beth's discharge, in a series of fierce whispers, Mom threatened Charlotte with the removal of the color television set from the hospital room if she did not say good-bye to the Sullivans the next morning. Charlotte knew that it was not an idle threat.

All of us stood in the hallway that Saturday morning waiting for Charlotte to speak to Beth, who was dressed in a hand-smocked blue jumper and a red turtleneck for her ride home. Mr. and Mrs. Sullivan stood with the luggage and their two adult sons, who held the family's coats, waiting for Charlotte's words.

"Charlotte," Mom said, in a voice that spoke of no nonsense, "it's time. The Sullivans need to drive during daylight. They can't be here all day. The roads are icy." Then she walked over to the television set and flipped off the Saturday morning cartoons that Charlotte had been watching while the Sullivans bustled through the room, preparing for Beth's departure.

Charlotte kept looking at the blank television screen as silence enveloped the room like a storm cloud. Seconds, then minutes, passed.

"Charlotte..." Beth said, reaching out to touch the blue hospital blanket at the foot of Charlotte's bed.

Charlotte turned her head away as she said, "Good-bye."

Mr. Sullivan promptly walked out of the room with his sons and Beth's luggage, bumping into Morgan without saying a word. Mrs. Sullivan hugged Mom and grabbed Beth's hand to help her into the wheelchair that the nurse had rolled through the doorway. And they were gone.

THE ROOM FELT big and empty to me. In her hospital bed, Charlotte seemed small and helpless, like an infant, with her face still turned away from our eyes. I felt a palpable jealousy of the Sullivans, who were making their escape east into Iowa with the hope that they would never visit Children's Hospital again.

The nurses made only the scheduled visits that day to Charlotte's room. Charlotte slept most of the day. We stayed through lunch and through the dinner hour, slipping out only to eat Bronco's hamburger sandwiches and French fries in the Studebaker, shielding Charlotte from the smell of one more thing she could not have. A little before seven she woke up grumpy, but asked for something to drink and wanted to play a board game. All six of us played a combative and unforgiving game of Monopoly. We spread the game board across Charlotte's blanketed legs while watching the NBC *Saturday Movie of the Week,* which was *The Nun's Story.* Morgan and Charlotte argued over the point of the movie.

Charlotte said the point was "that the nun was going to leave. Who would want to be a nun anyway, Morgan? Who would want to see a movie where the nun didn't fall in love? Who would want to see a nun stay? I passed Go. Give me my two hundred dollars, Fred." Charlotte pointed at me with the thimble that she always claimed as her playing piece. I was the banker.

Morgan harrumphed and lit a Marlboro, saying, "The movie is about the perplexities of life. How we don't always know what is going to happen. The nun thought her love was God, but Africa taught her something entirely different. Life throws us curves," he said, moving his silver hat onto the B & O Railroad, which Laurence owned.

"Don't forget to pay Laurence, Morgan," I said from my position as banker and Laurence's financial adviser.

"Movies aren't about life throwing us curves, Morgan," Charlotte said as she straightened her Monopoly money. "Movies are about people falling in love or fighting in World War II or Indian chiefs and cowboys, but they're never about life throwing us curves. Things happen in movies."

Morgan snorted as we all watched Sarah throw the dice. The intercom voice came on telling us visiting hours were almost over, but we kept playing into the evening news and long past when all the other visitors had left. Finally, at ten-fifteen, a night nurse came into the room to escort us out.

"Don't go," Charlotte wailed, as we began to put on our coats, "somebody has to stay. I can't sleep alone." She kept clenching and unclenching the hand that was bandaged to the drip.

It was her first allusion to Beth's departure.

"I'll stay," Mom said.

"I'll stay," Laurence said through the thumb in his mouth.

"No, he can't stay," said the night nurse at the door, "only a parent can stay." Laurence looked at the nurse over his thumb, and she looked away.

"I want him," Charlotte said.

"Charlotte, you know the rules," the nurse told her, reaching for the door.

"Could we bend the rules tonight?" Morgan asked.

"Only a parent can stay," the nurse said, opening the door halfway.

"But there's no Beth," Mom said.

The nurse blinked. No one said anything. We all waited. The nurse sighed. "There are reasons for rules."

"Life can throw you curves," Morgan said to her.

"Look, what's your name?" the nurse asked Laurence.

He pulled out his thumb, "Laurence," he told her, staring at her.

"Laurence, you can stay tonight because your mom will be here. And because of...well, just because, but not again. I could lose my job. We have rules. If anyone finds out, I didn't know about it. Do you understand?"

We all nodded.

IT CAME TO me on the afternoon of Beth's discharge that Charlotte had forgotten her former life and that to get well, she needed to remember it. For only in remembering it could she develop the will to fight for her health and the ordinariness of returning to our home on Thirty-eighth Street. Hetty was at the core of that life. Somehow, I believed that if we could bring Hetty to the hospital, Charlotte would have the thread back to her old world, and then she, like Beth, would go home. As I doled out the Monopoly money and ruthlessly collected my rents off Boardwalk and Park Place, the sense that Charlotte needed to remember what she was healing for took over my thoughts. It seemed utterly logical. It became more than the birthday present that Sarah and I had discussed in the attic. It became my mission.

I left the hospital with an energy that I hadn't felt in weeks, ready to call Hetty, despite the late hour, to formulate my plan. When I realized I couldn't wake up the household of a sleeping rector at eleven o'clock on a Saturday night, I began to clean our cluttered house to dissipate my fidgetiness and to keep my hands off the phone. I washed the dishes, swept the floor, and wiped the counters in the kitchen, which were sticky and discolored with the spills of condiments. I did three loads of laundry and would have changed the beds, but they were filled with sleeping bodies. Vacuuming was out of the question, but dusting was not, nor wet-mopping the kitchen floor. Finally, at about three o'clock in the morning, I carefully removed each ornament from our still-standing Christmas tree and spread them across the dining room table so I could wrap them on Sunday like Mom always did. I dragged the crooked trunk of the Scotch pine tree out the front door, down the cement steps, and across our snow-covered yard to the barrel in the alley. Handfuls of brown pine needles were scattered along the way. With relish I jammed the tree into the blackened barrel, lit my match, and tossed it onto the branches. With a whoosh the tree burned like a rocket while I stood there, watching it. All of my energy died with each orange lick of the flames. It was then that James walked out of the shadows.

"Hey, Fred," he said, "what the hell are you doing?"

I could smell beer and cigarette smoke tinged with the sour odor of vomit as he came up to me. He put his arm around me and stared into the fire, and I leaned into the charcoal gray of his coat. My face rubbed against the scratchiness of his shoulder. It was good to be close again to James, who had avoided talking to Sarah and me since his birthday party by singing loudly to the radio as we drove back and forth to school and disappearing from campus at lunchtime.

"I'm going to take Hetty to the hospital for Charlotte's birthday. We're going to break all the rules. She needs to remember us, that we're waiting here at home for her."

"Break all the rules. Break all the fucking rules."

James tossed the butt of his cigarette into the barrel and he put both his arms around me, our heads bumping into each other.

"I love him, Fred."

"I know, I know," I said, putting what I could of my arms around James, who held me like a vise.

"But I loved you Hollys first. All of you first, before Neil."

"I know, James."

And then he kissed the top of my head and my forehead, brushing my eyelashes with his lips.

"Let's break the fucking rules. I'll help you. We'll sneak old Hetty into the hospital."

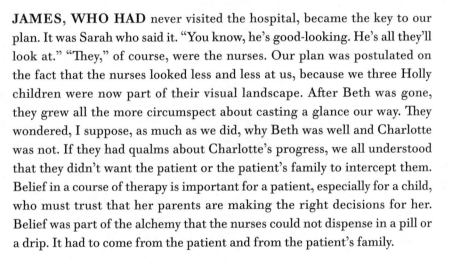

JAMES, WHO HAD never visited the hospital, became the key to our plan. It was Sarah who said it. "You know, he's good-looking. He's all they'll look at." "They," of course, were the nurses. Our plan was postulated on the fact that the nurses looked less and less at us, because we three Holly children were now part of their visual landscape. After Beth was gone, they grew all the more circumspect about casting a glance our way. They wondered, I suppose, as much as we did, why Beth was well and Charlotte was not. If they had qualms about Charlotte's progress, we all understood that they didn't want the patient or the patient's family to intercept them. Belief in a course of therapy is important for a patient, especially for a child, who must trust that her parents are making the right decisions for her. Belief was part of the alchemy that the nurses could not dispense in a pill or a drip. It had to come from the patient and from the patient's family.

WHAT I UNDERSTOOD about nurses in 1970 was more social than professional. They were, to a person, female, and they served at the beck and call of doctors. Doctors were accorded an almost reverential deference. Physicians were the white-collar class at the hospital and the nurses were accorded a more blue- than white-collar status. Nurses fell in love with both doctors and residents, but they always wanted to meet men, because most of the doctors were married and most of the residents were obnoxious and thought themselves a little too good to be dating a nurse. In James Day, we had a handsome eighteen-year-old-boy who looked older than his years. We had an attractive face that the nurses had never seen before. James would act as our nurse magnet.

Our plan may seem clichéd now, but of course there are truths embedded in every cliché. Sarah understood immediately that the three Holly children could form a screen around Hetty, hoping to keep her from an errant nurse's eye, while James could divert a vast amount of that attention by standing puzzled and in need of assistance near the nurses' desk. He could engage them in conversation for a few minutes before asking them for help in finding Charlotte's room.

We needed to hide Hetty because she did not look older than her almost eleven years, and where some children have the persuasive technique and the courage of a burglar in telling stories that adults want to believe, Hetty did not. Hetty was too earnest, too truthful. She couldn't lie her way out of a paper bag, so it was important to make sure that she had to lie as little as possible.

What surprised me about Hetty was how much she took to the plan. How she knew just what to say to her parents about what she would be doing on the night of Charlotte's birthday. "I'll tell them that you need me to be with Laurence, because he has a head cold and that he can't visit Charlotte on her birthday. I'll say that Mr. and Mrs. Holly don't want him alone at night." About this lie she seemed serene.

It became apparent to all of us that visiting Charlotte in the hospital was a great moment for Hetty. It was part group activity and part hanging out with what she perceived to be cool teenagers. Most of all it involved the risk of breaking rules. The joy in a tiny bit of vice, but for a good cause.

"You know," Hetty said to James, Sarah, Laurence, and me in the twilight chill of the attic, "Charlotte's been gone too long. She's forgotten what it's like to have friends or to go to school. She's forgotten the good parts of being well. She can't imagine it anymore. We have to remind her."

Hetty believed everything that I had told her. She had faith in my plan. "If this little girl Beth can get well, Charlotte can get well. Charlotte's a fighter." Hetty said this with a toss of her braids, and then she pushed her cat-eyed glasses farther up her nose for emphasis.

"Hear, hear," James shouted, making our plan official.

"Sometimes you have to break the rules for the right reason," Hetty said. "Like Gandhi or Thoreau or Dr. Martin Luther King. That's what my dad says."

"Hear, hear," James shouted again, punching his fist into the chill air of the attic.

"Hear, hear," the rest of us shouted back to him with Hetty smiling and blushing a deep pink.

It felt to me like we were planning a pantomime. James again was our leader, as he had been all those years ago; the attic, our rehearsal set; but the hospital was the staging point. In my bones I could feel Charlotte well and home again. I could see her walking down Thirty-eighth Street, normal and unswollen, redheaded, and wearing her go-go boots.

ON THE EVENING of January 21, 1970, Charlotte's eleventh birthday, the nurses quietly laughed at the handsome but befuddled James Day as he stood before them, lost and looking for Charlotte Holly's room. Sarah, Laurence, and I shielded Hetty past them into the room. We were silenced by its darkness, and by the black, still screen of the color television set on its mounted pedestal.

Charlotte was asleep, attached to the always-present drip, and in her nostrils were plastic tubes through which oxygen flowed. Mom stood leaning over the chrome railing of the bed, holding her free hand. Morgan sat perched on Beth's empty bed, staring at them. He looked up when the four of us walked into the room, lifting his finger to his lips. We stood in the doorway with our Shaver's grocery bag filled with party hats, noisemakers, and presents, not moving. Down the hallway the faint whistled strains of

"Happy Birthday" preceded James. I stepped out of the doorway to intercept him.

My finger to my lips, I imitated Morgan, whispering to James, "She's asleep."

For James, taller than the rest of us, it took a moment for his eyes to adjust to the darkness and for him to take in the scene around Charlotte's bed. His eyes narrowed and the smile broke from his face. Lips covered teeth. It was then that Hetty walked up to Mom's side to whisper, "Happy Birthday, Charlotte."

Morgan stood up from the bed, crossing the room to the rest of us to say, "I think you might want to come back another evening." His voice was quiet, but firm.

"Hetty," Sarah whispered, "we need to go now."

"I love you, Charlotte," Hetty whispered, looking at the blanketed form on the bed.

Morgan walked over to Hetty, taking her by the hand and gently leading her back to us. Hetty's head was twisted as her body followed Morgan, but her eyes continued to stare at Charlotte. Mom said nothing. We moved into the light of the hallway.

"Tonight is not a good night," Morgan said, bending down to Hetty, "but we appreciate your efforts."

"We're here for Charlotte's birthday," Hetty said to Morgan, her voice breathless, but strained with held-back tears. "We wanted to make her feel better. We wanted to help her get well."

"Thank you, Hetty," Morgan said from his crouched position in front of her. "She'll be so sorry when she wakes up that she missed you. But tonight, she is so tired. We're hoping that soon, she can come home for a day or two. Then you can spend time with her."

"I'm sorry, Mr. Holly," Hetty said, a tear spilling.

"Nothing to be sorry about, Hetty. Mrs. Holly and I appreciate your friendship with Charlotte. We appreciate you making the trip tonight. But Charlotte's is just too tired for company."

Hetty nodded.

"The boys will get you home safely," Morgan told her with a look our way and then he stood up and disappeared back into Charlotte's room.

The nurses didn't look at us as we passed their station. They didn't sneak glances at James Day, or take time to scold us for bringing Hetty into the building. I'm not certain they knew what to do with us. It was hard enough for them to figure out what to do for Charlotte.

It was snowing when we reached the car. James lit a cigarette and handed it to me before starting the engine. As the engine roared and the windshield wipers swept back and forth across the glass, I inhaled, holding the smoke deep in my chest and feeling it burn. I offered the cigarette to Sarah, who shook her head and then returned it to James.

"What was in Charlotte's nose?" he asked before inhaling.

"Oxygen," Sarah said from the backseat, where she sat between Hetty and Laurence. "She didn't have pneumonia yesterday, but I guess that was today's development."

"But it should be gone in ten days. Pneumonia is one course of heavy antibiotics," I said, looking out the windshield at the snow and all the wet blackness of the parking lot. "You know that, Sarah, Charlotte's had it before. One good course of heavy-duty antibiotics and the pneumonia will be gone."

"I'd never been in a hospital before," Hetty said.

"Me, either," James told her. "This was my first hospital visit. Eighteen years old, and I haven't been in a hospital since I was born. I didn't know what to expect. I thought Charlotte would be the same. I think of her as the same old Charlotte. I don't know why. It's the only way I can picture her. I didn't expect her to be sick."

"But kids get better," I said as James pulled out of the parking lot. "Beth got better, and then she looked normal again."

"Yeah, it was amazing when Beth got better," Sarah said, sighing. "I couldn't believe how the swelling went away and her color came back."

I turned around to look at Sarah. She was holding both Hetty's and Laurence's hands, and she was looking out the small triangle-shaped window on the passenger side of the Galaxy 500. Her eyes searched for something in the wet swirling snow spreading across the asphalt. They were tired eyes, bordered by brown-and-olive bags underneath, and streaked with red at the rims. Sarah looked like a very old young person. I reached out to touch her, my hand grabbing the hem of her coat, glad to feel something attached to her. I wanted to bring her back to all the hope and excitement of our planning in the attic.

As James turned onto Dodge Street, Hetty spoke: "My father says that sometimes, but not often, there are miracles. That every day we should pray for miracles. Just in case."

I didn't know what to say to Hetty. I didn't think in terms of miracles. No one else said anything. The only sound was the slap of the windshield wipers.

Finally Laurence pulled the thumb out of his mouth to ask, "What's a miracle?"

"It's when something really great happens, Laurence, that you don't think can happen." James told him. "It's a great big happy surprise."

"It's like a present from Jesus," Hetty added. "Jesus can do the impossible. That's a miracle."

"Like Santa Claus?" Laurence asked.

"Much better than Santa Claus," James said.

"I pray for miracles. They come from Jesus," Hetty told Laurence.

"Could you pray for a pony? Would Jesus give you a pony?"

"Ponies are like Christmas," Hetty said. "Santa can bring them, if you have a farm. Miracles are bigger than ponies."

"Then what's a miracle?" Laurence asked.

"A miracle's like Charlotte getting well," Hetty said.

James punched on the radio. The Supremes sang, "Stop in the name of love, before you break my heart. Stop in the name of love, before you break my heart. Think it over. Think it over." James sang in falsetto right along with Florence, Mary, and Diana, slapping his palm against the glass of the windshield on the word, "Stop." In the rearview mirror, I could see Sarah and Laurence join in on the chorus with the Supremes' hand gestures as Hetty watched. On the next go-around, I sang along, and James called out,

"Come on Hetty, sing." And she sang with us the six blocks home, crooning, "Think it oh-oh-oh-ver. Think it oh-oh- oh-ver" as she jumped out of the Galaxy 500 at the St. Barnabas parsonage.

Failing

A FEW DAYS later, the antibiotics kicked in and Charlotte's lungs began to clear. Sometime in January when I wasn't in class, and after the students had passed through the hallways and the teachers and hall monitors had relaxed their vigilance, I began to slip out the south entrance of Central High School, down its long flight of steps, to make my run into the refuge of the Joslyn Art Museum. There in the museum's galleries I found sanctuary, and the fierce beating of my heart would settle into a rhythm without pain. When a janitor or a docent saw me, they would say, "Hi, Fred," but ask me no questions as I stood staring at my favorite works of art.

I was not the first Central High School student to do this, nor was I the last. The policy on students in the museum was selective and biased toward the quiet and respectful truants, and the former art students who turned toward truancy in between their high school classes or on their lunch hours. Docents, curators, and security staff showed a kindness toward students who sought refuge in art, and they displayed a downright affection toward their own former pupils. They were merciless toward the noisy or uncivilized, calling the principal's secretary if any student dared to break the rules. Truants in search of high jinks knew to give the museum a wide berth and walk the three or four city blocks into Omaha's downtown, where they could buy a Coke and smoke their cigarettes, putting forth noisy judgments on passersby and department store displays. The museum staff was used to the constancy of the visits of Central High School classes, and could support a kind of feigned ignorance of the school's escapees by responding vaguely, when questioned about a truant, that they had assumed that the student was with a class. Even the Central High teachers leading classes through the building showed a rather benign indifference when they saw students like me, who were presumably absent without leave from study hall or the student smoking lounge. In 1970, kids who decided to hang out in the museum were thought to be good kids. Our teachers, like the adults at the museum, exuded an air of confidence in us, that we were good kids on the verge of being adults.

For me, almost eighteen years of age, the Joslyn was a sanctuary like the medieval churches of old. I believed that no one would hurt me there. I could not be overtaken by marauding forces or errant-knight warriors or be shackled by the soldiers of evil despots. The order and the presentation of the artworks reassured me in the belief that beauty could be made and difficulties, overcome. I did not feel alone in its corridors or overwhelmed by the pounding of my rushing heart. What I understood God to be—the presence of beauty and the equality of all spirits—was there. Unlike Hetty, I did not have the hope in miracles or the knowledge of Jesus Christ as my personal savior, only my family and art. Already a failed Catholic, I looked to religion not with a skeptic's eye but with the sadness about what I could not bring to it. I did not believe in the power of a faith, but I did not disparage what I could not believe in.

One Wednesday during the thirty minutes of my lunch hour, I stood before Claude Monet's *A travers la prairie–Across the Meadow,* wondering about the three children almost lost in the paint of the colored grasses. A tall girl wearing a feathered hat seems to be in charge of the tiny girl in a cloth bonnet and a small boy in a beribboned boater. The three of them walk toward the viewer through waves of grass and wildflowers. Behind them are trees and a blue sky dappled white. As I fell into the chunky strokes of blue and green and the daubs of yellow, sometimes gold, the painting's shimmering effect pulled me onto its surface and held me tight. There I hovered over the small figures of the children, seeing in the brilliant summer light Sarah, Laurence, and little Charlotte, and me, the human boy, skimming them like a bird on the crests of paint. I could smell the heat off the grass and the scent of crushed lavender and the wild bushes of rosemary. In their French voices, the children called out "*Viens, viens, Fred.*" In my heart, I heard, "Follow us, Fred, follow us." It seemed possible in the heat of the painting that we could be there together, children forever. Brushing the ridges of oil paint through the flowers and grass, I raised my arm to them to feel the weight of my watch and sweat pooling on the bridge of my nose, its steam clouding the lenses of my glasses.

"Fred, man, Fred, are you okay?" It was the voice of Micah Little, who grabbed my shoulder, pulling me back.

"Fred, you need some fresh air. You need to go outside." It was Arianna Isaacs.

The two of them led me past the curious gazes of security staff, the sweet old lady docents, and our fellow students, outside into the frigid air of January. It slapped me, freezing the moisture on my lenses into a lacy swirl of frost. I took off my glasses, unable to see with or without them, dependent on the voices and the steady arms of Micah and Arianna. Together, they chattered about me as if I were deaf and mute, and I could hear in their voices both concern for me and love for each other.

"Fred looked like he was going to dive into the painting," Arianna said.

"His hand was almost on it, in front of everybody. He could have gotten kicked out of the museum forever. When we were kids, Joshua and I used to watch him hug the statues. Fred thought that nobody ever saw him. He was the funniest little kid. My mom said he was crazy about the museum. It was a wonder he didn't sleep there."

I listened to them talk as the three of us walked across the gravel of the parking lot. The sound of the pebbles crunched beneath the soles of our shoes.

"You know, he needs to eat before class," Arianna said, stopping. She dropped my arm and began to rummage through her purse. "Here, try this, Fred."

She handed me a candy bar and took my arm again. The two of them navigated me around the packs of smoking students and pushed me through the school's west doors. We huddled at the base of the stairs as frost melted from my lenses and I tore open Arianna's candy bar. It was a Snickers—

peanuts, caramel and chocolate—gone soft and gooey in the heat of my hand. Micah took a quick look around to make sure that no one was watching us and then gave Arianna a kiss on her cheek. "Bye, honey," he said.

"I love you," Arianna whispered to Micah as he ran up the boys' stairs.

She waited with me while I finished the Snickers.

"Do you feel okay?" she asked me.

I felt like melted chocolate was running through my ribcage and as though the axis of the universe had slightly dipped in some fine direction.

"You're in love?" I asked her.

"I am," Arianna said.

"I've loved you for years," I told her.

"You don't know me."

"But I've loved you."

"I love Micah."

"I know. I'm happy for you."

Arianna looked puzzled.

"Are you okay, Fred?

"I love you, Arianna. But I understand about Micah. He loves you, too."

"Please don't tell anyone about us."

"I won't. I understand about secrets."

"I have to go now," Arianna said, tugging on the strap of her purse and running up the girls' stairs. Halfway up the steps she stopped and turned around to look at me. "Fred," she called down, "I'm sorry about your sister."

I nodded. "Thanks for everything," I told her, not wanting to say that I was sorry about Charlotte, too.

I LEARNED TO see Micah and Arianna as I slipped through the Joslyn during the last days of January leading into February. The two of them were in overlooked corners and in out-of-the-way points in the galleries. Often they were hidden in the shadows of unused stairwells. Arianna looked beautiful and Micah looked happy in those first weeks of the new year. Knowing that they were together gave me a sense that dragons could be slain and that the pureness of love would conquer all. Of course, I loved Arianna Isaacs, if not for loving me, then for loving Micah.

IN LATE JANUARY, only Morgan came home from the hospital, having left Mom with Charlotte after visiting hours. One day we returned from school to see the Studebaker parked far back on the driveway. Sarah, Laurence, and I walked inside the house to find both the kitchen and the sunroom empty. From the hallway on the second floor we could see that their bedroom door was shut and we could hear him talking to someone on the telephone.

"But we would like to bring Charlotte sooner, doctor. We're afraid she's failing," Morgan said with a quaver in his voice. The pause was long and in the interim of silence the only sound was the strike of a match.

"Yes, I see, I see," he said into the expectant air.

That night all of us visited Charlotte, who was cranky and out of sorts.

"I want salt," Charlotte told a young woman who was delivering snack trays.

"It says on your chart 'no salts,'" the girl said, putting the tray on the table, which swept across Charlotte's bed on a swinging arm.

"I want salt," Charlotte said, her voice rising.

"I'm sorry, I can't give you any salt," the girl said, looking at Charlotte.

"Then I won't eat," Charlotte told her.

"You have to eat," the girl said as she turned to push the deck of snack trays out of the room.

"You can't make me eat. Nobody can make me do anything," Charlotte said.

"That's not a very good attitude," the girl told Charlotte over her shoulder as the door closed behind her.

We all looked up then—Mom and Morgan, Sarah, Laurence, and me—to see the faint acridness left in the air by the girl's words and the wall of the closed door.

"You try being sick," Charlotte screamed at the door, "you just try being sick," and she threw the tray of carrot sticks and applesauce across the room with a vigor that she had not possessed for months, then hiccoughed and started crying. Her tears expanded into hopeless, heaving sobs.

"Charlotte," Mom said, frozen in her chair for a moment by the spectacle.

Sarah picked up the tray while Laurence crawled around the floor, grabbing the carrot sticks. Morgan wiped up the applesauce. Next to Mom, I sat frozen with Erich Maria Remarque's *All Quiet on the Western Front* open on my lap. It was early on in the novel, and the narrator was visiting his friend, Franz Kemmerich, in the hospital. Kemmerich has lost his leg. He dreamed of being a forester. Our English teacher said that we would learn about war, about its uselessness, from this novel. What bad things war did to men. It was a lovely, hopeless, sad book, he told us. Reading it made me nervous and my stomach anxious.

Charlotte sobbed as Mom reached for her. "Honey, it's okay. It's okay."

The tears became rivulets across the desert of Charlotte's swollen face. Her faint orange freckles glistened through the wash of saltwater. Mom held her, whispering, "Now, Charlotte, everything's going to be okay. Everything's going to be okay. It's just been a rough day."

THE ROUGH DAYS in February came more often. On the fourth day of the month, a resident heard the sound of fluid in one of Charlotte's lungs. This time, Charlotte had a reaction to the antibiotic. Hives covered the lower half of her trunk, and the nurses had to tape her hands into white cotton stockings to stop her from scratching. The hives complicated the inserting of all of Charlotte's catheters, including the I.V.'s.

The word "failing" played over and over again in my ears like a scratched record. The word's sound became a tinnitus that injected adrenaline directly into my bloodstream. Only the Joslyn could still the pain of my rushing heart. I skipped whole days of classes to stop the knifing ache that centered in my sternum.

SARAH CAME SEARCHING for me at the museum.

"Fred," she said, "the vice principal is looking for you."

"Why?" I said, not looking at her but at a portrait of Lydia Cassatt by her sister, Mary Cassatt, entitled *Woman Reading*. A pink ribbon holds a sleeping kerchief on the pile of Lydia's brown hair. Lydia's white dressing gown is ruffled and flecked with blues. Her back is bolstered by a green armchair created by rolls of paint strokes, the apostrophe curve, boldly utilized. Captured in oil, Lydia reads the morning paper. Lydia isn't looking at Mary or me, and I wouldn't look at Sarah. Lydia and I were both determined to ignore our observers.

"Fred, you can't live in the Joslyn. You have to go to classes. You have to go home."

"Why not? I said, turning to look at Sarah. "Why can't I live here? Why can't I be here forever? I love this place. It's my truest home."

"Because I need you and Charlotte's failing. That's why they're looking for you. Charlotte's failing."

I wanted to look away from the pain and sorrow in Sarah's face to stay there in the Joslyn Art Museum, where I could be sheltered and no one could harm me. Like Lydia Cassatt, I wanted to avoid the gaze of my sister. I did not want this news.

SARAH TOOK ME by the hand, walking me out of the Joslyn across the snowy parking lot and up the girls' staircase to the vice principal's office, where we were released to go home to Thirty-eighth Street to wait for more news from the hospital. We could not find James, so we walked home the two miles up and down Dodge Street's hills. We saw the Mutual of Omaha tower and its bronzed Indian head. The Indian surveyed us and the world from his point high atop the Farnam Street hill. Sarah and I were two figures lost in a snowy landscape. A point of reference for the viewer's eye.

A PRIEST CAME to Children's Hospital to administer Extreme Unction, the last rites. Sarah, Laurence, and I were not there. The nurses and doctors and residents did not want children—once again, the three of us were children—to see her fail. For four days after Extreme Unction, we waited at home, and Charlotte did not fail. Each day that she lived, our hopes grew that once again she would rally.

At five o'clock in the morning on the fourteenth of February, 1970, Morgan slipped into the space on the floor where James usually slept and zipped himself into the sleeping bag between Laurence and me. The sound of the zipper and the creak of the wooden floorboards woke me. Tiger Cat jumped down from Laurence's bed to brush his orange fur against Morgan.

"Morgan," I whispered, "How's Charlotte?"

"She's gone."

"Gone?" I asked, thinking of Charlotte, fleeing the hospital in search of salt—almost saying, "Charlotte ran away from the hospital?"

But Morgan interrupted me saying, "Fred, Charlotte passed over three hours ago. She died, son."

I did not believe him.

"Morgan, Charlotte's not dead," I said, knowing that his words were mistaken. Ill chosen. Charlotte might have failed, but she wouldn't die on us.

"Son, it was more than the kidneys. It was the pneumonia and the wear and tear on her heart. Nothing was working. They all began to stop. I'm so sorry, Fred. She tried so hard. But we couldn't get it figured out." And Morgan began to sob, and then I knew that Charlotte was dead.

For the days up to the funeral and for weeks afterward, Morgan slept there on the floor between Laurence and me. In the middle of these nights, he would reach out to take our hands, feeling first for Laurence's pulse and then my own, sighing before returning to his restless sleep. Mom slept in Charlotte's bed across from Sarah. Sarah told me that often Mom would leave the bed and open the door to the girls' shared closet, to sit, holding Charlotte's dresses, breathing her in.

Mom and Morgan stayed near us, but not together. They kept the three of us between them. They took us everywhere as they prepared for the funeral.

The Funeral

MORGAN MADE THE telephone calls in the kitchen. Each time he spoke into the phone, he searched for some form of the words "Charlotte has died." When he found them, his voice would crack and he would struggle for control. During those calls, Ronald Day stood at his side, handing him stiff shots of whiskey when the tears came too fast. I watched from a chair at the table with Sarah, Laurence, and James.

Neighbors began to arrive with food and condolences, pushing open the unlocked back door, touching or hugging Morgan, and then placing their gifts on the counters, in the refrigerator, and in the dining room. Cakes and casseroles, cookies and fruit salad lined every open space, with the expectation that they would be used after the funeral to feed the grieving guests. Food was piled up everywhere. One neighbor who brought a chicken casserole and a Bundt cake, both wrapped in aluminum foil, scanned the kitchen and said, "Ronald, I'm going to take these to your house." Ronald nodded, waving her on her way with a sweep of his hand.

The doorbell rang and Serena Day answered it. I heard her instruct the man from Janousek's Florists, "Please take the flowers to the John A. Gentleman Mortuary on Farnam Street. They'll know what to do." Serena then ran back up the front stairs to help Mom choose a dress for Charlotte's laying out for the wake. Sarah, Laurence, and I had given up on the ordeal of this choice. The green gingham of one dress, the blue ribbon of another, and the pink roses on a third—each dress all the more sacred than the one before—brought Mom to tears. As I sat on Sarah's bed, I could smell Charlotte's peculiar scent of playground soil and Dial soap. It lingered on in the fabrics.

With the strength of the war survivor that she was, Serena sent us away and took over at what she did best, helping people make things beautiful.

At a little past eleven that morning, the doorbell rang and I answered it. There in the bright sun of February's chill stood eleven actuaries in gray and brown suits under black-and-gray winter coats. Each man wore buckled galoshes and a black fedora, the hat made unpopular by President Kennedy because he refused to wear one. I opened the door to them, invited them in, and called out, "Morgan, it's for you." He and Ronald walked from the kitchen to see a minyan of actuaries waiting in the foyer. One man stepped forward, saying, "Morgan, we are so sorry," and the actuaries murmured as one body the word "Sorry."

One by one each actuary hugged Morgan, wordlessly, ending with Seymour Fineman, who said, "Morgan, just let us know what we can do."

"Thank you, Fineman," Morgan said, looking at these men, his comrades, calculators of the body's odds, feeling forever the weight of life's facts. The realities of the statistics that the rest of the world ignored. "I will let you know. Your support these months has meant so much to me."

As a body they nodded, and as a body they left, their party splitting between the Ford and the Buick parked beside the curb of Thirty-eighth Street.

HETTY CAME THAT afternoon with her parents. Reverend and Mrs. Carmichael stood behind their ashen-faced daughter. Seeing Hetty in the foyer made my stomach clench.

Morgan called upstairs to Mom, who was still going through Charlotte's dresses, "Eileen, please come downstairs. Hetty is here."

Mom came down the steps with Serena following her. When she reached the final stair she sat down, her arms reaching out to Hetty as though to a toddler.

"Oh, Hetty, Hetty, Hetty," Mom said, "I am so sorry."

Hetty slipped into Mom's arms and bawled like a small animal in pain. The rest of us stood outside of them, staring. At this raw time, it became apparent that Mom's loss was not Morgan's loss or Sarah's loss or Laurence's loss, or even my own. It was separate and stood alone, only to be shared with Hetty Carmichael, who Mom could be assured would love Charlotte as her shadow best friend for the rest of her life. The stabbing notion that whatever Sarah, Laurence, and I would do with our lives—our degrees, our successes, our children, our very being—would never make up for our mother's loss took root in me then, as I watched her hold Hetty. Mom had lost the child that she'd loved the best. The reality of that love was exposed in her grief.

IN THOSE HOURS after Morgan and Mom came back from the hospital, it was still not clear to me or Laurence or Sarah that Charlotte was gone, that somehow we were not dreaming it all. Sucking his thumb and holding Tiger Cat, Laurence followed Morgan around the kitchen that morning before anyone arrived, making him explain Charlotte's death over and over again.

"But where is Charlotte?" Laurence asked him.

"Charlotte's in heaven," Morgan told him as cold water splashed from the tap into the coffee pot.

"Where's heaven?" Laurence persisted.

"We don't know where heaven is, but we know God is there and Charlotte will be safe and happy."

"Can we go there?"

"Not until we die. We'll go there when we die, and then we will be with Charlotte."

"When will we die?"

"We won't die for a long time."

"Why did Charlotte die?"

"She was very sick. Her body quit working. When your body quits working, you die."

"But how can she go to heaven, if her body quit working?"

"What goes to heaven is your soul, Laurence. Your soul is the electricity that makes your eyes light up. It's what makes you Laurence and not Fred. So Charlotte's electricity went straight to heaven, but her body stayed here. We'll bury her body, but not her soul. Her soul's gone."

Laurence walked across the kitchen and pressed the black buttons that controlled the fluorescent lights, off and on, trying to understand what Morgan had told him. Eating cornflakes and trying to make sense of the notion that Charlotte was dead seemed beyond impossible to me. We would not be returning to Children's Hospital. Charlotte was not there. Her body, her corpse, her cadaver was waiting to be dressed for her laying out at the John A. Gentleman Mortuary. As Laurence flickered the lights on and off, I considered the blue electricity of our souls, but I only understood that Charlotte was gone.

~e~⌒~~⌒~

IT WAS SERENA who reached out to touch Mom's shoulder, saying, "Eileen, maybe Hetty would want you to put something of hers in the coffin alongside the go-go boots? Something to share with Charlotte."

Everyone looked at Serena, including Mom and Hetty.

"Something of us to go along with Charlotte. So we know that she won't be alone." Serena pinkened as she said this, her voice quavering.

Reverend Carmichael cleared his throat and then said, "Jesus was wrapped in a beautiful burial cloth. Having something of beauty and softness wrapped around her son, I'm sure, brought comfort to his mother and his friends."

Mom said, "Morgan do you think the mortician would let us?"

Reverend Carmichael replied instead of Morgan, "I will talk to them for you about this. I think I can make them understand. Just prepare what you want to be in the coffin with Charlotte."

Morgan looked relieved. "Thank you."

"When are you going to the mortuary?" Reverend Carmichael asked.

"In about an hour," Morgan told him.

"Get what you want ready, and I'll meet you there."

WITH REVEREND CARMICHAEL'S help we placed inside Charlotte's coffin her go-go boots, James's forty-five recording of the Beatles singing "Twist and Shout," Hetty Carmichael's hand-sized white children's Bible, dried roses from Morgan's garden, Sarah's bronze replica of Degas's *Little Dancer, Fourteen Years Old,* Laurence's favorite bubble pipe, and Serena and Ronald's recording of "Me and My Shadow," by Berkeley Thrive, from our first pantomime.

I picked up what seemed to be a thousand objects before I could find one to put in the coffin. Finally I took something that was not mine. It was a small black-and-white photograph of the six of us that Mom kept on the windowsill above the kitchen sink in a frame of Popsicle sticks painted red and blue that Laurence had made at the Madonna School. In the photograph, Charlotte was five and I was twelve. We were all leaning toward the camera and smiling a continuum of toothy and toothless smiles, Mom and Dad in the Camelot pose of the sixties, Jack and Jackie, forever. There were several copies of this photograph around the house. It was not unique and it was what I handed to Reverend Carmichael. So that we would be with her. Always and forever.

What we were doing felt pagan and peculiar, rebellious, but necessary. None of us wanted Charlotte to be alone, wherever she had gone, without the bits of flotsam and jetsam that made her one of us, and all of us part of her.

AT THE JOHN A. Gentleman Mortuary at the wake that evening, we said the rosary on our knees, repeating the litany of "Our Fathers" and "Hail Marys" and "Glory be's" as if they were a droning punishment. It was the tradition in Omaha for Catholics to say the rosary at the wake, the night before the funeral, and it was a tradition that brought comfort to Mom and control to the priest that led the affair. Thin and dressed in a black cassock, the priest, who looked barely eighteen years old but must have been at least twenty-six, spoke to Mom and Morgan with a forced confidence.

That afternoon, when Mom asked him, before the rosary began, the ominous question "Why Father, why did God let Charlotte die?" the priest turned into the boy he was, first stammering before turning a florid red.

"There is meaning," he said as though choking, "in all that God does. We just don't know why God took Charlotte now. He may have been saving her from a more painful life or some hideous burden in the future."

Mom stood silent, uncertain of how to respond to the priest's words. She looked over the sandy hair of the young man's head at Laurence, Sarah, and me. Her eyes moved upward and away from all of us as though she was contemplating what could have been Charlotte's future, and the terrors that the future could hold for her other children.

Morgan turned away from the priest and whispered, "Eileen, it was the disease. It wore her down. That's all. It was the kidneys, not God. They're all going to have great lives. They're great kids."

"Excuse me," Mom said to the priest, not looking at Morgan, "I need to go to the restroom," and she walked away from both of them.

The priest looked at Mom's back and then said to Morgan, "The Monsignor says that we can celebrate a Mass of the Angels for Charlotte. She is over the age limit, but the Monsignor says that in the spirit of Vatican II, we will do it. He says that Charlotte couldn't have committed serious sin. The Monsignor wants you to know that all of the Cathedral's priests will be there for you, Mr. Holly."

Morgan cleared his throat before saying, "Thank you, Father."

~ _e_ ~~

ON OUR KNEES in front of Charlotte's white casket lined in a silky white cloth, I looked at her hands, holding Hetty's Bible, wondering how long we could endure the mystery of the rosary and the foolish boy leading it. I could smell smoke and whiskey on Morgan's black suit, and mothballs and Jean Naté After Bath Splash on Mom's black dress. Mom knelt next to Sarah, who was on the other side of Laurence and far away from Morgan. I soon lost my place on the crystal beads of the rosary that Mom had handed me. My mind began to drift to somewhere outside of the mortuary's viewing room and away from the heavily made-up child's corpse in the casket in front of me. What remained of Charlotte's red hair had been carefully lacquered to give the appearance of curls. It was our last glance at what was left of her, but already I realized it was not her, no matter how many times people said, "She look's lovely, Eileen. Just as I remember her."

Words at death, I learned then, are the well-intended, often awkward, and sometimes stupid gestures that express a person's desire to help the living. It is impossible to calculate how many people said to Morgan and Mom, "Oh, the good die young."

In the place to where my mind had wandered, I responded, "Then there must have been a mistake, because Charlotte Anne Holly was never good. Sometimes she was great and sometimes she was a pain in the ass and sometimes she was kind, but she never was plain good. 'Good' is an adjective for another child, not Charlotte. If God had wanted good, he would have taken Hetty. Charlotte was not bad, but she was far too complicated to be good."

In this mental place where I was, far from the John A Gentleman Mortuary, I began to giggle in a slight and private hysteria. Choking back laughter, I began to cough, then cry. I stood up abruptly, breaking the line of the family to leave the viewing room and the mantra of the rosary. Pushing my way through the people still arriving to express their condolences and say a decade of the rosary with the family, I fled the building itself, making my escape into the frigid air and an inky night pierced with white stars.

Blocks away from the funeral home, I shoved myself into the glass phone booth outside the Blackstone Hotel, weeping my grief into the receiver to a Charlotte gone, as well-heeled Omahans passed me, their conversations clouds of frozen air. I didn't understand the permanency of death any more than Laurence did. All I wanted was for Charlotte to come home. My hope was that I would wake up from her death to find out that all of it had been a dream. The tape of our lives would roll back into the warmth of summer and possibility. To a place before illness, cold, and death. In this green place, I would say something to Charlotte that was permanent and loving, kind and big-brotherly. I would be a Fred that I had never been.

They sold me two shots of bourbon at the Blackstone Hotel lounge, which I sipped while smoking three cigarettes. No one in the bar spoke to me or asked to see my I.D. Afterward, I wandered back to the mortuary to find Sarah on its steps, looking up and down Farnam Street for me.

"You've been drinking," she said.

"Only a little. No one will notice," I told her, turning my head to avoid the sorrow in her brown eyes.

"Don't drink alone, Fred. Drinking alone is the beginning of a bad habit."

AT THE FOOT of the steps of the Cathedral of St. Cecilia, I stood with Morgan, Laurence, James and Ronald Day, and the Reverend Carmichael as the morticians unloaded Charlotte's coffin onto a dolly. Dressed in black suits, the six of us were Charlotte's pallbearers. Behind us in black veils and dresses were Mom, Sarah, Serena, Hetty, and Mrs. Carmichael, and Aunt Mary, Mom's sister from San Diego. We were the last to enter the church. The black cloth of our coats and clothing fluttered in the cold wind of February. Speaking to each other in the incomprehensible, monosyllabic language of sorrow, we must have sounded like visitors from a foreign country to the passersby on Fortieth Street. Our language more simile than metaphor, more sound than word. Black grunts of "What?" and "Where?" and "Grab Laurence's hand, Fred."

Like shepherds, the morticians herded us together and then hoisted the casket up the steep flight of stairs, before lining the pallbearers around the casket, which then rested on the dolly. Before sending the family, pallbearers, and casket down the vast aisle of the cathedral, the morticians whispered, "Are you ready, Mrs. Holly? Are you ready, Mr. Holly?" And I thought, "Ready for what?"

THE TWO BLACK-SUITED, somber men opened the bronze doors of the cathedral and sent us, the small tribe that made up Charlotte's family, into her funeral. As we stepped inside the darkened area underneath the choir loft, the organ boomed a processional, and all the people in the pews stood up. Stepping from the darkness into the main aisle, I was blinded by the electric lights that mingled with the sun streaming through the broken colors of the stained glass windows, leaving us blinking as we made our way down the marble flooring. Everyone, it seemed, was there. Charlotte's fifth-grade class from Saunders Elementary School and Laurence's class from the Madonna School stood looking at us with scared, expectant faces, their winter coats splashed across the wooden seats of the pews in the reds, greens, blues, and yellows of the primary colors. Herb Pepper, the head janitor at the Joslyn Art Museum, stood with Mrs. Reiko Kato, my origami teacher at the Joslyn and now head docent. With them were two dozen docents in mink and camel-hair coats, filling two pews in the middle of the church. Dressed in a dramatic black cape, Lana Beth Boyer from the dance studio sat with three rows of suited actuaries from Mutual of Omaha. Eight receptionists from the Medical Arts Building were wedged in with a group from Bogart's Drugstore and the barber from Thirty-third Street who cut Morgan's hair. Two bartenders from the California Street Bar were there. Six nuns from Duchesne Academy sat behind the receptionists, wearing newer and shorter gray habits that revealed wisps of hair at the white edges of their veils and nylon-covered legs in sensible Hush Puppy shoes. Classmates and students from Central High School filled up half of the cathedral.

Arianna Isaacs was there with her parents, Rabbi and Mrs. Isaacs. Joshua and Micah Little stood on either side of their parents, Annie and Abram. The neighbors who made up the village of the eight square blocks of our neighborhood in Omaha were there: the Spielmans, the Viponds, the Wilwerdings, the Kalkowskis, the Kenneys, the Langdons, the Kennedys, the Kirbys, the Mahers, the Mitchells, the Wrights, the Doolings, the Gilberts, the Watanabes, the Valentines, the Eischeids, the Howards—husbands and wives, children, widows and grandfathers, sisters and brothers in their Sunday best on that cold, sunny morning. Each was an individual part of the canvas of my life there, but I never experienced them as a whole until then. It startled me to see families together—fathers with children and mothers with husbands—who rarely seemed connected in my daily comings and goings.

For me they were unique and understood in isolation in the vision of my space. A man's particular limping gait on the sidewalk or the brand of cigarettes an elderly widow smoked as she raked her leaves were the memories of my connection to them. A woman stood out to me as the mother of the bully who had plagued me on the playground during fifth-grade recess. Both bully and mother stared out at me balefully as the organ blared the processional and our cortege passed them.

I FELT A chill when I saw Neil Mahaffey in a black suit, standing next to a beautiful blonde young woman in a trench coat. Mike Raven in his ski jacket and khakis stood next to them. Laurence recognized Neil and waved to him. When Neil waved back, Laurence broke our ranks of severity with an ear-to-ear grin. In the audience of Charlotte's funeral, Laurence had found a friend. Unlike weddings, I learned that morning, funerals, particularly Catholic funerals, are public and are celebrated as part of the daily ritual of the Mass. In the great universality of the Faith, anyone and everyone was allowed into the sanctuary for the mourning of the dead. Saints and sinners, friends and foes, lovers, strangers, and even pricks like Mike Raven and semi-pricks like Neil Mahaffey could come to mourn Charlotte, though they did not know her. They understood that we had suffered loss, and they came for the living, if not really for the dead.

My grief turned to shame when I felt the gaze of Neil Mahaffey and Mike Raven upon us. We had not saved Charlotte. We had failed her and her funeral bore witness to that fact, and their presence among us seemed witness to our failure. I should have thought better of them at that moment as we reached the altar, but I did not.

AT THE ALTAR were nine priests in gold-and-white vestments. The old monsignor in the center looked like a plump white hen among stately cranes and nervous terns. The priests raised the flapping wings of their arms to Charlotte's casket and the morticians whisked us out of the aisle and into the front pews. Massed together like a family of black crows, we looked on from our reserved pews as the white birds of the priests took over Charlotte's body and the story of her life as they made it up from the altar. Charlotte was good, they told us. She was a child wanted by God in her goodness, taken unto heaven among the angels, they squawked and clucked to us. Priest after priest, they told us that the Virgin Mary would rock her to sleep and St. Joseph the Carpenter would build her a lovely bed. They gave their audience children's stories and a peasant's comfort. For the priests, Charlotte grew wings and floated about in their altar stories, an angel child.

One could feel in the impassioned singing of "Panis Angelicus" that the audience yearned to see Charlotte as special, something outside and extraordinary to the daily routines of the village of our neighborhood that surrounded the Cathedral of St. Cecilia there in Omaha. It was important to the priests, and particularly to the mothers and fathers, to feel that Charlotte had been taken by God because of her specialness and not because she died of complications related to kidney disease. Not because of a disease spurred on by germs that existed among the collective humanity of our neighborhood, our city, our state, our country, our world.

In their peculiar goodness and in their attempt to assuage the pain and fear of their audience, the priests killed the real Charlotte in the neighborhood's memory that morning. In the memory of Mitchell Abington, who was Charlotte's ongoing grade school nemesis, the boy who compared her to Wilbur's spider and landed her in the principal's office when she bloodied his nose. For Mitchell, it would seem, Charlotte took on actual wings. Older and wearing red basketball shoes under his altar-boy black and whites, Mitchell was one of the four boys serving at Charlotte's funeral. The derision that he had shown her all the years of grade school must have melted from Mitchell's recent memory. We were told later that afternoon by a young priest as he ate potato salad and dribbled yellowed mayonnaise on his black blazer that Mitchell's mother had volunteered him to serve the funeral Mass that morning. What stayed with Mitchell, I presume, was that Charlotte was special, and that was why God took her. As the Mass proceeded and the nine fathers preached their story of Charlotte's taking, fear melted from Mitchell's face. I watched it melt. In his ornery ordinariness, I could see Mitchell feeling safer, ringing the bells with energy as the collective priests presented the Body and then the Blood of Jesus Christ.

People needed to forget the Charlotte of scabbed knees and screaming mouth and playground scrapes—the little girl holding hands with Hetty—so that they could get up the nerve to send their own children out the door in the morning. So that they could drive past Children's Hospital without feeling cursed. Only later, after we buried Charlotte at Calvary Cemetery, after hundreds of people passed through the front doors of our house on Thirty-eighth Street and ate the food provided by the neighbors, did I begin to understand. Only then, that night when everyone was gone, even Aunt Mary, and Morgan stood drinking a glass of bourbon in the chill darkness of his leaf-buried rose garden, did I understand that we were alone with Charlotte dead.

Afterward

ON THE MONDAY after the funeral, I scraped frost from the windshield of James's Galaxy 500 and watched Morgan walk south on Thirty-eighth Street. He was dressed in his galoshes and a gray fedora, his head muffled by a maroon woolen scarf wrapped around the collar of his heavy gray overcoat. Between his gloved fingers, a lit Marlboro trailed smoke in the frigid February air as he skirted ice and the unshoveled sidewalks of our neighbors. Morgan's starting up his walk back to work again, the walk that he had made for more than twenty years to the Mutual of Omaha tower, should have been a comfort to me, a signal of a return to routine. But it was not. An acute sense of anxiety came over me as his figure grew smaller. I held my breath, certain that when I no longer saw him he might truly be gone. I wanted to chase him, to beg him to hold my hand and never leave me. As the minutes demarcating a life lived with Charlotte and then a life lived without her turned to hours and then days, a kernel of fear grew within me that I could lose them all. Morgan could die. Mom could die. Sarah could die. Laurence could die. James could die. I had never believed in death. Now I did, and the thought terrorized me.

Instead of chasing Morgan, I scraped the windshield with a passion, obliterating each web of crystals frozen to the glass, until James walked out with the car keys, and Sarah, pulling on her overcoat, turned to shut our back door. I jumped into the front seat, sweating, wanting to go back into the house and call Morgan at the office and leave him the message that he must come home and never leave us again. Instead, I sat in the passenger seat, saying nothing, and listened to James hum along with Dionne Warwick singing "Do you know the way to San Jose?" on the radio, knowing that I did not know the way, and feeling that I knew nothing.

Walking up the boys' stairs and into my first class of the day at Central High School, I was amazed at how it was all the same. Charlotte's death had changed nothing there. The rupture in my universe was something that only Sarah shared with me, and that James tangentially shared with both of us. The most startling quality of my sorrow was that it was mine and mine alone. The kind nods of my fellow students that first morning back, the waves, and the gentle pats on the shoulder from my instructors did not alter my sorrow, although there was a comfort to the sameness all around me, a place where I understood the routines, and what the teachers wanted. Walking down the hallways, I blended into the packs of students who were slamming locker doors and rushing into classrooms.

FOR FIVE DAYS after the funeral, Mom and Serena wrote hundreds of notes, expressing our family's thanks for food, flowers, donations, and condolences. On the sixth day, with the thank-you notes finished, Serena opened the door to her sunroom office to return to her interior decoration business, leaving Mom to her first day alone. When Sarah and I walked into the kitchen that afternoon, we saw Mom in her housecoat, cradling the black receiver of the telephone.

"Twila," she said into the receiver, "this is Eileen. I think I'm ready to come back to work. Could you use me?" She stood at the counter, balancing on her left leg, while her right leg jerked up and down, flapping her fluffy white slipper as she listened.

"Thank you, Twila. Thank you," Mom said, pausing to listen again.

"Yes, yes, I understand I'll have to cover Thursday nights. Fred and Sarah can help Morgan watch Laurence."

Hanging up the phone, Mom turned to the two of us and said, "I'm going back to work." She kissed Sarah, and then me. As her lips brushed my cheek they felt light and dry, like onionskin paper. The sweet smell of port blended with the citrus of her Jean Naté After Bath Splash, floating off the flowers in the cloth of her housecoat. Her fingers on my cheek felt cold and feathery. "When Laurence gets home, give him a snack, kids. I'm going upstairs for a while."

⌇

FOR THREE DAYS, Mom stayed in bed. During that time Morgan slept on the floor between Laurence and me. On Sunday, Mom rose early to shower and dress in her black funeral suit. She attended seven o'clock Mass alone, returning a little after eight to pass through the kitchen where Morgan was serving bacon and scrambled eggs to the three of us. Her eyes looked straight ahead at some unreachable point far away from our gazes.

"Good morning, Eileen," Morgan said, "would you like some breakfast?" Mom's high heels clicking across the linoleum floor were her only response. She reached the back stairs and was gone.

Laurence put down his fork and stuck his thumb into his mouth. Morgan lit a cigarette, while Sarah broke a piece of bacon and crumbled it across the top of her eggs. Pushing his chair back, Laurence left the table to follow Mom's path upstairs. Sarah soon followed him. I stared at the empty chairs as Morgan inhaled softly on his Marlboro, putting the frying pan into the sink.

"She needs to go back to work," Morgan told a smoke ring. "She needs to keep those dogs at bay."

Not knowing what to say to Morgan, I pushed back my chair and followed Laurence and Sarah upstairs.

Mom's bedroom door was open. She lay fully clothed in bed, the black shoulders of her suit not hidden by the white chenille bedspread. Her black-leather-gloved hands gripped the edge of the bedspread as she looked up to the cracks in the coved ceiling. Curled up next to her was Laurence, whose left hand stroked the wisps of red hair that escaped from the jet prison of her velvet veiled hat as he sucked his thumb. Tiger Cat paced the surface of the bed, wailing a nervous meow from somewhere deep in his orange body. Sarah knelt beside the bed's frame. "Mom," she kept saying, "Mom," because there did not seem to be anything else for her to say. I stood in the doorway, not moving, not certain what I should do or what I should say. In her grief, I felt that Mom was gone from us, living on a planet to which I could not travel. A planet of grief not inhabited by any of the rest of the family's mourners.

I heard Morgan's footsteps in the hallway. He stood beside me, staring at the scene on the bed. Looking down on the crown of his head, I could see the pale pink of his scalp, tonsured like a monk and surrounded by thick, steel-gray hair. Morgan cleared his throat.

"Eileen," he called out to her, "you must get up. This cannot go on."

"Morgan, I can't," Mom cried from the bed. Tiger Cat yowled in almost harmony. "I don't know if I can ever get up again. I want her back, Morgan. I would do anything to get her back."

"Eileen, you are going to work tomorrow. You need to get up."

"I don't know if I can."

"Mom," Sarah said.

"Eileen, you have other children. You have responsibilities. You must get up," Morgan said, his voice shaking with so many emotions, I could not pick out only one.

"I can't," she wailed, her heels kicking up and down against the mattress, the bedspread jumping with them.

"I can't do this alone, Eileen. You must come back. You have to go to work tomorrow. We're two months overdue with Laurence's tuition at the Madonna School. The hospital payment plan begins next month."

"Why would God do this to us? How could God let Charlotte die?"

"I cannot answer for God. You know what you have to do. You have to live, if not for me, then for them," Morgan said, pointing at each of us. "Charlotte was not the only one."

Mom looked at him with eyes of blue ice, betraying the sting of Morgan's words.

"Go away, all of you," she said, her gaze retracing the path of Morgan's finger, falling on each of us. "Tomorrow you will have me, but today I'm mad at God and all of you and everyone."

Morgan signaled that we should go; we left only Tiger Cat with her, a sentry curled up on the foot of the bed.

ON MONDAY, MOM came to breakfast dressed in a black wool skirt, a gray turtleneck, and a maroon jacket. With her faded red hair pulled back and rolled under at the nape of her neck, she looked thin and severe.

"Good morning," she said, spreading a paper napkin across her lap and then pouring a cup of coffee.

I watched her eat a single slice of buttered toast and half of a bruised banana. My eyes peered over my bowl of cornflakes at her mouth and the deliberateness of her jaw as she tore the toast with her small, efficient teeth. My heart sang in a bitter gladness. "She's back, she's back. She's ours again." But I knew Mom didn't want to be there. While I wanted Morgan to stay home with me forever, I wanted Mom up and out in the world. I needed to see her move and eat and breathe, for she seemed to me to be the closest to death, because she so wanted to follow Charlotte into the world beyond. Even then, that very day, February 27, 1970, Mom's return-to-work day and my then-forgotten eighteenth birthday, I needed her to live for me, because I'd begun to understand death days and what they meant. All I knew on my eighteenth birthday was that I needed my mother, that I could not spare her yet.

BUNDLED UP AGAINST a freezing wind, Mom waited with Laurence on the steps cut into the lawn for the little yellow bus of the Madonna School. After her last wave to Laurence as he sat down by the fourth window of the bus, she walked alone down Thirty-eighth Street, not waiting for Morgan to accompany her as was their custom, to catch the eastbound Dodge Street bus.

"Mrs. Holly," James called from the drive, "would you like a ride to work?"

"No thank you, James," Mom told him, "I need to get used to it again, this idea of work."

I watched her black coat zigzag around the ice and snow, and then I watched Morgan in his gray coat follow her, wondering whether he would ever catch up to Mom, and if he did, what they would say to each other.

"Happy birthday, Fred," James said, breaking my concentration, reminding me that I was now eighteen and, in the eyes of our government, a draft-age male adult.

Bending down to pick up a textbook that she had dropped by the side of the car, Sarah said, "Oh, God, Fred, I'm sorry. It's the twenty-seventh. We've all forgotten."

"It's okay," I told her, having forgotten it myself.

"No, no, it isn't okay. I'll make a cake tonight and we'll celebrate it. We have to celebrate. Eighteen is a big deal."

"Don't forget to register," James said. That, too, I had forgotten. I'd forgotten everything—that I was eighteen, that in Vietnam a war raged. I'd even forgotten that Richard Nixon was president. I'd forgotten that I was supposed to go to college.

"We'll go drinking," James said. "For your birthday, we'll go drinking."

PEOPLE OFTEN REFER to a supposed fact, a fact that I have never seen in a reference book or a census statistic, about bars in Omaha. I have heard this fact quoted in derision, in pride, and in shock, depending on the speaker. Omaha, Nebraska, is supposed to have more bars per square mile than any other city in America. It might be true. I do not know. My experience in bars in Omaha began in earnest that weekend after my eighteenth birthday. I walked out of our house on Thirty-eighth Street that Saturday night with twenty dollars in my pocket, given to me by Herb Pepper, after working all day at the Joslyn. It was too much, and I said so to Herb.

"Just take it, Fred. Put it away for college. You're a good boy," Herb said, turning around to walk across the Floral Court away from me and back to the closet the staff called his janitor's office.

Within the walking miles of our houses were seemingly dozens of bars. The California Street Bar, the Saddle Creek Lounge, the Chicago Bar, the Licorice Stick, the Tropics Bar and Grill, each filled with regulars and strangers, all hoping to get a drink without much hassle. In 1970, eighteen was not the legal drinking age in Nebraska, but it was the age that young Omahans began to go to bars, producing fake I.D.'s or winging it without any identification at all, hoping, only hoping, that the bartender would not ask to see a driver's license.

I did not have to drink alone, nor even try to drink alone, for however much James, Micah, and Joshua lacked in knowledge about mourning, they seemed to understand that their role was to get me something to drink. Drinking in Omaha was the unspoken solace that the city offered for those celebrating a joy, or for those enduring great pain. It was what the boys knew to do for me, for we had seen our parents do it. In Omaha, people drink. It was the only language of emotional expression that they knew how to offer.

These were my Saturday nights those weeks after Charlotte's funeral–slipping out the front door with the boys to find bars where blacks and whites could drink together, and where no one would ask for I.D.'s. Usually they were storefront bars among and around the shuttered-up windows of businesses on North Thirtieth Street, the forever riot-scarred black section of the city. It was a slim selection, but we were loyal customers, well behaved in our innocence, and willing to flee on signal out the back door to an alley, if Omaha's finest made an appearance. In fact, though, visitations by the police were rare in a city with such a vast quantity of drinking establishments.

What I learned from drinking was that it could take me to a dark place beyond recognition, where my howling grief could be released. Each beer, each glass of bourbon, every sly rum and Coke lowered the elevator to all my pain. After last call, the guys carefully followed me down Omaha's streets as I slammed myself into glass telephone booths, pulling on the retractable doors, shutting out James, Micah, and Joshua in their green Central High letter jackets.

"Charlotte, Charlotte," I would say into the receiver, "come home Charlotte. Mom's crying and we miss you."

Standing cold and drunk in those glass and metal boxes, I believed that somehow Charlotte could hear my pleas in the place where she existed. For me, in drunkenness, there was a third reality of choice, the choice of Charlotte coming home. I believed as I walked down Omaha's streets in the early hours of Sunday morning, searching out phone booths, that Charlotte would pick up some pink telephone in the world of her new existence and respond to me. "Fred," I wanted to hear her say, and after that I didn't know what an eleven-year-old dead girl would say to her brother, but I knew that she would begin with "Fred."

My favorite phone booth—the phone booth that James, Joshua, and Micah hated—was across the expanse of lawn from the Children's Hospital. As they stood by, looking at the hospital's windows and shaking from the March cold, I howled my pleas to Charlotte into the receiver. On more than one occasion the security guard chased us away. My secret belief in the dark place where drinking could take me was that if Charlotte did exist in some spectral form, it would be there at her last home, Children's Hospital.

Always at the magic hour of 3 A.M. on Sunday morning, one boy, usually James, would take my hand in a locking grip as the other two stood close by to prevent me from bolting, and then the three of them would lead me home. When we reached Thirty-eighth Street, we would often see Sarah's silhouette in the attic window. Uninvited on our Saturday night drinking binges, Sarah found solace in the attic at her barre, practicing for hours with an imaginary ballet company. We would stand there watching her arms and the fluttering of her fingers in the harsh light of the attic's bare bulbs. One of the boys, usually Micah, would say, "God, Fred, she's beautiful," and the other two would chorus in, "Yeah, she's beautiful." Seeing Sarah was the blessing on our evening's end, a reminder of life's possibilities—girls, beauty, and love.

After handing me over to Morgan, Micah and Joshua would sprint down our driveway, whispering, "Good night, Fred. Good night, James," to run home and sleep the few hours before Annie would awaken them for African Methodist Episcopal Sunday school. James watched from his side of our driveways as I stumbled through the kitchen door and into Morgan's arms. At the bathroom sink, Morgan would silently wipe the vomit from my face. Then he would unzip my pants, forcing me to pee, after which he handed me two glasses of water, which I drank without question. Holding my hand, Morgan would lead me to my bed, tuck me under the covers with a kiss to my forehead, and whisper a prayer of thanks to God that I was home and safe.

On those Sunday afternoons, I would wake up to the banging noise of the piano and Laurence's laughter as Hetty played duets with him. After my shower, my head screaming with pain and my stomach churning from the abuse of the alcohol, I would first greet Hetty and then Laurence, then move to walk the sunlit path across the room to kiss Mom on the cheek.

Mom would point to the sofa and I would sit next to her. She would hold my hand and whisper, "Isn't Hetty kind, Fred? Laurence would be lost without her." Even through the pain of my hangover, which only increased as Hetty and Laurence banged out their raucous version of "Heart and Soul," I was thankful for Hetty. Laurence sucked his thumb less and spoke more when Hetty was around. Mom's shoulders lifted as she poured grape juice and served Hydrox cookies to Hetty and Laurence in the kitchen on those Sunday afternoons. When Hetty was in the house it felt as though Charlotte wasn't so far away.

Sarah

SARAH SUFFERED. AND she suffered alone. Like disease, suffering manifests itself in both acute and chronic forms, and Sarah suffered acutely during the months after Charlotte's death. Where I escaped to Omaha's bars, reaching into my sadness, Sarah floated in the sea of her sadness, of missing Charlotte. And she floated publicly. Unlike Eleanor Rigby, Sarah did not keep her face in a glass by the door. The starkness of Sarah's grieving was in the rising of her cheek bones as she lost weight. Sarah's soul disappeared, leaving her eyes vacant. Her electricity gone. I believed that Sarah's soul searched for Charlotte, it searched for the explanation of death. She wanted to know how someone so alive could be gone. Sarah's soul was a lonely soul.

If Sarah's first death had been that of a lover, a friend, or even Morgan, then Mom could have comforted her. Mom would have been at Sarah's side. But Mom was gone from Sarah, from all of us, in those first years after Charlotte's death, living in a Mom-world of work, housekeeping, and preparing Laurence for his transition into a workshop program at Westside High School. Mom became a sad flutter-bird in our lives, in constant twitch and twitter about going somewhere, about Mass, about Campbell's Cream of Mushroom Soup recipes. She was all wings, flying around the leaden feelings that might pull her into the doom of her bed. Mom talked, but not to us. Sarah swam alone in a world comprising a father, two brothers, and an orange tomcat. Morgan, by his very nature, gave the teenage Sarah great room. He knocked on bedroom and bathroom doors. He was extraordinarily careful about bathrobes and covering himself. When he hugged Sarah, he made sure that there were inches between them, that their father and daughter trunks never quite touched. He kept her safe from all things masculine.

Daily, Morgan lined the three of us up in the kitchen and kissed each of us on the forehead with soft, dry, closed lips. It was a good-bye kiss. A just-in-case kiss, a this-could-be-the-last-time kiss. A kiss of blessing, a kiss of warning. Those kisses were everything Morgan could not say. They were his worry. They were his fear. They were his love.

Talk of Charlotte's death, talk of Charlotte, came to seem forbidden. Like talk of sex, that place where Morgan and Mom could not, or would not, go. Sarah's grieving, the appearance of her bones, the plum-colored shadows under her eyes terrified me. It was as if she walked among us naked. Her starkness was beautiful. Men turned to watch her on the street— her black, straight hair pulled back into a dancer's ponytail, swinging in rhythm to her walk. A walk punctuated by poised shoulders, a chest out, and a spine straightened to an aching perfection. A body opened to the world with a face streaked in pain. When the well-meaning stranger would touch her arm at the bus stop, and ask, "Dear, is everything okay? Are you sick?" Sarah would answer, "My sister died," or "Charlotte died," or "My sister is dead," and the kind stranger would pull back, uncertain of what to say. For talk of death in 1970 was considered vulgar and intimate. People learned to give Sarah space. They learned to look away from her. Even Morgan, like Mom, seemed unable to see Sarah, to recognize her grieving. His eyes were averted. But mine were not.

During those sixty-one days of March and April, I could not keep my eyes off Sarah. I wanted someone to touch her. I wanted her to go to the prom. I wanted James to take Sarah to prom. At prom, Sarah could dance and James could hold her. Even if James did not love Sarah in the way Sarah loved him, he could hold her in his arms safely. He could move with her and in that movement, I believed, bring her soul back into her body, if only for a little while. I wanted James to do this for Sarah. I wanted James to do this for me.

$$\sim\!\!\sim\!\!\sim$$

THE LAST SATURDAY of March was warm all day and into the night. Annie Little had made Joshua and Micah promise to be home by midnight, which left James and me together, and only halfway drunk. We sat behind our garages, where lily of the valley was sprouting around fully bloomed crocus. We were smoking under a beam of light off the utility pole in the alley. James's back was against the brick wall of our garage and we were talking about nothing and everything. It was the night of the new moon. The white light of stars shimmered around the surface of the moon's silhouette.

"James," I said, "do me a favor. Take Sarah to prom."

"Fred," he said, looking away from me, "that's complicated."

"I understand it's complicated. But do me a favor and take Sarah to prom. You don't have to love and marry a girl just because you take her to prom. She needs this. She needs to dress up and dance. Please do this for me."

"What if Sarah thinks it's more than that? I can't deal with her being in love with me. She's so busted up over Charlotte, I couldn't take it if she were busted up over me."

"Look," I said, reaching out for his arm, "I think Sarah understands that. I can make her understand that. But she needs this now. I need you to do this for me."

My hand stayed clamped to his arm. I pitched my cigarette and cupped his face with my free hand, turning his eyes toward mine. "Please, James, do this for me."

"Fred, you don't understand," he told me with serious blue eyes. All of their boyishness had drained away.

"I do understand. You always think that you're a closed book, but I understand, I have always understood."

His face turned in my hand.

"James, please."

Turning back to me, James reached out and touched the bridge of my nose, tapping it ever so gently with his index finger, and then I kissed him almost on his lips, bumping his chin. James kissed me back. It was not like Morgan's daily kisses, or Mom's bedtime kisses of my childhood. It was open-mouthed and in no way chaste. I responded in kind, by falling on him. We rolled on top of the crocuses, tearing leaves and smashing petals. James burned me with his cigarette, but I did not stop kissing him. Sorrow and rage and desire were locked there between us, and I refused to give up his tongue, his lips, or his teeth. I tasted the rum on his tongue and the cigarettes on his breath. Neither of us would break. When James finally took his lips from mine, I could taste blood, and I began to cry. All of me spilled out onto the purple and yellow crocus petals and still, cold black soil. Charlotte spilled out and Sarah spilled out. My love for James, my years and years of love for James, spread out under the orange haze of the utility pole light.

"I'll take her."

"How could you love that bastard? I could imagine almost anyone, but him."

His blue eyes answered me wide and startled, "I still love that bastard, Fred."

"You should have loved me first. I am your best friend," I whispered to him, pounding my fist into the sprouts of lily of the valley. "I would do anything for you. You should have loved me better than him." I began to bawl, heaving, angry little-boy sobs. James grabbed me and locked me in his arms, rocking me back and forth.

"Fred, I'll take her."

"Charlotte's dead."

"I know, Fred, I know."

Then James kissed me again. It was a long sad kiss. His face glistened with tears.

Prom

SARAH SAID YES. In between classes, I stood in the Joslyn, staring at the bulbous hills of Grant Wood's *Stone City, Iowa,* and thinking of Sarah's yes. How it was a quiet "Yes." Mom, Morgan, Laurence, and I all heard her "Yes" in response to the formality of James's question in the sunroom early on that first Saturday morning in April.

"Sarah, would you go to prom with me?"

There was a pause and all the listeners in the house were suspended in its silence. In the pause, we considered, we feared, that Sarah might say no. She might say no in the self-punishment of her grieving. She might say no because she knew James was not in love with her. Even, I thought, Sarah might say no because she was too in love with James to spend time with him when he was not in love with her. But she said yes. Our house sighed in unison.

"I think we'll double with Joshua and Lily, and maybe Micah, if that's okay with you?" Again we waited in the great space of no words for Sarah's response.

"Sure," she said.

"Well, that'll be great," James told her. I could hear an upbeat note in the timbre of his voice. "We can dance, Sarah. I mean, we could even practice in the attic like we used to. We'll be the stars of the show." The sound of tapping floated upstairs to where I stood on the landing, listening, with Tiger Cat weaving through my legs. Sarah laughed.

"We were always the stars of the show."

After he left, Sarah walked up the stairs, passing me without a word as she made her way to the attic. There she practiced at her barre for an hour before leaving for Lana Beth Boyer's dance studio. Lana Beth had hired her as an assistant teacher and as the Saturday afternoon cleaning woman. I came out of my bedroom when I heard the Beatles' "Dizzy Miss Lizzy" pounding through the ceiling from above. The voices of John, Paul, George, and Ringo transfixed me. The song was a memory of happiness, of summer in a land where we once lived. The bathroom door across the hallway opened and Morgan stood in its frame, muttering the name "Fred." In his black and blue plaid bathrobe with his face covered in shaving cream, Morgan was working himself into a literal lather, preparing his lungs to yell my name up the attic stairs when he saw me.

"Who's playing the goddamn rock and roll, Fred?"

"Sarah," I told him. "Its sounds great, doesn't it?"

Morgan looked up and down the ceiling of the hallway.

"Well, I guess she's getting ready for this dance," he said gruffly, as though the music were some kind of school assignment that had to be completed before the prom. Then he turned back into the bathroom, shutting the door with a firm click.

"Dizzy Miss Lizzy" marked the first notes of rock 'n' roll to be played in the attic since the weeks before Charlotte's death. The song marked the beginning of moments of less sadness for Sarah. It marked something for me, too. A gift from James.

I OFTEN STARED at *Stone City, Iowa*. Its terrain was like nothing around Omaha. Grant Wood's compact hills pushed off the surface of the painting like bosoms out of a corset. Surrounded by fawn-colored hills, dappled by cloud shadow, and sprouting with corn, this village was not the Puritan and earnest world of *American Gothic*. To me at eighteen, *Stone City, Iowa* was all about sex. Its forms were breasts and buttocks that spoke of fecundity, and were part of the puzzle of my attractions to both. I stood there, nursing the cut to my kissed lip in the wonderment of my feelings for James and the still-yearning notion that I was in love with Arianna Isaacs. It was then that I heard someone say my name.

"Fred."

I turned from the painting to see Arianna Isaacs standing there in a red beret, a black cable-stitch sweater, and a green skirt, above the kneecaps but not enough to be a mini. Arianna's face looked grim. We had not spoken since before Charlotte's funeral. From a distance I had seen Arianna and Micah in the museum, but they were always headed to some dark corner.

"Fred," she said again, "I need a favor. I need a favor, a very big favor."

"Yes," I said to her as a deep blush spread up my neck and across my face, reaching to the deepest roots of my hair. My thoughts on Grant Wood's hills were still suspended in my imagination. Standing next to Arianna was an unsettling moment of reality. I was uncomfortable with her closeness. My affections were attuned to distance.

"Will you take me to prom? I want to meet Micah there. It's the only way I'll ever get to dance with him. Once I leave Omaha, I'll never see him again. It's killing me, Fred." With these words Arianna Isaacs started to weep. Her weeping was different than crying. It was not the sob of crying, but the bleat of weeping. I reached for the handkerchief that Morgan made me carry and handed it to her.

"Sure, sure, I'll take you. You can dance every dance with Micah. I'd be glad to take you. I love you. Of course, I'll take you." My words came out confused and in a rush.

"Fred," Arianna said, blowing her nose into my handkerchief, "you can't love me. You don't even know me. I've told you this before. I can't go to this dance thinking you love me, when you don't even know me. It's creepy."

"You mean we're not going to the dance together?" I asked, beginning to feel more confused and wondering why I shouldn't say I love her.

"No, I mean you have to stop talking about loving me. You can't love someone you don't know."

"I'm not certain of that," I told her. I have no idea why I said this. I felt a little crazy in her presence, reckless, like I wanted to debate her and win. "I love this painting," I said, pointing to *Stone City, Iowa.* "I have loved this painting for years, but I don't expect the painting to love me back.

And I don't expect you to love me back, but I do love you. And I have since September of junior year."

It was true, I did love Arianna Isaacs. I loved her laughter and her thick curly, brown hair. I loved the way she ruthlessly debated in contests and the way she pulled her turtleneck collars up and over her chin when she studied alone under the clock in the library.

"I am not creepy, Arianna. I will take you to this dance like a gentleman."

"But first you have to take me on a date so that my parents can meet you."

"What?"

"A date, a Coke date on Wednesday night, so that my mom and dad can meet you. They're uncomfortable with me going out with a Gentile."

"I'm gentle?" I asked her.

"No, you're a gentile," Arianna said, emphasizing the hard i. "It means not Jewish. My parents don't want me to date non-Jews."

"Then why are they letting me take you on a Coke date? Or to prom for that matter?"

"Your sister," Arianna whispered, her eyes widening.

"My sister? Sarah?" I asked her.

"No, Charlotte," she said in a hushed tone, blushing a deeper red than mine. "I told my parents that you didn't have a date for senior prom and that you asked me to go as your friend. I told them I was going with you as a mitzvah, because your sister died."

"What is a mitzvah?" I asked her.

Arianna looked at the hills of *Stone City, Iowa* and away from me. "A mitzvah," she began, "is an act of goodness. A good deed. It relates to moral conduct. A mitzvah is how we are supposed to treat one another. It is doing good for another."

"Oh, then, what you're saying is that I am doing a mitzvah for you and Micah. This has nothing to do with Charlotte."

"Yes," she said in a small voice.

For a moment we both stood, looking at *Stone City, Iowa*, not saying a word. Finally I said: "I saw you and your parents at Charlotte's funeral and that was a good deed. I appreciated it. Sarah appreciated it. That was a mitzvah for us. Thank you," I told her, while focusing on the horse and rider approaching the bridge in the center of the painting.

"Wednesday, the Coke date? Will you meet my parents?" Arianna asked.

"Would seven be okay, Arianna?"

She nodded.

"We don't know each other very well do we," I said, looking back at the hills in the painting.

"No, we don't," she said. "I'm afraid not knowing you will go down on my list of regrets, Fred Holly."

"You keep a list of regrets?" I asked her.

"Yeah, I do. I once thought I could live my life without regrets. I could organize everything so that I would have no regrets at the end. But then, I started talking to Micah Little in the parking lot and my universe tilted. I fell in love. I didn't plan on falling in love."

"At this point in my life, Arianna, I couldn't imagine a life without regrets," I told her. "Or not being in love. Every day of my life, I'm in love with you, or a painting, or something. Every day I miss Charlotte. I wish I had said the right things to her. But I'm sure I didn't. I know I didn't."

"You're a strange boy," Arianna said, "but in a nice way. You're strange in a nice way."

"But I'm the boy who will take you to prom."

Arianna looked away from me, blushing an even deeper red, a red only a shade lighter than her beret.

"Micah said to say 'thank you.' He said to tell you 'he owes you one.'"

"Tell Micah I say 'You're welcome.'"

"Here's your handkerchief."

Arianna's hand reached out to me with the crumpled, moist linen ball.

"Oh, no keep it. You might need it," I told her, feeling for a moment like the gentleman that Morgan wanted me to be.

RABBI AND MRS. Isaacs were small, gray-haired, and dignified. They both shook my hand and they both spoke English with refined German accents.

"Arianna tells us your father works at Mutual of Omaha," Rabbi Isaacs said.

"Yes," I told him, "my father is an actuary."

"And you, will you be studying business?" Mrs. Isaacs asked me.

"I would like to study art history," I said.

A look crossed between them. It was a look I would grow to know. It contained a concerned pity in an attempt not to be patronizing. I sensed that they felt sorry for my parents.

"And where will you go to college to study art history?" Mrs. Isaacs asked.

"I'm going to Stanford," I told them. It was true. Mom and Morgan had shown me the letter of acceptance at dinner that very evening. I encountered the Fred of Seymour Fineman's imagination. Morgan and Mom, Sarah and Laurence all kept repeating the fact that "Fred is going to Stanford." Mom said, "Mr. Fineman told Morgan that you need to apply for a college deferment. That even Republicans apply for college deferments." All I could think, but could not say, was that I didn't even know that I was a Republican. As far as I knew, I wasn't anything, only Fred.

"Stanford?" Rabbi Isaacs asked. "That's in California, isn't it?"

"Morgan tells me that the students are happy there," I said. "That he wants me in a school where the students are happy."

"Who is this Morgan?" Rabbi Isaacs asked.

"Morgan is my father, sir." It was the first time in my life that I added "sir." Again I watched the look that crossed between Arianna's parents. There was an intimation of fear. It seemed probable that their daughter was going to prom with a crazy boy. A boy who called his father by his first name.

"Have her home by nine. It's a school night," Rabbi Isaacs said, ushering us out the door.

It was a warm evening, and the smell of wet black soil floated in the air. We walked up to the Baskin-Robbins at Fiftieth Street and Underwood Avenue. I ordered a chocolate cone and Arianna ordered pistachio. We strolled out of the ice-cream store, licking our cones and looking into the shop windows.

Arianna spoke first.

"I love my parents, Fred. I understand that they want the best for me. I'm going to Brandeis University. I want to study medicine and save lives. I want to marry a nice Jewish man and have three children. I want to fall in love with a nice Jewish man."

"What about Micah?" I asked her.

"Oh," Arianna said with a small bleat. "Oh," she said again with a tremble in her voice. "If I could, I would marry Micah and move to Hawaii where everyone is of mixed race. We could have our babies there. We would go to the University of Hawaii and Micah could play football. The babies and I would watch him from a blanket in the green grass. That's my Micah dream. They would be beautiful babies. My parents would forgive me. My brother would forgive me. Annie Little would stop hating me. Our families would come live with us in Hawaii. It would be perfect."

"You would have no regrets?" I asked her.

"But it's a dream," she said. "If I married Micah, my father would be so sad he wouldn't get out of bed for days. Annie Little would chase me down and tell me exactly what she thinks of me. Micah would sigh in pain. I couldn't take my father's pain and my mother's tears. There would be crying and screaming and recriminations of all sorts. I would have only regrets. I'm no Juliet."

"I'm sorry," I said, watching a drop of green ice cream come to rest on her chin. I considered wiping it away in one deft movement. A suave, Cary Grant moment for me, but instead I took note of her feelings, and pointed to my chin.

"What? Arianna asked.

"There's ice cream on your chin."

She wiped her chin with a napkin.

"Is it gone?"

"You got it," I told her.

"What I hate is that I already regret not running away to Hawaii with Micah. I regret that I haven't had the courage to tell him that I dream of running away with him. That I dream of Hawaii all the time. I regret that I'm a Jew and he's a Christian. I regret that we both believe in our religions. I regret how much we love our parents. How much we hate to disappoint them."

Arianna sighed.

"So how do you feel about prom? Do you really want to go?"

Arianna's eyes were on the seed display in the hardware-store window. Seed packets of zinnias, marigolds, snapdragons, butter beans, pansies, portulaca, sweet corn, tomatoes, and lima beans were fanned out across hoes, ladies' spades, and the green coils of rubber hoses attached to yellow lawn sprinklers. She tapped her index finger against the plate-glass window as if to awaken something in the display, possibly a mole or a cricket or a field mouse that had taken refuge there until the real summer came along.

"Yes, I want this time with him. I want to be beautiful for him and I don't want him ever to forget me. I want him to have as many regrets as I do."

"I think you're as brave as Juliet, but in an inverse fashion. You are thinking about the families. She sacrificed her life and you're sacrificing your heart." I said this to Arianna in a rush of passion and she gave me that look again.

"You are the nicest, strangest boy, Fred Holly. Do you always tell people what you think? Do you always tell people the truth?"

"Don't you?" I asked her. "Aren't you worried about time? That you won't have enough time to do what you want? Why wouldn't you tell the truth? It's a waste of time not to tell the truth."

"Well, there isn't just one truth. There are many aspects to any situation, to any particular truth. It's like preparing for a debate—you have to know all of your opponent's arguments as well as your own, or you won't be able to counter them."

"Ah," I said, "Neil Mahaffey coached you well."

"Neil Mahaffey might be America's biggest jerk, but he knows his debate strategy. Neil is a complicated situation. He's both a bastard and a saint. A dramatic guy who yearns for his bright and shining moment."

"The priesthood?" I asked her.

"Well, first it was the Peace Corps and then it was law school and now it's the priesthood. But he will have to shed himself of his girlfriend before he's goes away to priest school. Like that's the big deal with priests, right? They're celibate?"

"What girlfriend?" I asked her.

"Did you see Neil at the funeral?"

"Yeah."

"Did you see the striking blonde with him?"

"I noticed her. She wasn't the first thing on my mind that day."

"Well, she isn't Neil's sister. She's Neil's girlfriend."

"But–" I stopped.

"But what?"

"Nothing, nothing. I just didn't realize that Neil Mahaffey had a girlfriend. Didn't he always pick on you and Sarah at the debate tournaments? I thought he was sort of toughening himself up to live without women." And I thought, but I did not say to Arianna Isaacs, "Poor James, poor James."

It was nearly nine o'clock when we walked up to her house. The streetlights were popping on and the night air had grown cool. I could see Arianna's father and mother sitting on matching chairs in the front room, watching a black-and-white television. Rabbi Isaacs was smoking a pipe.

"Well, I'll walk you to your door and shake your hand. I want your parents to think well of me."

"Micah will give you the plans for the prom. He has it all figured out."

I shook her hand and held the door for her. Her parents rose from their chairs to greet her. Arianna Isaacs was home safely.

THE PROM, STANFORD, my college deferment, and James's college deferment all took on an energy in April for Mom and Serena Day. An energy that was not related to Children's Hospital or Charlotte or Charlotte's dying. Mom worked herself into a kind of frenzy over filling out my papers for Stanford and making sure that I applied for my college deferment. She pestered Sarah endlessly about buying a dress, and she called Serena daily to confer with her on what James and I should wear to the dance and what flowers we should order for the girls. The nomenclature of prom and college and boyfriends and girlfriends, and the possibility for these two women that romance and marriage and grandchildren could be in a future nearer than they hoped almost left them giddy. If any of us mentioned Charlotte's name, Mom would freeze and walk into another room. She would not talk about Charlotte during those weeks before prom. The language of those weeks careened so far away from death and hospitals that I would work in the garden at night, uncovering Morgan's buried roses, whispering and savoring Charlotte's name, telling her the pieces of secrets that I held in my heart.

I was on my knees, scooping up muddied leaves, telling Charlotte, "You'll be glad to know, Charlotte, Sarah found her dress at the Goodwill. Mom said, 'Sarah, you bought a used dress? Honey, this is the prom.' So Sarah says to Mom, 'I love this dress. It's very Jackie Kennedy, 1962. I want that look, Mom. I don't want to pay a ton of money for a new dress I don't want. Besides, Fred's not the only one going to college. I need to save my money for college.' Charlotte, Mom looked like a snake bit her. She thinks that prom means James and Sarah are going to get married."

"But Fred, don't you think that James might marry her?"

"What?" I jumped back from the rose bush, tossing muddy leaves everywhere. My heart pounding so hard, it felt like it would split from my chest. I turned around to see Hetty standing on the path behind me.

"Hetty, what are you doing here? Aren't you supposed to be doing homework or something? Don't sneak up on me like that."

"Don't you think that the prom could be the beginning of everything for James and Sarah?"

"No," I said, still shaking, "I think it's just prom. James will go away to Purdue or Northwestern in the fall, and Sarah will go to some college the year after that. They'll meet other people and fall in love with them."

"Charlotte told me that Sarah was in love with James."

Hetty tossed one of her braids and kicked at a clod of dirt. Her cat-eyed glasses tilted southward off the bridge of her nose. In the weeks since Charlotte's death, Hetty had grown at least an inch. Her clothes were tighter and her chest was beginning to develop.

"Charlotte sure paid attention to us, didn't she?" I said, sitting back on the path, looking into the eyes behind Hetty's glasses. They were green speckled with brown.

"Yeah, she talked about you and Sarah all the time. All the time. You two were our stories."

"Sarah and I would talk about how lucky it was for Charlotte to have you as a friend."

Hetty sat down beside me on the path. I felt that I was about as close as I would ever get to Charlotte in a sober state. Hetty knew more about Charlotte than I did.

"She was mad at you, Fred."

I took a deep breath, my heart's beating, surging, painfully.

"You are a very honest person, Hetty Carmichael."

"Charlotte wanted you to pay attention to her."

"It was difficult last summer with Morgan and Vietnam. I needed to be anywhere but here."

"She wanted to be with you, to hang out with you and Sarah and all your friends. Sometimes I felt I wasn't cool enough for her. Charlotte wanted to grow up to be cool. To wear go-go boots and miniskirts."

"Hetty, you were the best thing that ever happened to Charlotte. She loved you. You were the only kid that she would let come over to the house when she was sick. You were the only kid that she trusted enough to let see her." My chest heaved. It hurt to think of Christmas and go-go boots.

"Your mom won't say her name, Fred. All she talks about is prom and Stanford. It's as if Charlotte never existed."

"My mom's a little crazy now, Hetty. She's just a little crazy now. Her sadness makes her so sad that she has to pack it up in a little bundle inside herself and pretend that it's not there."

"Can I talk about Charlotte with you, then?"

"Sure you can. I talk to Charlotte here in the garden where no else can hear me. It's a little one-sided. Sometimes I think she agrees with me, but other times, I'm glad she can't talk back."

Hetty pushed her glasses northward and smiled a sad smile.

"My dad says that Charlotte was full of life. He said that it was not her time. Even as a man of God, he knows that it was not Charlotte's time. And that's why we are all so sad. Because sometimes, it is a person's time to die. But it wasn't Charlotte's." Hetty bent over, picked up a clod of earth, and broke it through her fingers. "He says that when parents lose a child, they're never the same. Parents plan to die first."

I didn't know what to say to all of Hetty's words.

"Hetty, Charlotte's body was so broken down. Her body failed."

"But, it wasn't her time. How could God let her die?"

"Well, how does God allow wars and injustice and man's inhumanity to man?"

"Fred, I'm only eleven years old. I don't know why God allows all that. I just don't know how God could let Charlotte die. My life is terrible now. I'm lonely all the time. She was my best friend." And Hetty Carmichael began to cry. All I knew to do was to give her my handkerchief and wait it out. When she blew her nose and began to hiccough, I asked her, "Hetty, what was Charlotte like?"

Hetty wiped her nose and studied my handkerchief. It was one of Morgan's, Irish linen with his monogram in a tight thread of black script.

"Charlotte told me that she felt like an only child. You and Sarah were so much older. She didn't go to school with you and Sarah. Laurence didn't go to school with her, and—"

"And what, Hetty?"

"Some kids at school, even some girls, called Charlotte 'the retard's sister.' Boys called her 'Lucy Retardo,' because of her red hair."

"What?"

"It's the playground. On the playground, people can say just about anything and get away with it."

"She never said anything. I mean, Morgan and Mom would have done something." My eyes hurt, thinking of Charlotte defending herself, and Laurence.

"It wasn't all the time. Just sometimes. Charlotte would mouth off to kids who made fun of her on the playground. They would tease her, because they knew she wouldn't take it. Charlotte always put up a fight. She didn't want your folks to know what the kids said, or what she said back to them."

"Like Mitchell Abington?" I asked.

"Yeah, like Mitchell."

"Little prick," I said, making Hetty wince.

"You know she loved Laurence, but it was hard. Kids are mean to retarded people. They're afraid of them. It's hard to be cool with a retarded brother. Charlotte wanted to be cool, but the cool kids made fun of Laurence, and then she made fun of the cool kids."

"How did she make fun of the cool kids?" I asked.

"In third grade, Mitchell Abington had this Oscar Meyer Wiener whistle, and he'd only let certain kids blow it. And he would never ever let Charlotte blow it, because she was the retard's sister. He said he didn't want any 'retard germs' on his whistle. So Charlotte called him 'wienie.' Every time he pulled out his whistle, she'd say things like, 'Well go ahead and blow, you eeny teeny wienie, Mitchell Abington.' Finally all the kids began to say it when Mitchell pulled out his whistle, and then he left his whistle at home."

I knew then that childhood was over for me, because the cruelty of Charlotte's and Mitchell's words made me hurt. At the same time, family loyalty and my own peculiar sense of humor made me laugh.

"Charlotte didn't really say 'eeny teeny wienie,' did she?" I asked with a chuckle.

Hetty looked at me like I was a madman. "This isn't funny. She said it every time. And Mitchell called her the retard's sister all the time."

"You're right, it isn't funny, but it is funny and it's terrible and it's mean. And thank you for telling me, because I didn't know any of this about Charlotte's life."

And then I hugged Hetty Carmichael, and she told me story after story there in the garden, night after night into the summer, as I worked with Morgan's roses. Little stories of shared secrets and solemn vows, and one about Charlotte's crush on a boy I'd never heard of named Matthew Prunes. The sound of his name enchanted me. His purple-tinged, improbable surname.

"Charlotte loved Matthew Prunes," Hetty whispered to me, "and so did I."

"Did Charlotte know that you loved Matthew Prunes?" I asked.

"Yes, she did. So we made this deal. I would like Matthew on Mondays, Wednesdays and Fridays, and Charlotte would like him on Tuesdays, Thursdays, and Saturdays."

"What about Sunday?"

"On Sunday, neither of us liked him. But sometimes, I forgot not to like Matthew on Sunday, and I liked him anyway, especially when I was in church. My mind would just wander to Matthew in church."

"Well, that can happen. It's hard not to like someone you really like."

"But I wasn't supposed to like Matthew on Sundays and now I feel like I ruined it for Charlotte."

"You didn't ruin it for Charlotte."

"Are you sure?"

"I'm sure as I can be."

HETTY'S STORIES OF Charlotte were both a finite and incomplete group. It turned out that the irony of dying at eleven is that a child's stories are all partial rosebuds, or like three petals of the flower opening into the morning light, and then the light and the opening flower are gone, and only the three fast-browning petals are left. They were a fragmented, never quite finished group of tales. Charlotte's life as told by Hetty never changed. The stories have stayed with me like a scrapbook of language written in Hetty's voice. Hetty's voice and her images of Charlotte have come to me in dreams, during roaring nights of drinking, and in my California moments of mushrooms and blotter acid. My sister lives on in my world like an imaginary tamarin monkey that sits on my shoulder in a red-furred splendor. Or a golden Pomeranian dog who nips at the heels of my existence and only I know that she's there. Survivor's guilt, I have learned, can be offset when one shares one's senses with their ghosts and invites them along for the ride. That lesson, however, took me decades to learn. It is not a young man's lesson. There in the garden with Hetty, I was still a very young man. What we shared seemed complete and enough. Only later, years later, did Hetty let me know that her affections were swayed that summer. Matthew Prunes fell from grace. At least one girl from Omaha loved me. But that I didn't know for a very long time.

That Night

THE DAY OF prom was beautiful, warm, and clear. Late that afternoon, Sarah and I sat in our finery on the upstairs landing with Laurence, waiting for James to arrive for photographs. Sarah was beautiful in her used yellow Jackie Kennedy–style dress. Its fitted sleeveless bodice was embroidered with white silk, and its yellow chiffon skirt flowed straight to the tips of her white pumps. (In a series of careful repairs, Sarah had mended the slight rips in the bodice and then gently smoothed out the snags in the layers of nylon chiffon.) She wore white gloves that reached beyond her elbows, emphasizing her thin but muscled arms. Her impossibly thick black hair was pinned and frozen with hair spray into a French roll, displaying Sarah's face as all chin and cheekbone. With eyes accented by black eyeliner and her lips the cherry red of Marilyn Monroe, Sarah didn't look like Jackie Kennedy. Sarah looked like the Jackie Kennedy of 1962, as inspired by Holly Golightly as acted by Audrey Hepburn dressed by Givenchy. Sarah chose the part of the 1960s that she loved, when Camelot was still perfect and everything seemed possible. If James was never going to be in love with Sarah, at least Sarah could attend prom in the figment of her imagination that contained her love for him. On that Saturday night in April, Sarah was Jackie and Holly and Audrey. For her, James would be John Kennedy, George Peppard, and Cary Grant wrapped into one. And I would be the ever-present lone male stag, lining the side of the dance floor, taking it all in, performing for all of the lovers and nonlovers alike as their living memory.

A prom is, more than anything else, make-believe. I made believe that I was Arianna Isaacs's date. Arianna made believe that one night with Micah was enough, one night to last their lifetimes, that hours of dancing and fleeting kisses would be all the memories she would ever have or need of Micah Little. Micah made believe that he wasn't afraid. He made believe that he and Arianna would get over their feelings. They both made believe that they would not be hurt. James made believe that he was straight, a term I did not know at the time.

Moments before James arrived and Morgan shot the photographs, Sarah said to me, "Fred, thank you."

"For what?" I asked.

"Asking James to take me to prom."

I looked at her without responding.

"I wheedled the information out of James. I wanted to know. I wanted to understand why he asked me."

I continued in silence.

"Thank you, Fred. You're a good brother."

Picking up Tiger Cat, Laurence stared at the two of us. Slung over his shoulder, Tiger Cat meowed to be put down while Laurence sucked his thirteen-year-old thumb, waiting for Morgan and his Brownie camera to appear.

What, I wondered, standing there on the landing, is a good brother? In the midst of the three of us, I felt Charlotte gone. For Laurence and for Sarah I felt a love that I could not express in words. I did not feel like a good brother. I felt like a cigarette. I felt like a drink. Part of me felt like two Freds, one in my blue suit, white shirt, and maroon rep tie, and the other observing myself there on the landing in blue jeans and a black leather jacket, ready to disappear into some wild life as led by Mick Jagger or Marlon Brando. On the waterfront or in a rock band. The other Fred, ready to run away to some world where there was energy and movement and music, and on the morning after, I would awaken hungover to find Charlotte not dead.

～e～～～～

"THANK YOU, FRED," Arianna Isaacs said as she slipped away from me into the honeycomb of white windowed rooms that lined the dance floor where Micah Little waited for her. I stood there watching all the make-believe, while a South Omaha combo strummed an era full of sixties music into a danceable beat. Girls in paper minidresses and white go-go boots floated past me with their parted in-the-middle Peggy Lipton hair, straight out of Mod Squad, or a Marlo Thomas–style flip and bangs. More sedate young women sprouted beehive hairdos and long dresses that were in the polyester pastels of June weddings. There were the bold stripes of Betsy Johnson knockoffs and the home-sewn gowns of the 4-H girls. High heels, false eyelashes, cigarettes, and boys with hair feathering onto their collars paraded past me. Black boys with the beginnings of the giant Afros that were to come danced with Diana Ross look-alikes. The dancing was easy and relatively unsophisticated. They were the wonderful dances of the sixties that took no talent, only guts and verve, to rule the dance floor. Couples twisted and pogo'd, they jumped and they whooped. Arms flew and chests shimmied.

There on that warm April evening as stiff-backed teachers chaperoned us in the living dress of conservative Nebraska, the sixties paraded across that 1970 dance floor, where for a moment we experienced, in style and sound, the decade that had passed Omaha by. Tobacco smoke overhung with the first scents of patchouli created an exotic orange haze to the room's calculated dimness. From my incline against the wall, I watched as James and Sarah twirled through the clumps of flailing arms and grinding hips. Not missing a beat, they two-stepped and cha-cha-cha'd with the flair of the dancers they were. There was an elegance to the craziness that they embellished onto the formal movements of their patterns. A little bit like Fred and Ginger on acid. I watched as Mike Raven whispered into the ear of his shy date in a powder-blue dress and matching hair ribbon, pulling her onto the dance floor, where he danced into her and she danced away from him.

The Negro students, an island of a minority at Central High School, kept close together on the north wall of the ballroom. I watched Joshua and Lily bravely take to the floor, dancing south and then west before moving east and back to the safety of the north. The power and grace of Joshua's football player shoulders protected Lily's every swing, every twist. The Jewish students clumped on the south wall while the Wasps held the middle of the floor and the South Omaha Catholics hugged the periphery between the west and center. I stood on the western wall near the punch table opposite the honeycomb of windows that lined the eastern periphery.

As I stood against the wall, forever the intent observer, my memory receded. I forgot Charlotte was dead. Something in my soul lifted. The music and the movement and the girls in their finery shrouded in the haze of cigarette smoke made my world feel on the verge of summer and all its possibilities. My hopes for Arianna and Micah expanded. Summer would bring them all kinds of opportunities for the risk of love.

For the three hours of the dance, I did not see Arianna and Micah. Whatever their movements, they were not apparent to me there on the wall. At midnight, when I was scheduled to meet Arianna and Micah at the fourth white door of the honeycomb of rooms, I moved through the gyrating maze of bodies to see Arianna emerge alone from the door. Standing in her olive green satin dress with her thick brown hair loosened from its formal coiffure, she whispered to me, "Take me home, Fred, I need to go home now." In her voice I could hear the tears to come. I felt for my handkerchief before taking her elbow to shelter her through the crowd and into the cooling night.

In the safety of Morgan's Studebaker, away from our classmates, Arianna broke down, sobbing, nearly wailing, "He doesn't want me. He said, I'm crazy, and that we have to break it off. He laughed at Hawaii. He laughed and told me to grow up."

Under a gibbous moon, I handed Arianna Isaacs my clean linen handkerchief and then held her in my arms the way Mom did when we were little and scraped our knees, or Morgan did as he put us to bed. I held her like she was glass, as if Rabbi Isaacs was looking over my shoulder. I saw there at the base of Arianna's neck the red bruise of a hickey, that stain of a broken heart.

"He's going to Howard and I'm going to Brandeis," she cried into the shoulder of my blue suit, "and we will never see each other again."

"I'm sorry, Arianna, I'm sorry," I kept telling her over and over again, beginning to feel frightened of bringing her home in such a state, worried that Rabbi Isaacs would connect the hickey to my lips, to my teeth. For at that moment, I realized that I was her date, her escort, and it was my duty to get her home safely. When a girl attends a dance with a friend, she does not return home with her hair down, tear-stained, and bruised with hickeys, or at least that's how I understood it. My knowledge of Omaha's etiquette was that if Arianna returned home in this distressed state, Rabbi and Mrs. Isaacs would have the right to interrogate me at the very least. In some corners of Omaha, it would be understood that Rabbi Isaacs would have the right to beat the living shit out of me. In much of Nebraska, including many homes in Omaha, "shotgun marriage" was not a metaphor.

"Arianna," I said, "did Micah do anything out of line? Anything you didn't want him to do?"

"He doesn't want me," she wailed.

"What I am asking was, did Micah do anything wrong? Anything your parents would have to know about?"

"No, but..." She looked up at me, ready to cry some more. Out of the windshield of the Studebaker, I could see that the prom was breaking up. Dancers spilled out the doors, holding hands, many of them kissing passionately.

"Do you want me to get into trouble, Arianna? Do you want Micah to get into trouble?"

"No, but Fred–"

"Your parents can't know about any of this, Arianna. We broke all the rules. We told lies. You spent three hours with a black boy."

Startled, Arianna pulled away from me.

"Don't call Micah a 'black boy.' "

"Micah is black and he is a boy. I'm a boy. You are white and Jewish. Your parents didn't even want you here with me tonight. The only reason they let you go to prom with me is because Charlotte died. They felt sorry for me. It was your parents' mitzvah to me. They did it to be kind."

"Stop it, Fred."

"Current events, Arianna. Young men like Micah have been hung for less than this evening. You have to pull yourself together, go home, and pretend you went to prom with me."

"Shut up, Fred."

"If you go home like this, your parents will believe that I did something awful to you. And if you tell them about Micah, they will never trust you again. Kiss Brandeis good-bye."

For a moment we were both silent, and then Arianna opened her evening bag and took out a small comb. She began to French braid her hair with an almost vicious intensity.

"I need to wash my face."

"Cover that up," I said to her, pointing to the base of her neck. "I don't want your parents to think I gave you a hickey."

"Find a public restroom. Find a restroom where no one will know me."

I started the Studebaker.

~~~~~

WE STOPPED AT a 7-Eleven where we could see lights on. I banged on the plate-glass door until the clerk paid attention.

"We're closed," he shouted.

"My girlfriend needs to use the bathroom," I shouted in return, adding, "please."

The clerk shrugged, moving to unlock the door. "Hurry," he said, looking at Arianna as she walked past him to the restroom, and then at me. "School dance?"

"Yeah, prom," I said.

"She looks a little upset." He raised an eyebrow, flexing a muscled arm tattooed with a ball and chain. "Helen" was inscribed underneath it in a block print.

"We're late. Out after curfew. Her dad gets mad."

"Afraid the carriage will turn into a pumpkin? And you'll turn into a rat?" The clerk laughed.

"Something like that," I said, wishing that Arianna would hurry up.

The toilet flushed, and seconds later Arianna opened the door and moved toward the freezer case. She pulled out two Popsicles.

The clerk smiled. "Cinderella needs some nourishment?"

For a moment, I thought Arianna would burst into tears, ruining all of her efforts in the restroom.

"Thank you," she said stiffly, handing him fifty cents and walking out of the store.

"Good luck with that pumpkin," he shouted to her as he followed me outside.

The clerk stood under the fluorescent green light of the 7-Eleven, waving his tattooed arm at us, and laughing as he repeated his witticism. "Good luck with that pumpkin."

While everyone else was drinking, partying, and making their first- or last-ditch attempts at fornication with the one they loved, I drove Arianna Isaacs through Elmwood and Memorial parks as she held two orange Popsicles in their paper coverings against her swollen eyelids. I asked her the questions that her parents would ask her, "How was the evening, Arianna?" and "Did you have a nice time?" I made Arianna practice her answers so that they sounded natural to the ear. "Who did you see?" and "Who was her date, dear?" I reminded her to thank her parents for letting her go to prom. I reminded her to tell them how excited she was about going to Brandeis. Finally as we pulled up to the curb in front of her house, I said, "I've known Micah Little almost all my life. You can bet tonight will be on his list of regrets. He does love you. It was just too much for him."

Arianna handed me the now-melting Popsicles. I could feel the cold slush through the paper packaging.

"How would you know anything about love, Fred Holly?"

Her words stung as they were meant to sting. She opened the Studebaker door.

"Tomorrow, you will regret those words. You will put this moment on your list."

I walked her to the door, watching her breathe deeply before pushing it open. Neither of us said a word, not even good night.

As I walked back to the car, I hoped to hear a "Thank you" or an "I'm sorry" float down the sidewalk to me. But that exchange wouldn't come for quite a while. Of course, I knew about love. I loved her. I loved Charlotte. And now they were both gone. Summer seemed an impossible distance away once again.

~e~⁓⁓

THE PORCH LIGHT was on when I pulled the Studebaker up our driveway. It was my first sober Saturday night in weeks. I stood in the darkness of the rose garden, smoking one of Morgan's Marlboros, when I heard the putter of a Volkswagen engine slowly motoring down Thirty-eighth Street and then stopping. Staying in the darkness, I moved to the driveway to see James, still dressed in his gray suit with a red rose boutonniere pinned to its lapel, gently open and then shut his parents' front door behind him. Neil Mahaffey popped the passenger door open of his bug and James slipped into the bucket seat, kissing Neil on the lips in one fierce movement under the glare of the car's dome light. I watched them coast down Thirty-eighth Street toward Dodge.

I walked into the street, trailing the Volkswagen for a block, wondering about love and how many broken hearts this evening contained. Already everything about the prom seemed imaginary but the pain.

Kent State

NEBRASKA ALWAYS FELT, and still does feel, far away from everything to me. Omaha is in the heart of flyover country. I always believed that if something really bad ever happened, if I could make it to Omaha, the badness would be slowed down by the very vastness of the state. It would be halted by the daunting length of the pursuit. So often by the time things reached Omaha, they were already over. In my own subconscious, that hazy realm of my being, I assumed that even Vietnam would not come looking for me in Nebraska. But on May 4, 1970, after twenty-eight Ohio National Guardsmen shot thirteen seconds' worth of rifle fire to disperse angry student protesters at Kent State University in Kent, Ohio, leaving four students dead, Vietnam caught up with me. It caught up with all of us. The black-and-white images of their bodies were front and center in the *Omaha World-Herald* and on the evening news.

Central to the composition of these photographs was a howling young woman with streams of dark hair, kneeling in front of one of the bodies. The words "Kent State" said aloud will always retrieve the image of that young woman and her pain for me. She has never gone away. She lives in a core of my memory with the burning Buddhist priest, the Vietnamese officer shooting the head of a suspect, Lieutenant Calley, Henry Kissinger, Jane Fonda in Hanoi, returning soldiers being met by the scorn and spit of protesters, clouds and clouds of tear gas, and that naked little girl who ran down a dirt road in the searing burn of napalm. Each image part of my shadow gallery of the Vietnam years, something that seemed so far away from my boyhood in Nebraska.

The nation's already seething universities erupted into flames. Buildings used by the Reserve Officers' Training Corps—ROTC—that hadn't already been burned were burned. University and college presidents shut down the campuses, telling students that their current grades would be their final grades for the spring semester of 1970. The presidents then sent the students home. We watched it all on our black-and-white television screen with Mom weeping, "Charlotte, Charlotte, Charlotte," as she dangled the cut-glass beads of her rosary, asking, "How could they kill some mother's child, Charlotte?"

What the five Hollys understood, as we watched image after image of those Kent State corpses and the ensuing riots all over the country, was what it took to save a body. And what it meant when a body was dead. I remember thinking, "What a waste, what a waste, such healthy bodies." We understood not the public grief, but the private pain of losing someone. What seemed extraordinary, what seemed appalling to me, was that they were so healthy and so young, just like soldier boys in Vietnam. Who made the telephone calls? How do you tell a mother or a father or a sister or a brother that someone so healthy, someone not on a battlefield, someone on a college campus, had been shot dead? How do you live with that? Why shoot at bodies, I thought then, when you could aim at the sky?

I do not remember much of my high school graduation, but I remember Kent State and the grimy feel of the *Omaha World-Herald* newsprint as I read each word, each sentence, and each paragraph of its daily coverage. Turning the pages of the paper that week, I stumbled onto an engagement announcement that caught my eye in the middle of all the tragic news. There, in a sweater set and pearls, was the beautiful blonde girl who'd accompanied Neil Mahaffey to Charlotte's funeral. It announced their engagement: "John and Emily O'Meara are happy to announce the engagement of their daughter, Anne Marie, to Neil Francis Mahaffey, son of Frank and Betty Mahaffey. Their wedding will be at two o'clock in the afternoon at St. Margaret Mary Church on Saturday, June 21, 1970." It stood out not only because it announced the wedding of Neil Mahaffey, who had announced his acceptance to the Jesuit seminary at James's birthday party, but also for the brevity of the engagement. One might presume that the beautiful young Anne Marie O'Meara was pregnant. I did. I used the kitchen scissors to clip the announcement from the paper and went looking for James. My stomach lurched in excitement. I wanted to be the one to tell him.

AFTER PROM, JAMES and Sarah would sing to the radio all the way to school on our morning drives. There existed between them some new kind of peace, something Sarah had accepted about him. For Sarah, prom with James had been enough. It sealed their friendship and lifted her spirits. Even in the sadness following Kent State, Sarah seemed livelier. She looked less strained, her color clearer, her face less contorted. The plum stain beneath her eyes had begun to fade. She danced less and less alone during the wee hours of Sunday mornings. Strangers stood closer to her at the bus stop.

At school, Arianna and Micah would not speak to each other. Nor would they speak to me. Between classes, dodging the newfound rapprochement between James and Sarah, I would disappear into the Joslyn to settle myself so that I could make it through to graduation. So I could make it to Stanford. I wanted to have words with Arianna and Micah. I wanted them to understand the pain I suffered. But I could not blow their cover, nor say the words that bubbled in me like a filthy brew. "You two," I wanted to say, "used me ill." For in the face of their silence and in the pain of Kent State, I did feel ill used that they did not appreciate my loyalty. I longed to say, "You are worse than Romeo and Juliet. You are silly in your misery," but I kept my silence. The debacle that had taken place between them on prom night was not known to the general student body. The rush toward graduation and the panic-stricken public sentiment surrounding Kent State clouded over the visible change in the feelings between Micah and Arianna. They were not being noticed. Apart, they were safe in the secret that they had once been in love.

Standing in the Joslyn Art Museum, staring at Jackson Pollock's *Galaxy*,

I came to feel that romantic love was always Romeo and Juliet. Even when it worked out, at some point it would fall apart. The problem was what to do with the pieces. Pollock's canvas made a logic to me that love could not. Love was an inchoate mess, as far as I was concerned. Whether romantic love was inspired by fate, some god or goddess, or pheromones, we did not control it. We didn't control it when it overtook us, nor when it departed. Its intensity was viselike and it was evaporative as fog. Turned inward by fear, or by fear of repercussions, love became the icy stoicism, bordering on hatred, that now existed between Arianna and Micah. Met with common sense head on, love can be splattered, defeated, destroyed. Micah made the irreversible error of speaking to his fears, of calculating his losses, of telling Arianna the truth as he saw it. A truth she knew, but did not want spoken, at least not by him. It was far more painful to perceive oneself as the rejected than to do the rejecting. I should know.

For, daily, as Arianna passed me by in the hallways of Central High School without a word or a look in my direction, my heart hardened to her plight. My love for her narrowed, it turned bitter, it withered. I found myself longing to spend time with James. Alone. Not with James and Sarah who sang along to Beach Boys' tunes and Elvis crooning "In the Ghetto," laughing at their own silliness as we drove to school each morning with the convertible top down under new green leaves. I wanted to tell James in detail about prom night. I wanted sympathy. I did not want Joshua Little, stopping by my locker to say, "Give it up, Fred. They weren't meant to be. Don't judge Micah. You don't know what he's going through." I understood that Joshua spoke the truth, but that he had no understanding of my truth. My sister was dead. The girl I loved, the girl I had made sacrifices for, wouldn't speak to me. Kent State. The world was falling apart, and Joshua thought I didn't understand.

The engagement announcement of Neil Francis Mahaffey and Anne Marie O'Meara exploded in my chest like a star of hope. It was something I alone would bring to James. It would be a bond with him that Sarah could not make. Both of us rejected in love. We could talk things over; I would lend him a sympathetic ear, tell him how I always knew Neil Mahaffey to be a prick. There were other fish in the sea. He had his whole future ahead of him. I spun platitude after platitude inside my head. Our futures I saw as intertwined, zigzagging roads of intersection.

SERENA SENT ME upstairs to James's bedroom, where he lay sprawled across the bed, rereading Salinger's *The Catcher in the Rye*. I sat down at his desk to wait for him to come to a pause in his reading. James read compulsively and he only stopped when he came to a natural break in the story. I knew it might take ten or fifteen minutes before James put down his creased red paperback edition of the novel. My stomach rumbled, heaving back and forth in anxious anticipation of the news I was about to deliver. In my sweating hand was the engagement announcement. On the book shelf above James's desk were the hardcover books that Sarah and I had given him for his eighteenth birthday: *The Catcher in the Rye, Franny and Zooey, Nine Stories, Raise High the Roof Beam, Carpenters and Seymour: An Introduction,* all by Salinger, and John Knowles's *A Separate Peace,* along with Hemingway's *The Sun Also Rises* and Fitzgerald's *The Great Gatsby* to round out his collection. The books were held in place by bookend replicas of the New York Public Library's lions, Patience and Fortitude, which Serena had given James for his sixteenth birthday.

On the desk was a diorama of Holden Caulfield's Manhattan that James had built in ninth grade for a book review assignment. I loved this diorama. (When I think of *The Catcher in the Rye,* it is James's diorama that I remember.) I could see Holden's Manhattan like a bird, like God looking down. At its center was Central Park, but it included the Brooklyn Bridge, which gives Holden passage from Pencey Prep back into the city. James had built John Roebling's great suspension bridge out of thread and toothpicks, using craft paint to create its metal and bricks. With great detail, James had painted clay replicas of Mr. Antolini's apartment building and the high-rise where the Caulfield family lives. The Lavender Room, where Holden met Bernice, Marty, and Laverne, was, of course, lavender. There was the Radio

City Ice Rink, where Holden took his date, Sally. Its opaque surface was made out of shirt-collar buttons. A clay version of the Edmont Hotel was there, as were Ernie's, the Fifth Avenue Automat, the Wicker, the Museum of Natural History, the Central Park duck pond, and Holden's final stop in his journey, the park's Carousel. There was only one human depiction in the diorama. It was not Holden. It was a tiny clay figure of Phoebe Caulfield, Holden's little sister. James loved Phoebe Caulfield. "Someday," he would say, "I want a daughter just like Phoebe Caulfield." And I would always say back to him, "And not a son like Holden?"

James looked up. "Hey, Fred." His eyes returned to the page.

Next to the diorama was the paperwork for a dormitory room at Northwestern University, weighed down by a framed photograph of James in England with Serena and her brother, Ian. Young James presented an earnest smile to the photographer while Ian grinned and Serena waved. I studied the black-and-white photograph, still wishing I had gone to England with James that summer of 1962. I waited for him to come to a break in his reading. A bubble that felt like acid gurgled in my stomach. A sweat broke out on my forehead. I looked down at the engagement announcement. Anne Marie O'Meara's face was stained with the perspiration of my palm.

Finally the book went down. "What's up?" James asked me.

Without a word, I handed him the stained announcement, watching him read and then reread those few sentences. My stomach growled. Another bubble of acid exploded, searing through me.

"Please leave."

It was not what I was expecting. I farted, breaking a loud and smelly wind.

"James," I said.

"Not now, please leave."

James's face was white and his nose wrinkled as my gas passed by.

"I'm sorry. I just thought you would want to know."

"Go, Fred. Go now. Please."

The room reeked of my fart.

"James," I stood up and walked to him. I touched his shoulder and he slapped my hand away.

"Get out of my room. Go," he told me.

I reached for him again. James hit my arm so hard that I stumbled backward against the desk chair, knocking the diorama to the floor. The clay breaking sounded like bells. I could see a broken Phoebe in the corner of her smashed Manhattan.

"Get the fuck out of my room."

For a moment, as shame, pain, and more of my own putrid gas washed over me, I wanted to kill James Day. I hated him. I picked up the chair, ready to beat him senseless. In that movement, my stomach lurched in a grinding, down-swirling sensation, sparking my bowels. I pooped my pants. I held the chair against my chest as the mess of my own feces slipped out of my jockey shorts and down the left leg of my jeans. I put down the chair and walked out of James Day's room, leaving James in an acrid cloud of methane and the horror smell of my emptied guts.

UPSTAIRS IN OUR bathroom, I stripped off everything and sat on the toilet, shitting, shitting, shitting, until I could shit no more. Then I filed the bathtub with hot water and Mom's Jean Naté bubble bath. I cried there in the bathtub for James and for Charlotte, not understanding what had gone wrong. It had all gone wrong. I knew then that what Arianna Isaacs had said was right. I knew nothing about love. And I knew that I would always love James Day.

I rolled up everything I wore that day into James's room and burned it in the barrel in our alley—the shit, my jockey shorts, a T-shirt, my jeans, white socks, my favorite pair of Converse tennis shoes, one of Morgan's linen handkerchiefs, sixty-eight cents, three dollars, my Timex watch, a black Van Heusen sports shirt, a photograph of Charlotte at three that I constantly carried in my back pocket, my class ring, a note from Herb Pepper at the Joslyn, the towels, the washcloth, everything that had touched my skin and the possible killer that lurked in me. I was terrified that I might have killed James that afternoon. I wanted in that moment of pure anger to beat him to a bloody pulp with the desk chair. I understood not the feelings of the protesters at Kent State but the blind, tired anger of the righteous members of the Ohio National Guard. In the worst of my moments, I knew, I understood, I was saved by my own shit. Somehow I aimed my gun to the sky. I have supposed it was because I was so deeply, madly in love with him. But I did not understand then the fine borders between love and hate and anger.

⟿

JAMES AND I quit speaking. We didn't speak on our rides to school. We didn't speak at convocation or graduation. We didn't speak at the graduation party that Mom and Serena gave for the two of us. Everyone noticed, but no one knew what to say, because we would not speak about what had happened between us. The silence of days turned into weeks. I was speaking so little that people gave up speaking to me. They blamed it on Charlotte's death, and the fickle queerness that the adults in our world had branded on me. The boy who loved the Joslyn Art Museum. The boy who loved art. "What could you expect? He was different even before his sister died. And you know the other brother's retarded, don't you?" These were the explanations that an audience of teachers and neighbors could understand. Never in my life had I been so lonely. Never in my life was I ever so sure that life was not worth living. Most of all I wanted him to speak first. Sarah asked me, Mom asked me, and even Morgan encouraged me to speak to James. To their great frustration, I continued to say nothing.

⟿

IN MID-JUNE, AFTER a long day of mowing at the Joslyn, I walked into the garden to bathe the green leather of the rose bushes with a potent chemical solution to kill aphids. The smell of the wash overpowered the scent of the roses. It was Serena's smell of lemon and lavender that stopped me. It penetrated the cloud of the pesticide and I knew I wasn't alone.

"Fred"–I felt the English lilt of her voice more than I heard it–"you must speak to him. This is killing him. It's killing all of us. James can't take it anymore. I can't take it anymore."

For a moment I was glad to hear it was killing James. I was glad to hear how much he hurt, and then my stomach lurched. My bowels quavered. My left leg shivered in memory.

"Please, Fred. Speak to him."

In all probability, Serena Day was my first great love. She opened that door in my imagination to other worlds where boys like me existed without being different. She added polish and shine to the order of my world in Omaha. She confirmed the existence of a place not too far away where, eventually, I could go. Serena was my heroine. The princess that my knight could save. I would do for her what I could not do for myself.

"UNCLE," I SAID to him.

James was lying on his bed, hands behind his head, looking at the ceiling. His transistor radio was playing Peter, Paul, and Mary singing "Puff the Magic Dragon." He said nothing.

"Uncle," I said again. "I'm sorry. It was wrong of me. Forgive me. It was none of my business."

James did not move. His eyes were on the cracks in the ceiling. The song ended and the DJ at KOIL announced an upcoming dance at Peony Park.

I looked around the room for *The Catcher in the Rye* diorama. It was gone.

"I'm full of shit," I told him and turned to leave.

"Wait, Fred."

It was an uneasy reunion. A very uneasy reunion. Not a hugs-and-kisses, it's-all-water-under-the-bridge kind of get-together. We were just together again. In the car, I said, "Good morning." He said, "Are we going out tonight? Have you called Joshua and Micah?" We spoke the words we knew how to speak. We never talked about Neil Mahaffey. We never talked about our feelings. We talked about drinks and when we would leave for college. Decades later, I understood that if I had only told him that I loved him, that I was jealous and that I loved him, it might have been different. But even I didn't know that then.

Three weeks after my first "Uncle," James enlisted in the United States Navy. Both Ronald and Serena looked at me as though I had pushed him there. I am not quite certain that Serena ever forgave me for that period of my life. She went to bed for three days, and it took Mom three more days to get her to leave the house.

"Why the fuck did you do it?" I asked him. "Your folks think it's all my fault. They think I pushed you to do this."

"Fred, it's not all about you," James said, adding, "and don't yell at me."

"I wasn't yelling," I yelled at him. "You could get killed over there."

"I know that."

"Then why are you doing this? Why?"

"For once in my life, I understand that I want to do something that many people do. I want to face my fears."

"Well, can't you face them at home near your mom?" I yelled at him.

"No."

"You got into Northwestern. You got a goddamn deferment. Why are you wasting your life?"

"Don't tell me I'm wasting my life, Fred Holly. You don't know jack shit about my life."

"I know jack shit about your life and jack shit about shit," I told him.

James began to chuckle. The he fell on his bed laughing. He laughed so hard that I began to laugh, too.

Leaving Omaha

ONE BY ONE we peeled off that summer. Micah took the train to Howard University in Washington, D.C. Joshua took the Greyhound bus to Drake University in Des Moines, where he planned to study actuarial science, as Morgan had done. Joshua's Lily, Lily Valentine, was hired to be one of the first Negro clerical staff on the Mutual of Omaha night crew while she attended college at the University of Nebraska-Omaha; she would see Joshua on weekends and holidays, until they married, four years later. Sarah attended a going-away party for Arianna Isaacs. I was not invited.

James took the bus to Great Lakes Naval Station, not far from Chicago. Serena was certain he was going to die in basic training, or be killed in Vietnam. James's enlistment weighed heavily upon Serena. She lost ten pounds off her already thin frame.

In the garden the night before he was to leave, I kissed James again. Micah and Joshua had sprinted home an hour earlier and Sarah was fast asleep upstairs. Locusts were buzzing and fireflies danced up from the lawn. The evening was heavy with the scent of roses and we were drunk. Even in the stupor of my drunkenness, I felt James kissing Neil Mahaffey through my lips. I kissed James back as Fred. Entirely Fred. Somewhere that late-summer night, the husband of Anne Marie O'Meara Mahaffey was being kissed by James Day. Somewhere Neil Mahaffey awakened next to his pregnant wife, longing for James.

IN JULY, HETTY'S father accepted a position as rector at a church in Ann Arbor, Michigan. Mom wept when she learned the news. Alone in the garden, I cried for the loss of Hetty. I knew nothing about the mysterious Episcopal church, but that their God did not know how much we had come to rely upon Hetty as our link to memories of Charlotte. After the moving van rolled eastward down Dodge Street that hot August morning, Reverend and Mrs. Carmichael sat in their Buick in front of our house, waiting as Hetty said good-bye to us.

Laurence held Hetty by her right hand. Tiger Cat was sitting on top of the carrier that held his hissing mother, Mrs. Gamp.

"Don't go," Laurence said. "You can live with us, Hetty. Don't go."

For a moment, Morgan, Mom, Sarah, and I were silent, savoring Laurence's invitation. His idea seemed burnished in gold. Hetty could live with us forever. It was Morgan who broke the reverie.

"Years ago," he said, clearing his throat, "I visited Ann Arbor after an actuarial meeting in Detroit. It's a beautiful college town. Michigan is a great university." Then Morgan put his arms around Hetty, kissing the part between her braids. "Good things will happen there for you."

Mom stepped toward Hetty and picked her up as though she were a toddler and not the eighty-pound girl that she was. "Thank you, Hetty Carmichael. You were Charlotte's best friend and ours, too."

When Mom put Hetty down the girl's freckled face was florid with heat and tear-stains. Her cat-eyed glasses were skewed southward. Hetty handed Mom a small black-and-white photograph. "This is for you," she said to Mom. "My mom wanted you to have it."

It was a photograph of Hetty and Charlotte holding Mrs. Gamp's kittens. Grinning into the camera with a smile punctuated with lost front teeth, each girl held two squirming kittens. "It's a copy," Hetty told Mom.

"Thank you," Mom whispered.

Sarah handed Hetty a heavy box wrapped in pink and yellow paper with a white bow.

"Should I open it, Sarah?" Hetty asked.

Sarah nodded.

Hetty ripped off the wrapping and opened the heavy box. "They're Charlotte's forty-fives," she said, looking up with consternation in her voice. "I can't take these."

"It's good to start with music in a new place, Hetty," Sarah said. "You can sing and hum to the records. It will keep your mind happy even when you're feeling blue. You'll know we're thinking of you."

"I don't know if I should take them." Hetty looked over her shoulder at her parents in the Buick.

"Take them," I told her. "Charlotte stole half of them from me, so think of half of them as a gift from me."

Everyone looked at me. Sarah began to grin. Morgan chuckled.

"Fred," Mom said, "Charlotte only borrowed them."

"Charlotte was always borrowing my records, and somehow they always became permanent parts of her collection."

Sarah laughed and Morgan smiled.

Tiger Cat jumped off of Mrs. Gamp's carrier and Morgan picked it up and started toward the car.

Laurence said, "Don't go Hetty," as we walked down the steps to the Buick at the curb. "Don't go."

"I have to, Laurence," Hetty said. "I can't leave my mom and dad."

"Why not?" Laurence asked, grabbing her right hand again, following Morgan and Mom who had the cat carrier between them.

"Because I would miss them too much. I'm only eleven years old."

"I'm thirteen," Laurence said.

"I know, Laurence, I know," said Hetty.

IN MID-SEPTEMBER, MOM and Morgan, Sarah and Laurence took me to the Omaha train station. As we waited for my train to arrive, they stood guard around me and my honey-colored leather suitcase and the green duffel bag I had purchased at the Army-Navy surplus store. A janitor with his hair tied in a ponytail was mopping the floor. His transistor radio hung from a black strap tied to a belt loop next to his keys. As he pushed a gray mop head across the black linoleum of the train station floor, Crosby, Stills, Nash, and Young's "Four Dead in Ohio" sang from the radio on his hip. *Woodstock*, I thought, *James and I should have gone to Woodstock*. But we didn't even know about it until it was on the evening news.

For two weeks I had been without friends in Omaha. Everyone was gone. Even Arianna had departed. Rabbi and Mrs. Isaacs had driven her back east the first week of September for orientation at Brandeis University. She called me the night before she left.

"Fred," she said, "I'm sorry."

"It's okay, Arianna."

"I'm scared. What if I don't cut it? What if nobody likes me?

"You'll be fine. You'll go to medical school. Boys will fall in love you. You'll break hearts."

"Thanks, Fred."

"I'll see you at Christmas," I told her.

"Christmas," she whispered.

"The winter holiday. I'll see you at Christmas break."

"Good luck, Fred."

"Thank you, Arianna."

The receiver clicked. I did not tell Arianna what Micah had told me in mid-August while we sat against the garage door underneath their basketball hoop. Annie Little was playing a tune by Béla Bártok for Laurence. The piano notes slipped out the window screens over our heads and into the warm yellow air of a Sunday afternoon.

"Fred, I'm sorry. I just wasn't ready for Hawaii and marriage and babies on prom night. Arianna always thinks it's because she's Jewish and I'm black, but it's because I'm not ready. I'm not that in love. I'm young. I don't want to go to war. I don't want to get married. I don't want to change diapers. I want to go to Howard. But I love her. I mean she's Arianna Isaacs. She's gorgeous. You'd have to be deaf, dumb, and blind not to love her."

Micah was right. I would have to be deaf, dumb, and blind not to love Arianna Isaacs.

On the way to the train station, Laurence held my hand in the Studebaker until our palms were drenched with sweat. "Don't go, Fred," he kept telling me in a full, clear voice. Morgan kept his eyes on Dodge Street, passing the Mutual of Omaha tower without a glance. Mom touched her eyes with a handkerchief. Sarah sighed and then grabbed my other hand. Laurence kept up his chorus as Morgan parallel-parked the Studebaker and fed the nickels into the parking meter.

I did not want to take the train to Oakland, California, where I would meet Seymour Fineman's sixty-two-year-old second cousin, Esther Safer. Esther was to take me down the peninsula on still another train to Palo Alto. She would see me safely to my dormitory and enrolled as a student in Stanford University, class of 1974. Three weeks before I was to leave, Esther Safer called Mom to say that she would look out for me. Mom burst into tears, telling her everything. "Charlotte was only eleven," Mom said, as we all listened, frozen in our positions throughout the house. Mom spoke to Esther Safer for fourteen minutes, an unheard-of amount of time for a long-distance phone call in our family. I felt I needed to go to Oakland to explain my mom to this stranger, then I could get back on the train and return to Omaha, to my bed, my brother, and my room. But I could not think of one thing I wanted to do in Omaha other than sleep and hold Laurence's hand. And Sarah's.

Standing there waiting for the train, I reached into my jacket pocket to hold my trilobite. Herb Pepper, Mrs. Kato, and a group of the docents and gift shop volunteers had presented it to me on my last afternoon of work at the Joslyn Art Museum. "It's a fossil over three hundred million years old," Herb told me. "It's like you, Fred," Mrs. Kato said, "an old soul. You both have endured." Herb shook my hand and each of the ladies kissed me, smearing my cheeks in a continuum of red lipsticks. The heavy weight of the black trilobite eased my fear. I was terrified of leaving Omaha.

My train pulled into the station and Mom pulled me to her. "You know I love you, Fred. I don't know what I am going to do without you," she whispered.

"Don't go," Laurence said again, staring at the train. Then he asked,

"Can I ride the train, too, Morgan? Can I go with Fred? I want to ride the train to Stanford."

"Who would take care of Tiger Cat?" Sarah asked him, before turning to me. "I'll write every week, Fred. It won't be the same without you." Sarah began to cry.

"Morgan...," I said, wanting him to tell me I could stay.

"Fred," he said, "life's greatest regret is not having tried. You have a chance to try. Go and take your chance." Tears spilled down his cheeks. I handed him my handkerchief. And he handed me his.

My stomach lurched as first Mom and then Sarah and then Laurence and finally Morgan hugged me. Then each of them kissed me. I did not want to go to Stanford University. I did not want to leave Omaha, Nebraska. I did not want Charlotte to be dead. I picked up my bags and stepped onto the train.

After Mass

AFTER ALL SOULS' Day Mass, we cleaned the gravestone of Thomas's mother, decorating it with marigolds, the flowers of the Day of the Dead. They are a glorious orange and give off an astringent aroma. We eat our breakfast sitting around her grave. Claire and Ellen eat scones and granola, while Hetty, Thomas, and I eat tortillas wrapped around beans, chorizo, and scrambled eggs. There is a thermos of coffee and a thermos of orange juice. I touch lightly Mrs. Santos's headstone. From her came Thomas. It is also how I think of Hetty's mom in Ann Arbor, who feels that I have ruined Hetty. Our divorce has not set Hetty free, as her mother hoped, but has woven her ever so tightly into an ongoing friendship with me and with Thomas. In bursts of anger, Mrs. Carmichael has referred to Charlotte as the spider who entrapped "poor Hetty" in that "crazy Holly family." From Hetty came Claire and Ellen, I think, as I trace the name "Maria Santos," deeply engraved in granite. Without Mrs. Carmichael there would be no Hetty, no Claire, no Ellen. I have never paid much attention to Mrs. Carmichael's outbursts because I do have Claire and Ellen. And Hetty, too.

From Mom came me and Sarah and Laurence and Charlotte. My mother is dead and buried in Calvary Cemetery, in Omaha, where Charlotte is buried. They are not buried together. Charlotte is buried in the children's section, which appears to me to be filled up with babies and youthful victims of cancer and cystic fibrosis and many other illnesses that now seem so curable. When I visit the cemetery with Morgan and Laurence and Sarah, we can never quite remember where Mom and Charlotte are. We wander among the flat headstones, uncertain of our geography, taking heart when we see gravestones we remember, the names and dates and blessings of other people's dead that jog our memories.

Five years ago, Mom was killed in a car accident. The Studebaker was broadsided on Seventy-second Street by a Ford Explorer that had run a red light. Laurence was in the passenger seat, holding his new kitten, Bob. Mom had driven Laurence to Long John Silver's on his day off, so that he could show Bob to his fellow employees. The woman in the Ford Explorer was physically unscathed, Laurence was in shock, and Bob was lost. The police officer at the scene who took Laurence to Bergan Mercy Hospital, told Ronald Day, who had driven Morgan to the hospital, that it was like a tank hitting a sardine can. Morgan never drove again. The Studebaker was his one and only car, the pride of retired Mutual of Omaha actuaries. A car that had broken odds, surviving its contemporaries and its maker.

I miss Mom with a pain that the years only intensify. I thought that my heart had callused to grief. That nothing could take me unawares after Charlotte. This was false. Mom's death dropped me like a shot. I adored her.

After our picnic we go to the beach, where Thomas and I watch Hetty and the girls surf. They wear full-body wet suits. Hetty has joined a women's surfing club in San Clemente. Hetty's surfing is another reason Mrs. Carmichael hates me. She is certain that Hetty will die in a sport that she views as both Californian and self-indulgent. Learning to surf was Hetty's therapy after our divorce. She has surfed through the pain that I have caused her. I am amazed when I see her on a board. I am also terrified. I carry Mom's crystal rosary in my pocket, fingering it silently as my family soars on cold, angry Pacific waves with laughter and squeals. Thomas sleeps in the sun, wrapped in an old woolen blanket. My cell phone rings and I press it to my ear. Through the pounding noise of the ocean, I hear the whispered sounds of Berkeley Thrive singing "Me and My Shadow" and the staccato sounds of tapping. I listen to the tapping and the music and I am carried away.

He finally says, "Fred."

I say, "I love you, James."

And he says, "I miss you."

"Where did you get the record?" I ask him.

"Uncle Ian found it."

"Good old Uncle Ian."

It is a web, this life, of vast and sticky strings. Strings that weave each soul's story, pulling us together. That has always been my regret for Charlotte. It would have been wonderful to witness what she might have woven.

Acknowledgments

I WOULD LIKE to acknowledge Janet Wiehe and the staff of the Fiction Department of the Public Library of Cincinnati and Hamilton County, along with with my colleagues at the Edina Community Library. Also the Joslyn Art Museum and the catalog, *Fifty Favorites: Joslyn Art Museum,* by Graham W. J. Beal, Janet L. Farber, Marsha V. Gallagher, David C. Hunt, and Carol D. Wyrick, provided both setting and solace for this novel.

I want to thank Joan Drury and Kay Grindland of Norcroft: A Writing Retreat for Women. Many thanks also to Sheila O'Connor and Mary Rockcastle of Hamline University and Janet Harris, Jean Owen, and the late Fred Slater of the University of Wyoming. And with great appreciation to Stu Abraham and Juliet Patterson of Abraham Associates, and Joseph Pittman, Richard Fumosa of Alyson Books, and the copy editor, Kate Scott. Thanks to Marie Stolte, Joshua Wilkes, Sheila Lynch-Salamon, John Schuerman, Leonardo Johnson, Steven Anthony Smith, Eydie Cloyd, Lorraine Langdon-Hull, Lisa Dunseth, Mary Pierce, Maria Dominga de Smith, Nancy Greer, Andree Rollee, Rosemary Furtak, Faith Mullen, Cecilia Horn, Paul Horn, Lily Sharpe, Betsy Holloway, Jonathan Lyons, Josip Novakovich, Kathleen Mickelson, Patrick Clark, Ed Denn, William Hardacker, Patrick Jones, Jeannette York, Tierza Stephan, Judy Inwood, Paul Turgeon, Jean Housh, Mark Cole, Lucy Spielman, Joanne Fitzpatrick, RSCJ, Mark Puttman, Joan Luebering, Theresa Farrell-Strauss, and Matthew Blakeman. And to Christopher Jon Tlustos, Michael Coester, Camilla Warrick, and Tom Morehouse, all who were once here. My mother and father, brothers and sisters.